I KNOW WHERE THE BODIES ARE BURIED

I KNOW WHERE THE BODIES ARE BURIED

CHRIS BEDELL

Copyright © 2020 Chris Bedell.

This edition published in 2020 by BLKDOG Publishing.

No part of this publication may be reproduced, stored in a retrieval system, or transmitted in any form or by any means, electronic, mechanical, photocopying, recording, or otherwise, without written permission of the publisher.

All rights reserved including the right of reproduction in whole or in part in any form. The moral right of the author has been asserted.

This is a work of fiction. Names, characters, businesses, places, events, locales, and incidents are either the products of the author's imagination or used in a fictitious manner. Any resemblance to actual persons, living or dead, or actual events is purely coincidental.

BLKDOG

www.blkdogpublishing.com

Other titles by Chris Bedell

Burning Bridges

Cousin Dearest

NOW

TUESDAY, SEPTEMBER 15, 2020

Ambiguity was everywhere and nowhere.

An argument could be made that ambiguity didn't exist because it depended on looking for hidden clues. Like when someone had a crush, and interpreted signs to believe said crush would reciprocate. Or like right now while I stood in front of a coffee cart after scurrying across my boarding school's quad and my sneakers crunched against leaves.

"I'm sorry," I said, holding an empty cup.

The guy in front of me with combed back hair, gazing at his soaked shirt and pants didn't know my feelings or thoughts. Even if assuming the worst in people complicated life. Whether people realized the truth or not, they gave away trust without a second thought on a daily basis. An apology was a convenient way for wrapping up a social blunder.

He bit his lip. "Don't worry about it."

"Really?"

"Wasn't like you spilled coffee on me or threw acid on my face."

Believing the best in people wasn't the only thing that people dispensed with less effort than breathing. People also revealed a lot by what they said. The guy didn't have to drop some profound truth for me to understand him. Mentioning acid showed he entertained the possibility of horrific events happening—like inventing problems that didn't exist.

"I'm Carson," I said, offering my hand.

He chuckled. "I know. We have several classes together."

I gasped. "Oh…"

Perhaps his continued focus on my hand while sweat clung to my brow was the universe's way of punishing me for spilling water on a classmate. Something about that law of physics where every event had an equal and opposite reaction. Only an optimist would've understood how something bad could happen to me after making a mistake—even the tiniest of mistakes that wouldn't matter later.

"Relax. I give everyone a hard time. Anyway, I'm Dean." He took my hand, and gave him such a firm handshake that my arm almost detached from my body.

"I know. I just introduced myself to be polite."

"Why are you carrying around a cup without a top?" Dean asked.

"I just came from the cafeteria."

Dean winked. "Couldn't have finished your beverage there?"

So much for having an easy conversation. He just had to continue giving me a hard time.

"It was another joke. I don't care where you drink your water," he continued.

"Why don't I buy your coffee?"

Some people might have chastised me for being polite. But anything proved better than letting the conversation deflate faster than helium leaving balloons. The conversation had to continue—almost as if talking to Dean was more important than oxygen.

"Sure." Dean turned around, and now faced the salt and pepper haired man behind the coffee cart. "I'd please like a large Caramel Macchiato."

I snickered even though sounding like a hyena ensured nobody liked me. Some comments warranted a reaction. Like a grandmother who only drank gin and nibbled on a few ice cubes and grapes during the day as opposed to eating two or three hearty meals.

"Something funny?" he asked.

"A Caramel Macchiato is my favorite coffee beverage."

Yeah. My comment was true. Nothing more alluring than the mixture of the bitter espresso flavor and sweet caramel flavor electrifying my taste buds. The drink revealed the perfect mixture of sweetness as opposed to some sugar packed Frappuccino beverage, which left people with parched throats while they searched for water.

"What a coincidence," Dean said.

I wiggled my eyebrows. "Coincidences are for amateurs. It's only an innocuous detail that reveals a nice similarity."

Reading into every detail might've annoyed some people, but my statement remained true. Coincidences were too convenient, and usually revealed something more. Like how Dean and I could've had more in common than the average onlooker might've thought. Having the same taste in coffee revealed our brains must have been a little similar despite how the factor shouldn't have been the only test for a friendship or relationship. The point was, we had something in common. And I wouldn't lie about something as insignificant as my coffee beverage.

Nope. Lying over something simple wasted both time and energy.

The man punched several buttons on the cash register. "That'll be $4.95."

I took my frayed leather wallet out from my pocket before grabbing a five-dollar bill. Then, I handed it to the cashier.

"Did you buy the wallet in 1952?" he asked.

Perhaps Dean had a future as a comedian. No offense to him, but he tried too hard with his latest joke. Almost as if seeming funny was more important than getting straight A's or into an Ivy League college.

My gaze narrowed. "My mom bought me the wallet for my fifteenth birthday, which means it is only two years old."

"I see..."

"You were teasing, weren't you?"

"Yeah, but don't worry. A lot of people don't understand my humor."

"Too bad," I said.

He drew in a breath. "Anyway, you aren't the only one who owes someone a polite sentiment."

"I don't understand."

"I'm sorry about Billy; I know you two were close."

My throat tightened despite how my surroundings weren't spinning around me. Saying a fellow classmate committed suicide by jumping off a cliff behind the school's woods would never roll off my tongue. Teenagers were supposed to read the news in a newspaper, on the internet, or even witness a soap opera worthy headline plastered on a cable news channel, not make the news. Not when Billy was only 17 years old.

I nodded. "Same. I know he was a part of your club."

Dean sipped his drink. "Well, he was no longer part of Charity Now when he died, but that doesn't matter. He didn't deserve to die."

Interesting. Dean's remark once again revealed more than he realized. Some people might not have chosen kindness, yet Dean had. He had no qualms about being positive, and I wouldn't forget that fact.

I averted my gaze. "It's like a nightmare I can't wake up from."

He patted my shoulder. "I know it doesn't seem like it now, but life will get better."

Grabbing Dean by his shirt collar while screaming because of him sounding too positive might've tempted anyone else, yet I counted to ten in my head. Starting trouble would only make me roll my eyes. No explanation needed about how drama sometimes hurt people more than it helped.

"Agreed," I forced out.

Sunlight glinted against his watch, accentuating its gold color. "I should leave, but thanks for the Caramel Macchiato."

Whether Dean realized the truth or not, he gave me further insight into his life. In this instance, the information had nothing to do with what he did or didn't say. It was about the bling that remained wrapped around his right hand, and the churning sensation in my stomach—even though Dean hadn't done anything offensive. Going to a boarding school meant dealing with people whose families had disposable incomes. My family might not have been struggling financially, yet I only attended Grand Preparatory because of my scholarship.

"No problem. See you in class later," I said.

"Sounds good. Maybe we could even hang at some point." His pupils dilated while he scanned me over before strutting away in the opposite direction.

My mind drifted back to his gaze.

Dean didn't have to do anything scandalous for me to remain in my current location in front of the coffee cart. Some people might've thought he shouldn't have stared at me so hard that his eyes would've made me bleed to death if they were knives and repeatedly cut my flesh. A curious person would've even speculated if Dean's behavior revealed he flirted with me.

I grinned. Small victories deserved praising as much as larger accomplishments. I was now in Dean's orbit, and nobody could take that fact from me. Not even the universe, and its twisted sense of humor.

THEN

FRIDAY, NOVEMBER 1, 2019

Having a stable group of friends didn't mean I had a perfect life. I somehow managed to be standing alone in front of the beverage and food table inside a barn—which must have been ten times bigger than my dorm room—on my boarding school's property. Music also blasted through the air from an iPhone plugged into a speaker while some teenagers danced—some even spilling their drinks on the ground—and others remained scattered at various locations inside the Barn, gripping their red Solo cups and munching on miscellaneous snacks while indulging conversation.

Someone snickered. "No offense, but you look lonely."

Billy could make his comment once or one-hundred times, yet the truth wouldn't change. He was correct. Freddie, Chelsea, and Amanda dragged me to the party, but hadn't kept me company after we arrived. They just told me to make a drink before Amanda scurried away to chat with a guy, and Freddie and Chelsea went off to have alone time (which was just code for them not being able to keep their hands off each other) at the opposite end of the Barn

I tilted my head. "I might leave."

Billy tugged at the sides of his leather jacket. "Have one drink first."

"I can drink in my dorm room."

"What's wrong? Never been to a party?"

I let out forced laughter. "That obvious?"

He winked. "Always answer a question with another question?"

"I've seen one too many cop shows."

"On Friday and Saturday nights that you spend alone in your dorm room watching TV."

Billy didn't have to make a damning remark for me to have an increased heartbeat. Not taking myself too seriously was good advice, yet Billy and I weren't friends. So, he couldn't say things Freddie, Amanda, and Chelsea could.

"Sorry. Didn't mean to offend you," Billy continued.

Perhaps I was wrong about Billy. Even if my opinion wasn't harsh since everyone knew Billy from the various whisperings about him on campus. The whisperings that revealed how he must've slept with at least half the girls in our sophomore class. The whisperings that mentioned how most girls in the sophomore class hated him. And the whisperings that said he'd fuck anyone with a pulse. Acknowledging his error meant he was more self-aware than most teens, though. Teachers were lucky if students cared about turning in homework or studying for a test.

I sighed. "Don't worry about it."

"Would you like me to make you a drink?" Billy asked.

"I'm not sure."

"Okay. Whatever." He poured some Margarita mix into his cup before adding a more than generous serving from a bottle with the name PATRON plastered on its label.

"Fuck it. I'll have a Margarita, too. Not like I'm driving; I'm just walking back to my dorm" I grabbed a cup from the table in front of me before grabbing the Margarita mix and Jose Cuervo bottle.

However, Billy grabbed the bottle while I almost added a splash of tequila to my cup.

"What the hell?" I asked.

"Don't use the Jose Cuervo; it's shit. Besides, you're at the party, and should take advantage of everything.

I laughed. Whether Billy was aware or not, his comment contained a sexual undertone. Anyone would've inferred that "everything" could've included sex.

"Good idea." I placed the Jose Cuervo bottle on the table after Billy released his grip before I poured some of the Patron tequila into my cup. Except Billy took the bottle from me when I was about to place it back down on the table, and poured more tequila into my cup.

He smirked. "Didn't use enough tequila."

"I didn't realize you were the tequila police."

He chugged his Margarita. "My job is to make sure everyone has fun."

"Mind if I ask a question?"

Billy rolled his eyes. Although he should've saved his energy. Life might not have been a nineteenth century romance novel, yet decorum mattered. Including asking if I could ask a question. I would've fretted if someone asked me an invasive question without considering whether the question was nosey.

"What made you talk to me?" I asked. "You could

chat with anyone."

My inquiry didn't reveal a self-esteem problem. Amanda, Chelsea, and Freddie still hadn't checked up on me, so I had nothing better to do than to continue talking with Billy. Even if sweat might've clung to my brow from the possibility of running out of topics to discuss with Billy.

Billy's eyes widened. "No fun in talking to everyone else when I've already chatted with them before."

"Good to know."

"I was kidding again."

I sucked in a breath. "Sorry. Must've been having a blond moment."

Yeah. The town of Violetwood wasn't only home to my boarding school. There were two universities within a couple of miles of my boarding school. And that meant living in a college town, and having access to a salon I frequented every seven to nine weeks to get my roots retouched back to their platinum blond glory.

And no. Poking fun at myself also didn't imply negativity. Being blond meant I could make an occasional blond joke. It wasn't like I said terrible things about other blonds. A difference also existed between hair color and reclaiming a slur—somebody only needed one second to figure out which issue was more serious.

"No worries," Billy said. "This conversation isn't a pop quiz, so you should drink up and have a refill."

I raised my eyebrows. "Trying to get me drunk?"

"You aren't driving."

"True."

He licked his lips. "The light hair color looks good."

A lump lingered in my throat. Billy's remark was one of those times when life wreaked of ambiguity. The writer in me questioned whether or not Billy was being polite or the hair color comment was his lame attempt at flirting.

I nodded. "Thanks."

"What? You won't give me a compliment?" Billy demanded.

"The leather jacket, white T-shirt, jeans, and sneakers is a good combination for mixing casual and formal wear."

"I was teasing..."

"Oh. Anyway, do you want to tell me a little about yourself?" I asked.

He finished his drink before making another. "What do you want to know?"

"Likes? Dislikes? Hobbies? Favorite television shows?"

"I like to party."

Scratching my chin would've happened if I didn't want to spill my drink. One minute Billy had no problem making small-talk, and the next minute he was vague. He could've revealed more than mentioning partying. That remark didn't tell me anything new since I could've inferred he liked partying from tonight's event at the Barn.

"Cool," I said.

Billy and I stared at each for a beat, yet neither one of us spoke. Instead, my teeth chattered, my body shivered, and a thick cloud of condensation left my mouth after swooshing wind trickled into the Barn. I rubbed my hands together, attempting to create friction. Even if some people might've thought I had myself to blame for the cold sensation that washed over my body since I sported basketball shorts.

"Maybe you shouldn't wear shorts in November," Billy said.

"Maybe." I downed more of my Margarita. The mixture of the lime and tequila lingered on my tongue, and I licked my lips. Being well acquainted with Billy wasn't mutually exclusive with not believing he had good taste in alcohol. A Margarita was my new official party beverage.

"Don't be too hard on yourself. Not like the Barn

is heated," Billy said.

"True. However, it's nice your father paid for the Barn."

"It was under the guise of wanting space for Charity Now," he touted.

"Still a clever idea."

"It's an excuse to party."

"I can't believe the school let you build the Barn." I sipped my drink, licking my lips even louder this time. Almost as if the Margarita tasted better with each subsequent sip.

"It helps when you have a parent who makes multiple endowments each year." Billy paused for a second. "Although that'll stop soon."

"What do you mean?"

"Can you keep a secret?" Billy whispered.

"Sure."

"My father lost his job as president of his hedge fund company. But you can't tell anyone."

Time for someone to pinch me. Billy couldn't have said what he had. Having empathy for someone going through a difficult financial time was one thing, yet telling me something so personal entailed vulnerability. Billy didn't owe me anything—including telling me something humiliating.

He ran his fingers through his spiked, black hair—although the gesture appeared vain. There wasn't much hair to grab. "Anyway, I have an idea. Why don't we stop talking? I could show you a good time in the woods behind the Barn."

"You'll have to be more specific. Not sure what you're getting at."

"Fine. I can give you clarity if you want." Billy leaned into my left ear before mumbling something.

Billy and I placed our cups on the wooden snack and beverage table before we darted towards the Barn's rear entrance. Except Amanda accosted us right when we were about to step outside.

Amanda smiled. "Hi, Billy."

Billy folded his arms. "Carson and I are preoccupied."

"It can wait; I need Carson," Amanda said.

He huffed. "Fine."

Billy shuffled away without having a fit before pouring himself another drink at the beverage and snack table and joining a conversation, which consisted of two guys and girls.

"What the hell was that for?" I asked.

Being best friends with Amanda entailed giving her more latitude than a stranger. However, she still intruded into a situation that was none of her business. I only imagined how she would feel if I begged her to chat while she flirted with a guy.

Amanda twirled a strand of hair around her finger. "I was being a good friend."

"I can look out for myself."

"Don't be stupid. You know about Billy's reputation."

"Your point?"

She tugged at her purse strap, which remained wrapped around her right shoulder. "I'm not an idiot. I can infer what you and Billy were about to do."

Perhaps Amanda should've been a detective. Having good deductive reasoning skills was required for being a cop. Anyone would've understood how a cop wouldn't solve a murder case without making the occasional logical inference. Especially if said police officer needed to go undercover to solve the case. In that instance, reading people would've meant life or death.

"So? I only had one Margarita."

"Not my point. What you and Billy were about to do means more to you than him."

Wow. Sex being a natural part of life didn't mean teenagers had to have graphic conversations about the topic or even discuss the issue in the first place. It wasn't like doing so would bring world peace.

"I see."

Amanda wrinkled her nose. "Don't be angry. I'm trying to look out for you."

***

MONDAY, NOVEMBER 4, 2020

My eyes lit up after I bought my Caramel Macchiato from the coffee cart on the quad. Billy just started walking in my direction, and an opportunity presented itself since we could finish what we didn't start at the party on Saturday night.

"Hi," I said.

"Hi," he murmured before strutting away.

I must've been having a fever dream. Billy couldn't have spoken in an almost inaudible tone. The universe couldn't have handed me something, only to take said thing away.

"What? Don't tell me you're angry because of Amanda interrupting us?"

He whirled around. "We just talked at a party once. Not like we're friends."

"Sorry to bother you…"

Billy scurried away without another word.

Ouch. So much for making new friends at a party. I should've been more realistic about life. The universe never missed an opportunity to drop a pile of shit on someone's lap.

The cashier lifted his gaze off the cash register while nearby birds screeched. "How about I treat you to a pastry?" he asked.

Sure. Anyone could've inferred he meant well. But he couldn't have overhead my conversation with Billy. Dread couldn't fill my body this early in the morning. Not when Billy contradicted himself because of how he generally acted nice at the party, yet couldn't even be bothered to say five words to me a few moments ago. It wasn't like Billy was my boyfriend because he indulged a conversation with me. It just wouldn't have been the end of the world if I had a new friend.

"Rain check—I'm not hungry. But thanks for the offer," I said.

"Sure," replied the cashier.

Someone tapped my back. "Everything okay?"

I cocked my head. "Hi..."

"I saw you frowning all the way from my dorm building," Amanda said.

Props to her for not starting the conversation in an awkward fashion. I would've ran to Timbuktu if Amanda didn't feign politeness. Having flushed cheeks wouldn't help me since Billy's aloofness and curt behavior proved to be problem enough for the rest of the month.

I averted my gaze. "Billy wasn't too chatty."

She patted my shoulder. "Sorry. But maybe it's better to be disappointed now then after you sleep with him."

"Who said anything about sleeping with Billy? He was just going to blow me at the party."

Yup. No qualms about being blunt existed this time. Amanda already knowing about the Billy situation meant discretion wasn't needed. Besides, it wasn't only too early in the morning for drama; it was also too early in the morning for lying. A person shouldn't have been concerned about self-preservation before having at least two coffee beverages.

"Okay. Thanks for sharing." Amanda looped her arm around mine. "How about I walk you to class?"

Getting emotional support didn't make me weak; Amanda's coddling made me human. I challenged anyone not to need help when disappointment happened only to have to put on a mask and pretend that life was okay. Everyone had pain—some people were just better at hiding it than others.

"Sure. That'd be nice," I said.

NOW

THURSDAY, SEPTEMBER 17, 2020

"**D**oing okay, Carson?" Freddie asked.

Specs of moonlight shimmered through the windows while Amanda, Chelsea, Freddie, and I sat at a table in the back of the dining hall. The chattering of numerous voices also filled the air because every table was occupied. However, I hadn't had one bite of my breadcrumb coated pork chop and Parmesan cheese topped penne. And my reasoning wasn't because we just sat down a minute ago. Nope. Freddie's, Amanda's, and Chelsea's plates were almost empty.

I put my fork down, and rested my hand under my chin. "I'm fine."

Chelsea flipped her black hair over her shoulders. "We don't need a 4.0 GPA to understand how Billy's death must be upsetting."

Amanda squeezed my hand. "Maybe we shouldn't force Carson to discuss Billy until he's ready."

Thank goodness for Amanda. Being best friends with Amanda, Freddie, and Chelsea didn't always entail honesty. Not if I wasn't ready to chat about Billy. At least not about everything regarding our "relationship."

Chelsea snorted, and soda dripped out of her nose. "No offense, but it's better to deal with issues."

"Forget I said anything," Freddie said.

No disrespect to Freddie, but he shouldn't have waffled. Offering an apology—whether indirectly or directly might've proved someone was decent. However, ambiguity only muddied life. If Freddie had a point to make, then he needed to either standby said point or not mention it.

Amanda glanced at Chelsea. "You're the one who waited till the night before your Biology final to study for it last May."

Kudos to Amanda. Some people wouldn't have stood up to a best friend—even over a minor issue like sounding hypocritical. Amanda didn't have to say anything, yet she had, proving people could learn from her. Liking or loving someone didn't mean that person wasn't capable of doing something wrong.

"I was just lost," Chelsea said.

Freddie looked me in the eye. "Sorry if I upset you."

"Don't worry about it because Chelsea is right. I can't wish away the pain, and I'm dealing with Billy's death," I said before picking up my fork and breaking off a piece of pork chop.

Amanda's eyes bulged. "And what's that supposed to mean?"

I sipped my Sprite Zero. "Just what I meant. I'm dealing with my feelings."

Someone hollered. "Hi, Carson."

The universe might've been a lot of things, yet I

couldn't accuse it of being boring. Not every surprise had was a crisis. A bunch of things would've been worse than Dean and I crossing paths again after I accidently spilled my water on him the other day.

I looked up at him. "Hi."

Dean took in a deep breath. "I don't mean to interrupt, but I wanted to let you know you're invited to a party at the Barn on Saturday night."

Perhaps I had been too hard on the universe all of these years. Dean didn't have to invite me to one of his parties, but he had. And I wouldn't complain. Dean and I hadn't talked since the other day. So, I would've had to stage another encounter or invent some other reason so we could interact again if Dean hadn't just approached me.

"Thanks," I said.

"Your friends can come too," Dean said.

Politeness deserved recognition despite how the idea wasn't complicated. Most people might not have invited my friends to the party if they were in Dean's position. No law existed that said Dean had to invite them.

Freddie nodded. "We'd be happy to go."

"Fantastic. Anyway, see you around, Carson." Dean glanced at me a second longer than he should've before darting by our table and towards the food section part of the cafeteria.

Freddie chewed on the inside of his lip. "Do I wanna know what that's about?"

"I'm handling the situation," I interrupted.

"What does Dean have to do with Billy?" Chelsea munched on a cookie, and a crunching sound echoed. Although I wouldn't criticize her. I wasn't my parents or Grandma, and that meant not giving a flying fuck about manners. Even if etiquette and manners might've made for an interesting story.

"Dean both was, and remains part of Charity Now," I said. "Because Billy was also a member of Charity Now before he mysteriously left the club a couple of days before his death."

"What are you saying?" Amanda asked.

"His suicide seems too convenient." I finished the last bite of pasta before grabbing a napkin and wiping away the sauce on my lips.

Chelsea picked her nail. "Suicide isn't meant to be understood; it's a tragedy."

My eyebrows inched up. "Do you really think Billy is the type of person to commit suicide?"

"I shouldn't have mentioned the Billy thing," Freddie said.

Gazing around the dining hall was all I needed for a scorching sensation to spread through my stomach. A guy with hair that extended to his eyelids sat at a table alone.

Sure. I knew nothing about the guy's personal life and could only fill in details based on my imagination or what unfolded in front of me. However, I wouldn't. The beginning of freshman year was only two years ago. No amount of wish fulfillment would've vanquished the constricted feeling in my throat from not having any friends during my first week of school. Because Freddie, Amanda, and Chelsea befriended me, not the other way around.

"Don't tell me you're using Dean to see if Billy's death wasn't suicide?" Amanda asked.

Perhaps Amanda had a future as a psychic, because I wasn't throwing shade at her. My comment was completely serious. Not requiring any effort with knowing what I thought reinforced how she might've been more perceptive than I gave her credit for—even though I was the writer, and she was the one interested in science. Between the two, being a writer lent itself to observing and understanding humans better as a result of picking up on the little details that most people ignored without a second thought.

"They found a note, not a body," I said.

"Some things deserve to be buried," Chelsea said.

I shook my head in a vigorous fashion. "Not if Billy didn't kill himself."

"You don't have proof," Amanda said.

She might've been my best friend, but Amanda needed to watch the next thing that came out of her mouth. It wasn't like I squashed her desire to be a doctor even though I couldn't wrap my head around four years of college, four years of medical school, an internship, and a residency.

I guzzled my remaining Sprite Zero, then belched. "I'm allowed to have a theory. Not like I'm running around accusing people of killing Billy."

"Okay." Amanda paused for a second. "Make us understand. I get your motive, but what are you expecting to accomplish? Dean is a real person."

"I'm just being friendly—not leading him on," I said.

Amanda's eyes narrowed. "I'd be careful if I were you. You're supposed to be making your life less complicated, not more complicated."

Good thing I hadn't just sipped Sprite Zero, because it would've trickled out of my nose and mouth if I had. Amanda's disapproval made her seem like my mother no matter how much contempt might've flared through my body because of this conversation getting me into trouble when I wasn't even asking for it.

"We're not judging you. We just want you to be happy, and think that can only happen if you focus on being more positive," Freddie said.

"Would you really accept Billy's death if you were me? Because if I find a body, I'll drop the matter without hesitation," I said.

Amanda sighed. "Fine. Let's say you discover a person or more than one person from Charity Now is responsible for Billy's death. What would you do?"

I shrugged. "I don't know. It'd depend on the context."

Amanda slurped the rest of her fruit smoothie before speaking. "You better figure it out before the situation gets ahead of you."

"I knew it!" I exclaimed. "You do think it's possible Billy's death wasn't a suicide."

"Okay. There's a small chance you might be correct, but don't let that go to your head," Amanda said. "Nothing worse than false hope."

"I won't. Although if you're so concerned about me, then you can take me clothes shopping in town tomorrow after class," I said.

Amanda grunted at me. "Fine. You win."

Good to know Amanda offered unconditional support. Some people might not have enabled the situation if they were in her position. But no. Amanda set her feelings aside—at least for the moment. Taking me shopping revealed our friendship was more important than winning an argument. And that was something to grin about for one fleeting moment. Being right and continuing to be friends with Amanda weren't the same. I could criticize her while making sure not to ruin our friendship for good. Because that would've been awful.

"It's a shame you and Dean are only talking because of the whole Billy situation. He would make a cute boyfriend." Chelsea broke bits of a napkin apart, just leaving them in front of her on the table. "He's one of the few out LGBTQ students on campus."

Freddie rubbed his forehead. "You know I hate when you're messy."

Chelsea giggled. "That's not true, and you know it. You mentioned enjoying my messy side when we were in bed together the other day."

Freddie elbowed his girlfriend. "Chelsea!"

"I can't help it. I'm being honest," Chelsea said.

My tongue made a clucking noise. "Thanks! I think I'm going to be sick now. The idea of you and Freddie in bed together is just the visual I need."

Yup. Even I sometimes had a lighter side. Not like Chelsea and Freddie's relationship induced vomit. I just had to do my best friend duty and hassle them like they would've done to me if I had a boyfriend or girlfriend.

***

FRIDAY, SEPTMBER 18, 2020

"I wanted to apologize for last night at dinner," Amanda said while we stood in front of rack of clothes.

Perhaps tomorrow was the end of the world. That event was the only thing I could think of that would make Amanda feel contrition.

"Really?" I asked.

She exhaled a long breath. "In the future, I'll talk to you in private if I'm concerned."

Okay. At least Amanda was capable of correcting herself. I had to credit her for acknowledging a mistake when some people would've rather died than admitting an error. And I wasn't exaggerating; I was being completely serious. Some people just had too much fucking pride.

"Don't worry about it," I said.

"I'm not stupid. Nobody likes being ambushed. It can be overwhelming."

I continued sifting through the clothes on hangers in front of us. "Thanks."

Yup. Sometimes the simplest answer was the best one. Especially in light of last night's dinner conversation. All we needed was for one of us to make even an offhanded remark for trouble to start.

"I want you to know I won't stand in your way. If you need closure, then that's okay. It's not my place to judge," she said.

"You don't think I'm crazy, do you?"

"Nope. Anyway, how'd you even meet Dean?" Amanda asked.

I pulled a short-sleeved collared shirt from the rack that had a bunch of flamingos embroidered on it. "I staged an encounter by accidentally spilling water on him."

"I'll give you credit for having guts."

"At least he wasn't pissed." I held up the shirt at Amanda. "What about this shirt?"

"I like it."

"You can be honest. I won't be offended."

My comment had nothing to do with trying to read Amanda's mind. I meant what I said. Liking the shirt wasn't the same as giving me a hard time. There were much more serious aspects to get worked up at in life—like Billy's death. Besides, there were only a couple of other individuals in the boutique shop, proving looking for another shirt wouldn't have been a big deal as a result of having space to search.

She pushed a blonde curl behind her ear. "The shirt is fine. Although I have another question if that's okay."

"Go ahead."

"How much about Charity Now did Billy tell you?"

Way to ask a loaded question. I so needed to contemplate how many of my classmates might have been flawed or sociopaths. There was just no spinning some facts no matter how positive I pretended to be. And that was why this conversation wasn't the right time to dwell on what I did or didn't know about Charity Now.

"Enough to be curious," I replied.

"Oh. Okay. Anyway, do you wanna pay for the outfit now?"

Perhaps Amanda was more impatient than I realized. Nothing wrong existed with talking for a few minutes before buying my shirt. It wasn't like we'd get into trouble for not returning to campus at a certain time. Nope. Having our parents sign a permission slip allowed us to leave campus and come into town anytime we wanted. And no elaborate explanation needed about how getting off campus was important. I just couldn't fathom being stuck on campus from September to Thanksgiving. No thanks. Life was complicated enough without enabling claustrophobia. Someone didn't have to be buried alive in a coffin for a constricted throat. A boarding school that didn't let teenagers come and go meant the school resembled a prison.

"Sure," I said.

"Next on line?" asked the cashier a couple of minutes later.

I shuffled up to the cashier as Amanda trailed behind me.

Morgan took the shirt from me, and scanned it. "Hi, guys."

"Hi, Morgan," I said.

"Didn't realize you worked here, Morgan," Amanda said.

Morgan gritted her teeth. "Yeah. Working during junior year might not be ideal, but I need to save money for college."

Poor Morgan, because she was correct. Balancing schoolwork with working seemed like a sick joke. The type of prank the universe would've loved to pull on someone. Yes. There was nothing wrong about having a job and going to the school at the same since a lot of people did that regardless if they were in high school, or at the undergraduate or graduate level at college. However, people—especially teens could only handle so much stress at once. Teens ultimately weren't dolls to be used for amusement. They were real people, and that meant adults might've often expected too much of them. Because no shame existed from admitting when something proved too much to deal with.

"Fair enough," Amanda said.

"That'll be twenty dollars," Morgan said.

I gave Morgan a twenty-dollar bill before she took it from me, placed it in the cash register, and stuffed the receipt and shirt into a plastic bag.

Morgan handed me the bag. "Sorry for your loss, Carson. I can't imagine losing a friend."

"Thanks. I appreciate the support," I said.

Morgan scratched the side of her head. "I just can't believe a classmate committed suicide, and how I might've come across the body if I walked at a different location in the woods that day."

"What?" I exclaimed.

Morgan leaned closer—so much so that she might've broken her neck if she stretched her body any further. "You can't tell anyone this, but I was buying pot in the woods on the south side of campus that day."

Amanda beamed her eyes. "Don't worry. We won't tell anyone."

"Although I did see one curious thing," Morgan said.

"And what's that?" I asked.

"I couldn't make out everyone's faces, but I saw a few members of Charity Now walking through the woods a little while before Billy's note and sweater were discovered," Morgan revealed.

"Go ahead, and just say what you want to," Amanda said a moment later after the bell on the shop's door jingled when we opened it and stepped onto the sidewalk.

"I think we got a clue without even knowing it," I said.

She grimaced. "Fine. I'll give you that."

"But don't worry. I know it's only one piece of information since those guys could've just gone to the woods to smoke pot."

Amanda ruffled my hair. "Relax. I meant what I said. Even I'm not petty enough to burst your bubble."

Yup. Only a good friend could get away with messing up my hair. Because I'd have to kill anyone else who even thought about ruining my hair. Sure. My hair was short. Yet I couldn't forget its thickness and how I took a good five minutes to style my hairdo each morning.

"Remind me to spend extra money on your Christmas present this year," I said.

"I'll also give you one more thing. I think Charity Now is kind of a sexist club since they don't let girls in."

I chuckled. "Yeah. You have a point. It's not like Charity Now is a fraternity."

"It might as well be with their partying. In fact, I don't even how they have time do charity let alone school work."

I tilted my head, then laughed again. The neon OPEN sign glowing on the boutique's shop window almost appeared nonsensical. A clothing store seemed like the last place where a neon sign belonged.

"Wanna skip the cafeteria tonight, and grab a bite to eat somewhere in town?" Amanda asked.

Food was the one time I wouldn't curse the universe out of existence for giving me a surprise. There was nothing like the comfort of a good meal. Eating a favorite dish had the same cathartic effect that exercise had.

"Sure," I said. "I'd be fine with that, but I want you to know I really am thankful for you taking me shopping."

She nudged my shoulder. "No need to be formal. I'm not going to let one minor disagreement stop me from being your friend."

"It's not even entirely about that. I just know you have a lot of homework."

"It's only Friday," Amanda said. "I'll do my homework on Sunday night like almost everyone else. Besides, I didn't tell you guys this, but becoming a doctor no longer interests me. I want to be a photographer."

* * *

SATURDAY, SEPTEMBER 19, 2020

"I'm so glad you guys made it," Dean said.

Freddie, Chelsea, Amanda, and I just approached the Barn while tree branches shook in the howling wind and stars lit up the night sky while the moon glowed. Music also reverberated through the air—like the night I met Billy for the first time.

"We wouldn't miss the party for anything." Amanda unzipped her purse, grabbed a hair tie, and ran her fingers through her hair, putting it up in a ponytail.

Some people might've given Amanda a dirty look as a result of her fresh subtext. But I shoved the thought to the side. This party wasn't about my pulse drumming in my ears because of every single concern that popped into my head. Not when my hunch had a fleeting chance of being correct as a result of Morgan's tip yesterday.

Dean snickered. "Anyway, if you don't mind, I'm going to steal Carson from you. But help yourself to booze and food."

"What are your intentions with Carson?" Freddie asked.

I shrieked at him. "Freddie, please!"

"I had to go for the joke; it was right there," Freddie said.

"Well, you're going to have find other material. Because I will not provide fodder for your jokes again," I said.

Freddie's smirk expanded—as if that were even possible. "Whatever you say."

"Come on, Carson. Let's get you a drink." Dean grabbed my arm before I could respond, and he dragged me over to the beverage and snack table.

No offense to Dean, but he had more guts than he realized. His touching might've been limited to my arm. However, I never gave Amanda, Chelsea, or Freddie a pat on the shoulder let alone tugged at their arm. I just wasn't that type of person.

"Anyway, what's your poison?" he asked.

"I'll have a Margarita."

He almost choked on a gulp of his own air. "That was Billy's favorite drink."

"Sorry. Didn't mean to bring him up. Although Billy introduced me to tequila."

Perhaps I might've had a future in the CIA if I wasn't destined to be a writer. Embellishing on a moment's notice was a trait the agency must've valued when recruiting new agents. I only imagined how situations must've arose when a CIA agent's life depended on telling a good lie. No explanation necessary about how I really would bring Billy up again—I just had to be subtler.

Dean eye-fucked me. "Anything you care to share?"

"Nope. But please use the Patron tequila."

"Yes, sir!"

He grabbed a cup from the bag on the table before scooping ice, pouring in the Margarita mix, and topping it with what must've been two shots of tequila. Although I wouldn't complain. Dean's good host behavior proved accurate. Going to a party meant taking advantage of free food and booze.

"Here." Dean handed me my cocktail before making a Margarita for himself.

"Thanks." I raised my cup against Dean's cup so we could have a toast once he finished concocting his cocktail.

"What are we toasting to?"

"To new friends," I said.

A guy sporting a blazer, Polo shirt, khaki pants, and loafers—who also happened to have his hair parted to the left grabbed a beer. He then locked eyes with me for a second before darting away in a matter of seconds—like he was never here in the first place.

"What was the intense eye contact with Jonathan about?" Dean asked. "Don't tell me that I should be jealous?"

"Hardly. He doesn't like me because I had a higher average than him in Geometry last year. But please don't say anything since I don't want to cause trouble," I lied.

Yup. This conversation was one of those times when framing dishonesty as a kindness didn't make me a bad person; it made me practical. I wasn't obligated to disclose every detail about my past.

"Relax. I can keep a secret," Dean said.

"That's good to know. But I had one question if you don't mind. Why did Billy leave Charity Now?"

"He had a difference of opinion about what way the club should go in, and was voted out. But if it's okay with you, I don't want to chat about Billy tonight."

"Of course."

Agreeing with what Dean said almost made me curse. He was still the president of Charity Now, and associating with him was the easiest way to have access to the club. Subtlety also remained important whether Dean wanted to drop the Billy issue or not. Scaring him away ensured not finding out shit about if Billy's death really was a suicide. Besides, Dean's response provided a clue whether he realized the or not. I now didn't just know that Charity Now members walked through the woods before Billy died. I also knew exactly how Billy left the club, and that was a concrete fact worth holding onto. Only an optimistic person wouldn't have known the difference between quitting and being kicked out of a club or organization.

"Tell me about yourself," Dean said.

"Like what?"

"What do you want to be when you graduate?"

"I want to be a writer."

Dean's laughter echoed, yet he didn't respond. And I needed all of one second before the idea of pacing back and forth popped into my mind. He didn't have to say anything cruel for me to question what he really thought of what I just said.

"Not mocking you—just shocked. A hot and smart guy like you seems destined for something more difficult," he said.

Okay. The CIA should've also recruited Dean. Going from seriously fucking up to saving the conversation alluded to how he might've been able to handle high pressure situations. If someone asked me to bet my life on whether he would've come up with a quick save, then I wouldn't have been able to do so.

Wait. I glossed over a pretty important fact. It wasn't like I could ignore how Dean mentioned me being hot. Nope. The response was a specific comment as opposed to one of Billy's remarks.

"What about you?" I asked.

"I'd like to play professional baseball, but I doubt that'll happen."

Some people might've thought they were dreaming if they were in my position, and I wouldn't have faulted said people for their reasoning. Dean couldn't be the type of person that might've flirted with me one minute, only to have a negative attitude the next. Even if being a writer meant understanding people had contradictions.

"You never know," I said.

Yup. Unraveling the possible truth about Billy's death didn't only entail subtlety. My operation also involved flattery. No harm in trying to make Dean feel good about himself—not if I needed to get more information from him.

He sighed. "That's kinder than my parents. They're begging me to drop baseball."

"Doesn't baseball start in the spring?" I asked.

He took another swig of his Margarita. "Yeah. But you know parents. It's never too early to start campaigning about an issue."

"Good point."

"Anyway, would you like to dance?" Dean threw a gaze a few yards away from us. A few of our fellow classmates, which consisted of both boys and girls, happened to be dancing. A mahogany table—with a speaker and iPhone plugged into the speaker—also remained propped up in front of the dancing teens while the music just switched to a Taylor Swift song.

"Maybe another time. I don't dance much," I said.

"Live a little. It's not like dancing will kill you." Dean put our drinks down on the food and beverage table before taking me onto the dance floor, and moving his arms and legs.

Lucky for Dean, he only insisted on dancing, as opposed to having sex. A difference existed between wanting to dance and wanting to have sex without mutual consent. I would've thrown him or anyone else through a glass door if I was forced into having sex when I didn't want to.

Dean started moving his arms, legs, and back even faster after inching closer towards me. I then inhaled the deepest breath of my life and jiggled my arms, legs, and back as quickly as Dean did.

"Isn't this fun?" Dean asked.

"Yes. Although I might have to kill one of my friends."

Nope. My comment was neither an exaggeration nor offensive. The sound of an iPhone's clicking camera echoed in addition to how Amanda needed to pray for mercy if she even thought about posting the photo of me dancing on social media. Letting go of myself was one thing, yet the rest of the world didn't need to see my impulsive side.

"I'll give you props for one thing," I said, raising my voice even louder because of how the iPhone connected to the speakers just started blasting a rap song.

"And what's that?"

"You've got a lot of guts to be out."

Life might not have been a morality play, but I sometime had to acknowledge corny facts. Being out meant Dean was living his truth, and that was more than could be said about Billy when he was alive.

"I can't help who I am," he said.

"Don't take my comment the wrong way. I just meant it takes a lot of courage to be yourself in a world where people are always waiting to knock you down," I said.

"Anyway, do you wanna go back and finish our drinks?"

"Sure."

I trekked after Dean while we cut through the crowd. Sweat even dripped down my back. There was barely an inch of free space inside the Barn as a result of how many fellow classmates were now here.

"Smart of you to pour us new drinks," I said.

"I couldn't take the risk of someone drugging our drinks since we left them unattended."

"Exactly."

Nope. No regret existed in my mind from contemplating how someone could've drugged our drinks—even if someone might've accused me of sounding like I was on a soapbox from thinking that adults didn't just need to warn their children about drinking and driving being dangerous. They should've also warned their kids about people drugging drinks and how people could be raped at parties. Stranger things happened, after all.

Dean's eyebrows knitted together. "Hope I didn't cross the line by making you dance with me. If I did, I apologize. Don't wanna make you uncomfortable."

I raised my hand at him. "Don't worry about it. You'd know if you fucked up."

"Cool. Anyway, tell me more about yourself. Are you writing any new stories?"

THEN

THURDSAY, NOVEMBER 7, 2019

Freddie and I sat under a tree on the south side of campus while afternoon sunlight radiated from the sky and a squirrel grabbed an acorn before climbing up an adjacent tree. Several students flocked by—although no voices echoed, proving it was the quieter time of the day because of only having to wait around eighty minutes before the dining hall served dinner.

I lifted my gaze off my book. "Nice of you to take a break from your constant sex sessions with Chelsea so we can have some bro time."

"Don't worry about it." Freddie scribbled something in his notebook before flipping the page in his math textbook, revealing yet another yellow colored page. Almost as if the school should've sprung for new Algebra 2 textbooks already. "I always have time for you. Although

I'm sorry you attended the party by yourself last night."

"There's a difference between going to the Barn, and going to Las Vegas."

He snickered, yet the tone was soft as opposed to a high-pitch raspy sound one expected from an evil witch. "I know. But I didn't peg you as Mr. Social."

"I don't understand why Billy wasn't there. It's his barn, and he's the president of Charity Now."

"Don't ask me."

Fair enough. It wasn't like Freddie was Billy's guardian or could read Billy's mind. Only Billy knew what he was thinking.

I inhaled a deep breath. "I need to ask you something, but it has to stay between us."

"Absolutely."

"What's the deal with Billy?" I asked.

Yup. Now wasn't the time to give a flying fuck about how dwelling on an issue was unhealthy. Feelings couldn't be turned on and off with a switch. And that meant sometimes talking an issue to death. I was only human, and needed occasional coddling. It wasn't like I always expected people to baby me. I just had to get beyond this one particular issue. Whether I was honest or not, Billy was also the first guy or girl who gave me romantic attention. A big difference existed between making out with a guy or girl—which was something I had done (with both guys and girls), and having someone in my life who would've been an intriguing boyfriend.

"I don't understand," Freddie said.

I picked at my nail. "One minute he flirted with me, and the next he didn't give a flying fuck."

"Might be best to forget about it."

Interesting. Freddie's response balanced being supportive with firmness. Freddie hadn't blamed me, yet he also hadn't encouraged the subject. And I didn't blame him for that despite how I had a million years to go before understanding with how letting go was sometimes neces-

sary and following through with said idea were two different things.

"He really did flirt with me at last week's party," I
said.

"I know, and I believe you. However, if he's anything besides straight, then he isn't out."

Good save. We might've gotten into a fight if he
hadn't watched his response. There was a polite way to
disagree with someone, and then there was just plain rude
behavior.

I closed my book, and shoved it into my backpack.
It didn't matter if the book was a pleasure book as opposed
to a school textbook. I wasn't gonna get anymore reading
done, and that was fine. If Billy would be on my mind for
the foreseeable future, then I could at least talk about him.
"Amanda thinks I should forget about him."

"Maybe you should," he said.

"Maybe."

Freddie gritted his teeth. "Although don't look
now."

Tears almost dotted my eyes the second my gaze
shifted. Billy stood a few yards away from us. Being in
close proximity wasn't why my heart pounded faster,
though. He was holding hands with a girl. Almost as if our
flirtation meant nothing. Or if it did mean something to
him, it was just something he indulged out of boredom.

Billy shot a smile. "Hi, guys. Beautiful day, isn't
it?"

Demonizing pot might've been unfair, yet Billy
must've smoked a shitload of marijuana. I never saw
someone happy enough to use clichés.

"Yeah," mumbled Freddie.

"What's wrong with you, Carson?" Billy asked,
holding the girl's hand.

"He got a bad grade on a test, but will be fine,"
Freddie said.

"That's too bad. But see you around, Carson." Billy winked at me before strutting by while his hand remained attached to the girl's hand.

"You saw how he looked at me, right?" I asked.

"Yes. It's not just you." Freddie wrote something else down in his notebook before closing both it and his textbook.

I ran my fingers through my hair. Damn. My hair couldn't have been that dirty that grease now stuck to my fingers. "Maybe I'm a fucking idiot."

"Don't be hard on yourself. Everyone has trials and tribulations. The important thing is not to let them define you."

Throwing shade wouldn't have gotten me far, yet I clenched my fists. Trials and tribulations didn't seem like a strong enough expression to describe how I could've been the next Taylor Swift. I didn't have to know Billy that well to appreciate how the situation provided good fodder for a song.

Someone cackled. "What a beautiful sentiment."

So much for Billy's appearance making me wish I was a snake and that I could shed my skin. A guy sporting a blazer, buttoned down shirt, tie, khaki pants, and black shoes that sparkled a little bit as a result of the sunlight glinting against them now stood before us. Although the idea of wearing formal clothing was bullshit. My boarding school abolished its dress code three years before my freshman year. Something about not inhibiting creativity, and how adults needed to let kids make their own choices.

"Hi, Jonathan," Freddie said.

"Jonathan," I mumbled.

Jonathan scowled at me. "Something wrong?"

"He got a bad grade on a test," Freddie said.

Wow. I'd have to give Freddie an extra special birthday present. Some best friends wouldn't have covered during an awkward situation.

Jonathan's eyes widened. "It was fun meeting you at the party the other day, Carson."

"You two met at the Barn party?" Freddie asked.

"I'm a member of Charity Now," Jonathan said.

Freddie nodded. "Cool."

"Anyway, see you around." Jonathan waved goodbye before scurrying towards the nearest academic building.

He tilted his head. "Wow. Maybe today isn't your day. First Billy, and now Jonathan. Although Jonathan gave me the creeps."

How articulate of Freddie. And I wasn't being sarcastic this time. I was being completely serious. Getting a read on Jonathan proved he was a lot savvier than I or anyone else might've ever considered.

"No kidding," I said.

"You met him at last night's party?"

"That's what he said."

His eyebrows knitted together. "Did something happen?"

Goosebumps clung to my back, arms, and legs. Having good intuition was one thing, yet it wouldn't have killed Freddie if he was dumber. If I wasn't lucky, the truth about the party would come out, and I couldn't have that. Nope. Last night never happened, and that was final. Nothing good would come from reliving last night, which was yet another reason yesterday's memory should've been erased.

"No. I just think he's a douchebag from the way he dresses," I said.

He looked me in the eye. "I'm only asking you this since we're friends, so please don't get mad. Did something sexual happen between you and Jonathan last night that you didn't want to happen?"

The cruelest moments in life weren't because of physical pain. They occurred when something so bad happened and a person couldn't talk despite be given the opportunity. A little push to open up would've been all that I needed in a perfect world. However, this was real life, and that entailed learning to bury the pain—or even at least learning to live with the pain if I couldn't deceive myself.

I looked away. "Don't be absurd. He's just a douchebag."

"Forget I said anything."

***

FRIDAY, NOVEMBER 8, 2019

A banging noise echoed while I was in bed with the covers pulled over me. One quick glance to the left, and I almost cursed. The glowing red numbers on my alarm clock resting above me on a wooden shelf revealed it was only 6:00 P.M.

The fist returned, and this time one knock was followed by five.

Fuck. The person wouldn't go away, proving I had yet another reason to flip the universe off.

"Coming!" I jumped out of bed before slipping into my bathrobe since answering the door with only my plaid boxers on didn't seem appropriate. In fact, I also slid my feet into my slippers on the floor in front of my bed. Walking barefoot wouldn't have killed me, yet I couldn't risk stepping on a random bug that might've been scurrying across my floor.

"Took you long enough," Billy said after I opened the door.

My jaw trembled. "What do you want, Billy?"

"Is that anyway to speak to the hottest guy in the sophomore class?"

He needed an attitude adjustment like yesterday. No offense to Billy, but everyone at school wasn't lining up to suck his dick. He just wasn't that special.

"I'm tired, and would appreciate it if you left," I said.

His gaze narrowed. "Aren't you going to invite me in?"

"Why would I do that?"

"Because we need to talk."

"We have nothing to discuss."

Being firm with Billy didn't make me an asshole. I was only looking out for myself. It wasn't like I called Billy a dick to his face. I just couldn't deal with him. Not when last Wednesday night meant staying in bed for the rest of my life was ideal.

Billy pressed his hands together. "May I please come in? I'll only take five minutes of your time. In fact, you have my permission to throw me out on my ass if you don't like what I say."

A scent containing a mixture of earthly and sweet smells wafted through the air. But I couldn't scoff—not this time. The aroma resembled a hug for my nose as opposed to making my eyes burn. Although if Billy sprayed more deodorant on his body just for chatting with me, then he might've been a bigger tool than I realized. Looking your best was the type of thing someone did for a date—unless Billy had a date lined up after our conversation. That conclusion was a real possibility because of him seeming in love with that girl he was with the other day when Freddie and I sat under the tree.

I hesitated. "I don't know."

Making Billy work for it didn't make me a cruel person; it made me cunning. Seeming too eager only enabled flushed cheeks as a result of resembling a fool. It wasn't like I wanted to harm Billy. He just needed to know I wasn't a pushover.

"I said, 'please'," he replied.

"What? You expect a medal because you do the bare minimum when it comes to politeness?"

"I mean no harm."

"Fine. But you only have three minutes." I gesticulated at Billy, and he entered my dorm room without another word.

The door's slamming echoed after I shut it, yet now wasn't the time to worry about etiquette. Not after Wednesday night. It wasn't like I streaked through my dorm building. I just had no more fucks to give about anything.

Billy glanced at the floor as soon as we stood in front of my desk, which was behind my bed. Crumbled tissues seeped out of the top of the garbage, proving one movement might've sent all the tissues flying. A few crushed tissues also remained scattered on my desk.

"Don't tell me that you've been jerking off a lot?" he asked.

I glared. Billy didn't have to say anything cruel for the contempt radiating in my eyes. Any comment that was remotely crude proved reason enough to grab him by his shirt collar and shove him out of my dorm room—even if just giving him his several minutes proved easier as a result of how sometimes giving people what they wanted created less drama. Unless the person came back for more.

Billy looked at my face, then my eyes, then back at the tissues, then back at my face. "Have you been crying?"

"No!"

Lying once again proved best. Billy wasn't psychic, which meant he had no way of knowing whether I just told the truth or not. Although I should've spoken with a louder inflection in my voice so that he'd actually believe what I said.

"Liar!" he said.

"Tell me what you want."

Billy coughed into his right arm. "I wanna apologize for blowing you off on Monday in addition to how I might've hurt your feelings the other day when you were with Freddie. That girl was just a flirt, nothing more."

Wow. Billy might've been a lot of things, yet he wasn't stupid. Mentioning both occasions meant he was more aware of his behavior than I or anyone else might've realized, and that thought was therefore more than a little sobering. Being aware of his behavior meant Billy could've had a manipulative side since he might've known exactly the right thing to say.

"Okay," I said.

"That's all you have to say?"

"I don't know what you want from me."

"Anyone with half a brain can tell I acted like an asshole, and I wanna apologize for my behavior."

"You don't owe me anything."

He stomped his feet against the floor. "Why do you have to be so stubborn? I'm trying to do the right thing."

Perhaps Billy had more depth than anyone gave him credit for. I would've never guessed that some flirt from a random party would be this upset over someone not letting him have his way by giving the attention he so desperately craved.

"I appreciate your effort, but I don't have time for this."

"I should've been more mature. I blew you off on Monday because of a phone call with my father the previous night about needing to cut back on money because of his losing his hedge fund job while yesterday was just an unfortunate coincidence."

Billy surveyed all the used tissues in front of us, almost as if another glimpse proved the tissue boxing resting on my desk wasn't empty. "You really have been crying, haven't you?"

Damn him. He just couldn't be oblivious like the majority of students and teachers here. Because I so needed to the universe to give me what I wanted at the wrong time.

"Don't be ridiculous," I said.

"I'm not an idiot."

"I never said you were."

Billy stepped forward, leaving only about an inch

between us since he might as well have been on top of me. "Is it about the test you bombed?"

"Yeah," I murmured.

His head swayed from side to side. "No. I don't think your demeanor has anything to do with a bad test. I've failed my fair share of tests, but I've never come close to being so upset before."

Law enforcement had to recruit Billy the second he graduated from here. Impromptu dishonesty wasn't the only trait valued in a police officer. Tenacity was also required. I didn't need to be a police officer in order to understand how cases weren't always wrapped in a timely fashion like they were in one episode of television.

"Maybe I care more about school work than you," I said.

"Nah. My sister has also bombed a few tests despite her having a super brain, yet she also hasn't gotten upset."

Someone needed to alert the media ASAP. I hadn't realized how he had a sister, proving I really was capable of learning knew information—both inside and outside of the classroom.

I yelled. "Just go!"

Raising my voice wouldn't make me stay awake at night, staring at my ceiling. Nope. Giving him a few seconds while I pondered his sister reveal was one thing, yet he hadn't taken the hint. And that meant acting so tough that even I wouldn't have wanted to be friends with myself.

"Not until you tell me what's wrong," Billy said.

"Why?"

Shit. Asking a question would've only prolonged our conversation, and I therefore should've known better than to invite another tangent into the discussion—even if life once again contained ambiguity because of how he should've left my room. Like yesterday in addition to really wanting to know an answer to his question.

"I'm not gonna ignore someone in pain," he said.

"Fine. But I want to know something first. Was I just a flirt at the Barn party or did you actually enjoy chatting?"

"I was supposed to be getting a friend a refill, but your loneliness seemed like the more pressing issue."

Wow. Another example of ambiguity because life was always anything but simple. Billy couldn't have just wanted to get his friend another drink or only wanted to have talked to me. Both answers had to apply.

I forced a grin. "Okay. Thanks for your honesty."

He locked his arms together—almost as if his posture tempted me into revealing the reason behind my mood. "I'm serious. I wanna know what's wrong."

"Leave!"

"No!"

"Don't make me get my RA."

Billy sneered. "Go ahead. I'm not afraid."

I screamed even louder this time. "Fine! You wanna know what's wrong? Your friend, Jonathan, raped me at the Barn party this past Wednesday. The party I went to on the off chance of talking to you. But I must be a fucking idiot."

His mouth gaped. "What did you just say?"

"Yeah. You aren't dreaming. I just revealed your friend raped me. Apparently, talking in private behind the bushes in front of the trees outside the Barn doesn't have the same innocent connotation it might've had back in the eighteenth century."

He sobbed. "I don't know what to say other than I'm sorry."

This conversation was one of the few times when not uttering an articulate response didn't make Billy foolish. Not trying to tell me how to think or feel, or pretending to know what I was going through proved best. Nothing Billy said changed what happened Wednesday at the party.

"Don't worry about it. You weren't the one who

raped me. Now will you please go?" I asked. "Because it'd be great if I could go back to bed.

"It's not even seven o'clock on a Friday night."

Damn him. He couldn't let the issue go and live with not getting his way for once in his life. Whether he realized the truth or not, he'd eventually have to get smarter. The universe wouldn't always be kind to him.

"Go!" I bellowed.

Billy couldn't swallow the lump in his throat. Nope. It just lingered—almost as if someone told him his mother or father died. "No."

I stabbed my fists through the air despite how there was nothing for me to technically grab. "What do you want from me?"

"Let me help you. I might not understand what you're going through, but I can be a friend."

My face drooped. "It's okay. You don't owe me a fucking thing—nobody does."

"What kind of attitude is that?"

My back hairs rose, yet discussing my rape wasn't the sole reason for how I once again must've been buried alive. A spider caught my attention from the corner of my eye while it crawled along the floor, and the fucker was now so close to my right foot that it might as well have been on said foot.

Freezing during an unpleasant situation couldn't happen again, though. Like at the party two evenings ago when Jonathan pinned me against a tree while his hands grabbed my hips and his boxers and pants remained around his ankles. My boxers and shorts also hugged my ankles, and the room might as well have been spinning now despite how I wasn't high. One second could pass or a century could pass. However, his lips being so close to my ears that the scent of whatever mouthwash he used prickled my skin would always make my body shudder. And I couldn't forget about the grunting. His lips being only less than an inch from my ear meant he shouldn't have been so vocal, because I didn't just have to live with the actual moment. My ears would always ring from the hearing damage he probably caused.

"Where'd you go just now?" Billy asked.

"Doesn't matter. Just leave."

"I'm not trying to piss you off—especially in light of how people should be paying attention to your boundaries right now. But I can't pretend that you never told me Jonathan raped you."

The wind rattled against my dorm building so loud that the windows should've broken. Sweat dripped down my back while my chest expanded and contracted. The reality was, a series of roaring gusts of wind would no longer only be a series of loud breezes. The wind's loud volume meant I might as well have still been pinned against the tree as Jonathan kept jerking his body forward while thumping against his body against mine.

I didn't even fight back the tears. "You can't tell anyone Jonathan raped me."

"I won't. But I don't think you should be alone tonight."

"Where does that leave us?"

"I don't know. You tell me," he said.

I rolled my eyes, but didn't speak. Perhaps Billy wasn't cleverer than I thought he was. He really should've known better than to make the comment he did. It wasn't like I expected him to solve my problems. Billy just needed a little tact.

"Sorry," Billy continued.

"You're the only one who knows."

"I inferred that. But I have discretion, and won't out your secret."

Great to know Billy had discretion. Because I was thankful for anything to go right at this point. It wasn't like I dreamed about the school knowing I was raped. Nope. That event would've been worse than someone forcing me to walk across naked.

"I should've done something differently."

He pursed his lips. "No offense, but Jonathan is several inches taller than you."

"Being shorter than him doesn't mean I'm weak."

His Adam's apple throbbed. "I never said that. I just meant you need to focus on healing, not what you didn't do. Although please don't think that means I'm telling you what to do…"

"Thanks."

"Have you eaten anything today?" Billy asked.

"No"

"Well, let's change that. I'll order us takeout for dinner. Anything you want. Just name it, and it's yours."

I wiggled my eyebrows. "What about your dad losing his hedge fund job?"

"I still have my trust fund that I can access any time through my debit card."

Billy's cleverness might've been TBD, yet I couldn't accuse him of being extravagant. Showing restraint with his trust fund revealed another example of smaller moments defining character. Because I only required five seconds for contemplating how most teens in his position would've spent their trust fund faster than a kid with an endless supply of money buying candy from a sweet shop.

"I like General Tsao's Chicken," I said.

"Sure. I know a place."

"Cool. That'd be great. Although please get extra rice. I never get enough rice when I order Chinese Food."

He laughed. "You've got it."

Good move. Criticizing me for wanting extra rice would've only wasted his time, it would've wasted his energy. A difference existed from wanting more rice and wanting a Mercedes and a mansion.

"And thank you," I said.

"You don't have to thank me for being a decent human. I'm doing what anyone would do."

"I'm not sure about that. But let's not dwell on it."

Billy scrunched his fingers against mine, yet I didn't recoil from his touch. Enduring a trauma meant having said event remained etched in my brain. But I could still tell the difference between a compassionate gesture and inappropriate touching. If anything, Jonathan raping me clarified the two ways physical touching could go.

"I really wasn't flirting with him. I honestly thought he talk somewhere quieter as a result of the music being so loud," I said.

"This doesn't change what happened to you, but it's a shame we all have pain. Most of the time I can't even talk with my father on the phone and we just resort to communicating through email."

This conversation was one of those times nostalgia pangs wasn't sentimental bullshit. Life really had been simpler in elementary school because of anything being possible—even Santa Claus existing. However, elementary school didn't even resemble one person trying to pull another individual off a cliff and their fingers almost touching. At least then elementary school would've been tangible. But no. My mother's dusty photo album in my family's attic back home was the only reminder that elementary school happened. Jonathan raping me in the woods made innocent moments such as elementary school impossible to occur again. I might not have physically died, yet I died on the inside.

"You don't have to reveal your misery just because I embarrassed myself by revealing my own pain," I said.

His shoulders jumped up. "I'm telling the truth."

"Do you think life will get better?" I asked.

"One day."

"Thank you for not judging me."

"Don't worry about it."

"I really should call the Chinese restaurant now." Billy let go of my hand, yet I jerked him forward.

Our faces were now only an inch away from each other—especially our lips, which were close enough that might as well have been pressed together.

Billy sighed. "I don't think we should kiss…"

"Oh, sorry. Did I misread the signals?"

He pulled away from me. "No. There really has been a spark between us despite how I'm not out. This is just a fragile time for you, though…"

How nice of Billy to be delicate with his phrasing. Because someone people might've used the other R-word without any hesitation—even if doing so wouldn't have been smart. Not being psychic didn't mean being oblivious to social cues. One accidental offhanded comment might make a rape victim—or any other victim of trauma—have an emotional moment.

I licked my lips. "I can be raped and still want sex or a date. So, go ahead. Kiss me."

He looked at me so long that it might as well have been graduation time by the time he whisked me into his body, and he kissed me.

And no. Making out with Billy didn't make me impulsive. Romance and sex didn't deserve to be tainted for the rest of my life. And that was why blood pumping through my veins faster while his hands cupped my cheeks didn't make my stomach twist in ten different directions. I was taking an active role in my own happiness, and that detail was the only thing that mattered in this moment.

***

SATURDAY, NOVEMBER 9, 2019

Freddie, Amanda, Chelsea, and I sat at a table in the dining hall overlooking the windows. And there wasn't even one cloud in the sky while a bird remained perched on a tree branch, yet the usual ruckus didn't permeate the dining room air. And no complaints would come from me.

Only so much time could go by before an ache jolted someone's head from too many voices talking during peak dining room hours.

"It's a shame we were all too tired to do something fun last night." Freddie slurped down the rest of his cereal's milk.

"We could go clubbing tonight," Chelsea said.

Amanda played with a strand of her hair. "No way! I want to get a head start on homework."

Chelsea scowled. "Don't be a buzzkill."

Yup. Now wasn't a time to play devil's advocate—even if being a rambler meant considering the possibility. A person could only be responsible for so long, and that was a concept Amanda needed to understand like yesterday. She would only be young once, and no point existed in her having regret fifteen or twenty years from now when reflecting about boring weekends at boarding school.

"Everything okay, Carson?" Freddie asked. "Because please don't tell me Billy has caused you more grief."

"No. Things with Billy are fine. In fact, they're better than fine," I said.

Amanda blinked. "Really?"

"Yup," I said.

"I thought you're pissed at him?" Freddie asked.

"Dynamics change." I shoveled cereal into my mouth, and my teeth soon grinded against my food, making a series of crunching noises. Because it didn't matter how much effort someone put into eating cereal without making too much noise. It was just the type of food that couldn't be eaten quietly.

"Is he still in the closet?" Amanda asked.

Chelsea giggled. "No offense, Amanda, but you're a buzzkill. If Carson wants to have fun, then let him. It's not like he's superman and wants to jump off a building because he thinks he can fly."

"Don't put words in my mouth," Amanda spat.

"What about the girl from the other day? What's

to stop Billy from playing games again." Freddie grabbed a tissue from his pocket, and blew his noise.

Okay. Good to know I wasn't the only person who didn't pay attention to proper etiquette because I would've bet my life on Grandma having a meltdown if she sat at our dining hall table right now. Something about how blowing your nose too loudly—or even at the dining table at all—was worse than the crunching sound people made when eating.

"I deserve an epic romance," I said.

Amanda nibbled on a piece of melon and took a sip of water, only to cough so loud that she might've lost a chunk of melon in both of her lungs. "Nobody is saying you can't be happy. It's just very important to think about the people you associate with you."

"Like you guys?" I asked.

Freddie flicked the spilled Cheerios at me. "Very funny. But no need for cynicism. We know you enjoy our friendship."

Chelsea unzipped her purse, and coated her lips with a violet shade of lipstick. "Don't pay attention to Freddie. He's jealous because being in a committed relationship with me means there are no surprises in the bedroom now."

Freddie banged his fist against the table. "Chelsea, please!"

"No shade, but you two are wrong. Billy kissed me. In fact, he kissed me three times last night," I said. "And that proves the situation isn't in my head."

"Nobody accused you of being delusional. You just need to be careful," Amanda said.

"Don't pay attention to them. You'll be having fantastic sex in no time," Chelsea said.

Amanda finished the last piece of fruit in her bowl. "You say that like everyone should be having sex."

"That's because it's true. Everyone deserves a good fuck," Chelsea said.

"Chelsea!" Freddie exclaimed.

Chelsea's inappropriate comments were better than if Christmas morning and my birthday were on the same day. Amusement meant the return of normalcy. Being a teenager entailed making a few raunchy comments so long as they didn't imply harm. Anything that prevented me from having flashbacks to Jonathan pinning me against the tree while he used me to fill some physical need also deserved a parade. Because the tree's creaking from Jonathan's forward movements couldn't be so audible that I thought the incident was happening again. Nope. Not today.

NOW

MONDAY, SEPTEMBER 21, 2020

Taking several deep breaths and counting to ten in my head would always be necessary in certain situations no matter obvious the reaction was. Doing certain things—like standing outside Billy's dorm room—had to be done no matter how much I wished I was elsewhere.

And no. Hovering by Billy's dorm room didn't make me silly, it made me clever. Billy wasn't alive, yet he had a roommate, and said roommate might've known something about Billy. It wasn't like I could press the Billy issue with Dean so soon after he insisted on dropping the topic. Nope. Even I wasn't that impatient. Nothing good would come from alienating Dean before I got my first substantial clue. Morgan seeing some of the Charity Now members in the woods before Billy's suicide note and sweater were discovered in addition to how Billy was kicked out of Charity Now didn't count as major clues since they didn't really prove anything. They just hinted I might've been on the right track. Like when someone was sneezing, congested, and just wanted to clothes their eyes. Those symptoms might've pointed to the flu or they might have pointed to how said person might've had a cold.

Enough stalling.

So, I did the only thing I could do. I made a fist, and knocked on the door. Except nobody answered, and I knocked again.

Damn. The universe just couldn't have something positive happen to me, because the blue waning from the sky meant Billy's roommate, Otto, couldn't have been at classes. Also, he didn't belong to any clubs outside of Charity Now.

"What can I do for you, Carson?" called out a voice.

I glanced down the hallway. A guy with spiked hair and an earring in each ear shuffled towards the door I stood in front of.

"I was wondering if we could talk," I said after Otto arrived at his door.

He smiled. "I'm sorry for your loss. Losing a friend can't be easy."

"Billy is the reason I wanted to chat."

Otto tugged at his backpack straps. "Okay. What did you wanna know?"

"What was his demeanor during his last few days?"

"No disrespect, but it was hard to tell. The school year just barely begun before he killed himself."

"Fair enough."

The stench of smoke wafted through the air, stinging my nostrils. Three guesses as to where the smell came from as a result of how I'd seen Otto light up cigarettes numerous times on campus.

I couldn't judge Otto, though. Remembering the real reason for chatting with Otto proved more important than getting a good night sleep. I also wouldn't get anywhere if I lectured him about smoking.

"I don't mean to bother you. I'm just hoping to get some sort of closure," I said.

"No worries. You aren't bothering me. Because you just didn't lose a friend. You lost your on-again-off-again boyfriend."

My eyebrows swung upward. "You knew?"

"You would've had to have been oblivious not to realize he liked romantic attention wherever he got it."

"But he never came out."

"You have his conservative father to thank for that."

Ouch. Another reminder of how the world was far from perfect. Otto's comment the last thing that would've made me whistle across campus. And no need for contemplating whether the thought sounded too preachy. Some truisms deserved consideration—whether verbal or mental—because of their profound truth they revealed. In Billy's case, his father should've accepted him for who he was.

"Yeah, I know," I said. "Anyway, I need to ask you something else, and I apologize if it's upsetting, it just needs to be dealt with."

"Go ahead."

Smart move. Being prepared to argue and actually arguing were two different things. No reason existed why I should've been tempted to pull every last strand of hair from my head when a civil conversation was still possible.

"A friend of mine says some Charity Now members might've been in the woods on the south side of campus before Billy's note and sweater were discovered."

Yup. Subtleness only got people so far in life because I would have to be a little direct if I wanted to probe the matter more. It wasn't like I accused Otto or the rest of

Charity Now of murdering Billy, and making his death resemble a suicide. Nope. Even I wasn't that ballsy—at least not without more proof.

He hung his head lower. "I was the one who discovered the note and sweater."

"Really?"

"Yup. But the police and school administration didn't release that fact because they wanted to give me privacy since I'm a minor."

"Okay. But you didn't answer my question," I said.

Otto's lips curled—almost as if what he was about to say was worse than eating something sour. "Yes, we were in the woods on the south side of campus before Billy's sweater and the suicide note were discovered. Hell, we even ran into Billy. However, there was no indication of him being upset."

"Even though Billy was kicked out of the club and Dean became president?"

He snorted. "I didn't realize you were a detective. Besides, him leaving the club wasn't personal. Billy just wasn't a good fit for the club."

"I'm just trying to understand. He's gone, and I can't make sense of any it. I mean, it's not like I think he'll come back from the dead."

"Sometimes it's best to let go."

Perhaps Otto and Amanda were friends. Because they could've fooled me. It was like they shared the same brain as a result of implying my effort was frivolous. At least Otto had a little more tact, though. He used the indirect approach whereas Amanda had no qualms about telling me what she thought.

"Thanks for telling me that you guys chatted with Billy," I said.

Appearing formal by thanking him wasn't about sounding like a character out of a nineteenth century novel or even resembling my grandmother. More people would've done well with sound formal every now and then. No rule or law said Otto had to indulge me in conversation, yet he had, and I wouldn't forget that fact. Especially if I needed to talk him further down my inquiry.

"No problem," he said.

"One more thing, though. Please don't tell anyone about our chat, especially not Dean. Causing trouble is the last thing I want."

Overzealous planning didn't just qualify me for most likely teen to get away with a murder. Covering myself was a matter of survival. Just because Dean hadn't provided more information didn't mean he didn't know things, and might be more useful in the future.

"Relax. I'm not stupid," Otto said.

***

TUESDAY, SEPTEMBER 22, 2020

Gray clouds remained stacked together in the sky while I sat on a bench on the south side of campus reading a book, yet blood wasn't shooting through my veins faster any faster even though a murder of crows cawed through the sky a moment ago. Getting out of my dorm room was sometime a good thing. Because I couldn't spend the several hours between my last class of the day ending and dinner in an empty room with just me and my possible overactive imagination.

Hands covered my eyes before I could contemplate the weather anymore and I almost jumped ten feet into the air.

"I'm sorry," Dean said after removing his hands. "I was just joking."

"It's fine. Just don't do it again."

Leniency didn't make me wimpy—it was only fair. Being raped might've meant having a less favorable attitude towards surprised, but Dean didn't know about what happened between Jonathan and I in addition to how I couldn't have a meltdown over every little event. Pretending to be a strong person might even make the idea stick because of the concept of faking it until making it. I couldn't even remember the last time a bitter feeling lingered in my mouth because of my mind drifting back to Jonathan restraining me against the tree while his body jerked forward, and his moaning and groaning continued while he was so close to me that his mouthwash scented breath didn't just rub against my skin. His sweat dripped onto me too.

Dean sat next to me on the wooden bench. "Anyway, I wanted to get your opinion about something."

"Sure. You can ask me anything."

"I was wondering if you'd like to go out on a date with me."

Too bad I couldn't get one minute of reprieve from life's complications. Because Amanda's offhanded comment about Dean maybe falling me for me couldn't come true. Even if I was less oblivious to the possibility because of how we danced together at the Barn party the other day.

My lips quivered. "Dean…"

"Sorry. Was my question out of line?"

"I just haven't thought about dating in a while."

"Don't worry about it. Forget I asked. It was a silly idea, and I'm sorry if I offended you; just please know I meant no harm." Dean stood.

"Please don't go," I said, grabbing his hand.

Touching him wasn't about sending mixed signals. Used sparingly, physical contact had a place in life. Dean couldn't think I was robotic because not dating him didn't preclude me from being friends with him or us hanging out.

He exhaled a long breath. "If you aren't interested, then I shouldn't waste our time."

"We can still be friends."

"I knew about you and Billy, and how you weren't just friends," he blurted. "I mean, it was kind of obvious because of how you two spent so much time together.

"Excuse me?"

Yup. Just because Otto clued me in about how my "relationship" wasn't as secret as Billy might've thought it was didn't mean the muscles around my lips couldn't be a pinched constipated expression. That was just what happened when a "relationship" never got the opportunity to thrive in public.

"I didn't mention that to upset you. You just need to know that I'm here if you ever need to talk. No judgement. I might not have lost a boyfriend, but I did lose my grandfather in the seventh grade, and it sucked."

"I'm sorry to hear that, but thanks. I appreciate the support."

"Don't mention it. However, I have to give you something first." Dean unzipped his backpack before yanking out a pen, his notebook, and tearing a sheet out. He then jotted something down on it, and handed the paper.

I surveyed the sheet. "What's this?"

"My cellphone number, and you can call it anytime you want. No pressure. We could grab a coffee or go clubbing if you ever feel like going off campus."

"I'll keep that in mind. I do have one question for you, though. Why are you so drawn to me?"

His shrugged. "I don't know. I just want something different."

"Makes sense."

Humoring Dean about his interest in me proved harmless. Knowing how he thought would be invaluable because I would be able to handle him better—and the thought had nothing to do with malicious. It was just a fact. If I could avoid trouble, then I would.

"Have a good day," he said.

"Wait!" I said when Dean almost scurried out of earshot.

He titled his head. "Did you forget something?"

I got up, then darted towards Dean, and gave him a quick hug. Yup. I had to be a little bit of a tool regardless of the tingling sensation in my stomach. It wasn't like I kissed him—or worse, slept with him. He just needed to leave with a positive impression.

"What was that for?" he asked after we detached from our embrace.

"For not judging me, and offering support without any hesitation."

"No thanks necessary."

"Anyway, I've gotta do a couple of things, but please call at some point. Or hell, strike up a conversation with me in class."

"Will do."

Dean shuffled away without another word, but the emptiness in my stomach only grew. Just because I couldn't alienate Dean didn't mean I enjoyed faking sincerity. A good chance existed that we might've even dated if circumstances were different.

Shit. I should've known better than to have the type of thought I just had. Entertaining the idea of Dean and I being friends for even one second only meant trouble. Sure. Dean couldn't think I was robotic, yet I still had to be robotic on the inside. Getting answers about Billy's death was what mattered, not finding my next boyfriend.

"Still cozying up to Dean?" Amanda asked after her, Chelsea, and Freddie approached me.

No offense to Amanda, but she should've known mentioning Dean was a bad idea if she (or even Chelsea and Freddie) were going to give me grief about how I needed to accepted Billy was dead. My friends didn't have to mention the Billy issue every second of every day in order for a possible conflict to exist. Just the idea of Amanda's disapproval meant more conflict could ensue. It wasn't like she magically changed into a different person since first finding out about my theory. So, I'd have to be careful. I couldn't lose both Billy and my friends.

"It's not what it seems like," I said.

"Sure," Freddie said.

Chelsea's hair bounced after a gust of wind howled. "We should leave the issue alone. If Carson wants a new friend, boyfriend, or girlfriend, then that's his business."

Way to go Chelsea. And my opinion had nothing to do with seeming like I was too polite. Just because my sexuality didn't always need mentioning, didn't preclude Chelsea, Amanda, Freddie, or anyone else who knew I was bisexual from making an inclusive statement. Chelsea's comment just illustrated how the remark didn't have to be serious. Just a little statement that didn't erase my identity like how they would've been pissed if someone tried changing their "straightness."

"How were classes today, guys?" I asked.

Amanda crossed her arms. "Nice try, but you can't change the subject that easily. We need to talk about the Dean thing."

"What happened to keeping your opinion to yourself?" I asked.

"I changed my mind," Amanda said.

Forget about only Amanda having to choose her next words with more care than a neurosurgeon making an incision during brain surgery. Watching what I said next would've behooved me too. Having an opinion was one thing. But no reason existed for me to alienate Amanda—not when neither of us had said something that couldn't be taken back.

Chelsea pulled at the ends of her scarf, which had the dozens of Santa Clauses etched on it. "We should go off campus to Starbucks and grab coffee. There's nothing like a good coffee to make life less stressful."

Amanda's nostrils flared. "Not this time."

"For your information, Amanda, I'm not full of shit," I said. "I recently discovered Otto and other Charity

Now members weren't just in the woods before Billy's sweater and suicide note were discovered. They talked to him."

Nope. I wasn't going to lie to myself in this moment. A small amount of glee radiated from my body as a result of being the one to give Amanda a "lesson" since I was privy to information she wasn't.

Amanda scoffed. "That doesn't mean his death wasn't a suicide."

"Look, I'm sorry that you don't like Billy because you slept with him one night during freshman year, and he never talked to you again. But I deserve answers," I said.

"Why are you so intent on idolizing a guy who treated you like shit? Have you forgotten all the times he dicked you around?" Amanda asked.

Nope. Amanda couldn't have said what she just did. Doing so meant getting into more trouble, and Amanda had to have been smarter than that.

"Chelsea's right. We should all go to Starbucks in addition to venting about how our teachers give us too much homework," Freddie said.

Sure. No reason existed about doubting Freddie, yet we were a little beyond coffee. Intellectualizing not starting trouble and defending myself were two separate issues. Amanda's behavior couldn't go unchecked. Not this time. Not when she brought the criticism upon herself since she had to have her way with proving she was right. Being my friend meant she wasn't my parent, and shouldn't have bothered correcting my flaws.

I pointed my right index finger at Amanda. "You wanna know why I give a flying fuck about Billy despite all his bullshit? Because he was there for me after I told him Jonathan raped me."

"What did you just say?" Amanda asked.

She really should've known better than to steal one of my trademark comments. Surprise wouldn't make her less than favorable attitude okay. I annunciated when I dropped the Jonathan bombshell on her, and that meant no excuse existed for her response. She hadn't experienced someone demanding she took her clothes only to pin her against a tree and force himself inside her moments later. Nope. That was me.

"You heard me," I said through gritted teeth.

Freddie's jaw twitched. "Jonathan really raped you?"

"Yup. Around the time you and I sat under the tree last November and I bitched about Billy blowing me off," I said.

"I'm so sorry, Carson," Freddie said.

Chelsea rubbed her right cheek. "I can't believe that happened to you."

"We could've helped you. Why didn't you come to us?" Amanda demanded.

Amanda once again needed to check herself. There was no way that she could've been making my trauma about her. That option wasn't just misguided; it was foolish. Because I couldn't imagine her being happy if I was so insensitive to her.

"We're here for you now," Freddie said. "Anything. Just name it."

"It's too late because the damage is already done. But you know what really stinks? I never judged you for sleeping with Billy, Amanda. Even when you harped on it for several weeks." Holding back my tears wasn't only about not wanting passing students to witness my pain. I couldn't allow myself to be weak about anything—no matter how justified my anger was. Wallowing in my own despair just created an empty feeling no matter what way I spun the situation. "But you know what? I'll see you guys around."

Walking away at a brisk clip might've been a trademark soap opera move, yet even dramatic television shows had merit. There was just no other reaction worth having. Especially in light of the rain pattering against the ground, and how I didn't have an umbrella or raincoat with me since sunlight still shined when I first sat down on the bench earlier. I could either have my clothes be drenched in water or I could be pissed off. But I couldn't have both. That would've just been too cruel.

THEN

SUNDAY, NOVEMBER 10, 2019

I shuffled by the rust coated gate on the north side of campus while rays of sunlight beamed from the sky.

Yeah. I wasn't delirious; I got up at seven o'clock on the weekend. Something exciting existed from having alone time before people flocked around campus, en route to their various activities.

Except I shouldn't have counted on the universe letting my life remain drama free while I walked across the grass and past some the various academic buildings. Billy held Jonathan by his shirt collar in the distance in front of a maple tree, yet it wasn't only Billy's tightened grip that caused my blinking. Billy kept punching Jonathan's nose, and small specs of blood stained the left side of Jonathan's otherwise pale face.

"What's going on?" I asked after rushing towards

them.

Billy lifted his gaze off Jonathan. "You shouldn't be here, Carson."

"Why are you doing this?" I asked.

Billy chuckled at me. "I couldn't let Jonathan get away with raping you."

Deep breaths might not have guaranteed a perfect life since problems would always exist. However, focusing on my breathing was the only thing I could do. A good chance existed that I might've screamed if I didn't relax. Sure. Billy meant well by defending my reputation and beating the shit out of Jonathan. But I told him about what happened with Jonathan in confidence. Besides, I was the rape victim; not Billy. And that meant handling the situation was my prerogative, not Billy's prerogative.

Jonathan rolled his eyes. "Rape is a pretty strong word. Carson was begging me to fuck him."

An elephant might as well have crushed my windpipe.

Doing something despicable was one thing, but Jonathan shouldn't have lied. Jonathan was the one who lured me into the woods under the guise of talking alone. Jonathan was the one who heckled me into taking off my clothes. Jonathan was the one who pushed me against the tree and told me to spread my legs. Jonathan was the one who rammed into me without any warning while profuse amounts of sweat dripped down my back. Damn. And I only thought Jonathan might've just been a little skeevy. There was just no way my classmate was a rapist. Not someone who always wore a tie, buttoned down shirt, blazer, frayed belt, khaki pants, argyle socks, and either loafers or black dress shoes when he wasn't required to do so. Hating someone was a lot easier when said person had yellow teeth—or even missing teeth—an unshaven cheeks and neck, a foul stench coming from him, ripped clothing, or was lazy.

"You bastard." Billy decked Jonathan in the nose

again without flinching.

"Go ahead. Give it your best shot. But you'll be expelled when I tell the headmaster about this," Jonathan said.

Billy shrilled at Jonathan. "Fat chance.

"Yeah. You can't prove I did anything bad," Jonathan said.

"I can always lie and say that I saw the whole encounter, but was too afraid to do anything," Billy said.

I laughed, yet the reflex didn't make me morbid. The reaction made me human. People often couldn't help their reactions. I couldn't have predicted that Billy's theatrics would've amused me. Concocting a phony story was the type of thing someone did on a nighttime soap opera, not in real life.

"You'd really do that?" Jonathan asked. "Being in Charity Now means we're brothers."

"A real brother doesn't let his brother get away with rape," Billy said.

Jonathan pouted. "Fine. I won't tell the headmaster about you beating the shit out of me if you two will keep quiet about that night."

Billy looked at me, and I nodded. Speechlessness once again couldn't be avoided. Exerting too much energy about Jonathan would've only made me crawl into a fetal position in the corner of my dorm room. A person could only handle so many difficult situations at once before having an emotional meltdown.

"Okay," Billy said. "But you better leave Carson alone, including if he ever goes to a party at the Barn. Because if you even so much as sneeze in his direction, then you won't have to worry about Carson and I going to the police. Instead, I'll take a blowtorch to your balls and dick and burn them off."

Jonathan might've deserved every bad thing that happened to him for the rest of his life, yet even my body shook at Billy's comment. Threatening to burn someone's dick and balls off wasn't even the type of fucked up situation one would see on some cable television show that was rated TVMA. A small amount of glee rushed through my body for one fleeting moment, though—even if violence wasn't ideal. The scent of burnt flesh trickling through the air meant Jonathan would never be able to have sex again. Even the thought of him never using his dick again made me almost throw a party.

"Fine," Jonathan said.

Billy released Jonathan, and Jonathan's back thudded onto the grass where he remained for a beat before getting ready to stand. However, Billy unzipped his fly, and Jonathan studied his crotch—almost as if Billy would be Jonathan's next victim.

"I hope you like piss, Jonathan." Billy peed on Jonathan's face, yet Jonathan didn't wince. He remained on the ground with his back arched a couple of inches off the grass. Billy's zipper then squeaked as one jerk of his hand zipped up his pants. "You can go now, asshole!"

Jonathan stood—without even brushing the dust or dirt off his clothes—before running away. He was soon out of sight.

Billy's lips curled. "I hope you aren't angry."

Wow. Billy could've won a Nobel Peace for self-awareness as a result of how most teens wouldn't have been aware about the ramifications of a negative behavior.

"Forget about it," I said.

Forgiving Billy proved best.

Punishing Jonathan might not have been his place, but I would've been lying if I said I never contemplated Jonathan raping me again. If he raped me once, then there was no stopping him from repeating said action. Because Jonathan didn't have to say Billy succeeded for me to know Billy succeeded. Some emotions couldn't be faked no matter how good a liar someone was—there was no feigning the look of horror in Jonathan's eyes.

"Really?" Billy asked.

"Yes. It's nice that someone defended me. However, don't let the outburst happen again, though."

Yup. I qualified my statement. Billy might not have been blatantly mean to me, but I couldn't seem weak—especially since I still hadn't gotten a read on Billy's personality. Because he could spin as many stories as he wanted, but neither one story nor ten stories changed how he acted evasive towards me. People just didn't change into new people overnight regardless of how many mitigating factors existed—like with Billy's father revealing they had to cut back on money as a result of losing his hedge fund job.

"I don't know what I would've done if you hadn't stopped by my room on Friday night," I said.

"I hope that's not your way of saying you're suicidal?"

"No. I just meant I would've sulked in bed."

"Okay…"

"How did you even get Jonathan up at this hour?" I asked.

Billy smirked. "I texted him, and told him I could use a friend to chat with. And the move was genius. The brotherhood of Charity Now means never blowing someone off."

Maybe, just maybe, Billy would win an Oscar. Telling a fib was one thing, yet having no visceral reaction proved he was the type of person who could spin a story. Concocting phony scenarios just wasn't normal behavior for most teens as a result of the convoluted level of behavior doing so included.

"Cool. Anyway, would you want to grab breakfast at the dining hall?" I asked.

"I would love that, but I'm just going to have breakfast in my dorm room. How about a raincheck, though?"

"Sure. And thanks again for everything."

"Don't worry about it. But don't please don't fret

because I can't hang out with you this morning." Billy glanced around our surroundings, but nobody else was in sight—not even public safety or another student who might've gotten up early. His lips grazed my right ear. "Because I've been thinking about those three kisses all weekend."

Damn. My pediatrician needed to prescribe pills for me if the commotion of Billy and Jonathan fighting erased the three kisses from my mind. I was way too young for memory problems. In fact, maybe I would start taking my vitamins again on a regular basis in hopes of them also boosting my memory.

"Good. Because I'd hate to think I bored you," I said while my heart fluttered Making out with guys and girls in the past still didn't compare to how Billy brushed up against me. The fact that blood pumped through my body so fast that I no longer felt my fingers and legs proved my chemistry with Billy wasn't something that only existed in my head.

"Never." He pulled away from me. Then, scanned our immediate surroundings. Nope. Nobody else was around. Not even a chipmunk, squirrel, or gust of wind pushing a pile of leaves against the luscious, green grass. Billy wrapped his hands around my face before giving me a quick peck on the lips. But I must've been dreaming. Guys like me didn't get moments of happiness.

"There," Billy said a couple of minutes later. "Now you have a little something to hold you over till our short story class on Tuesday."

Billy strutted away from me.

I moved my fingers around my mouth—almost as if the soft texture of Billy's lips lingered. Although I couldn't lie. At least not to myself. Not even a kiss stopped my head from shaking as a result of Billy being unable to take twenty minutes for me by eating a quick breakfast in the dining hall. Almost as if he was once again the guy who blew me off last Monday in addition to parading a girl in front of me.

***

MONDAY, NOVEMBER 11, 2019

I scrolled through *Twitter* on my iPhone while standing in front of a door on the first floor of one of the academic buildings. Except a glass vase could've fallen onto the floor, and I would've been the only one to grip my chest. Apparently, it wasn't cool to be in the academic buildings once classes were done for the day.

The door opened a few students trekked out of the classroom I stood in front of. Including Chelsea who waved at the redhead before the girl dashed away in the opposite direction.

Chelsea giggled. "Maybe you need a new pocket watch like the White Rabbit in *Alice and Wonderland*. Chess Club starts at 2:20 P.M., not 3:20 P.M."

"I didn't come for Chess Club."

"Then why are you here? There's still plenty of time before dinner."

"I needed to chat about Billy. You're the only who won't judge me."

"Anyway, my advice would not be to overthink. The point is, Billy kissed you and said he was looking forward to seeing you tomorrow," Chelsea said while her arm remained linked around mine a couple of minutes later while we strolled across the grass.

Yup. I hadn't misspoken. Chelsea might've been dating Freddie, but she was still my friend. And that entailed being comfortable with showing platonic affection. It wasn't like Chelsea and I ever kissed.

"Yeah. You're probably right. I'm my own worst enemy, "I said."

"Don't be too hard on yourself, Carson. You're a baby when it comes to dating."

"Good point. So, how was Chess Club? Did you learn any good moves?" I asked.

"Not really. We're just getting ready for a big tournament with a rival school in a couple of weeks."

"Hopefully, you guys will win."

"We better," Chelsea said.

Whether Chelsea knew the truth or not, her personality provided humor. One wouldn't expect someone to both be fun and involved in something serious. The two traits just didn't go together since I couldn't even fathom what winning Chess must've entailed. Playing chess wasn't like playing a card game. A person had to think several moves ahead if he or she wanted to win. And that was the type of thing most people might not have been capable of—even if someone was smarter than the average person.

"Also, I hope you don't think I'm trying to self-sabotage myself by questioning Billy's motives. I just can't help myself since I'm a writer," I said.

"Stop apologizing for being your own authentic self. Not all writers are quirky. But you are, and you need to own that trait by being the best quirky version of yourself that you can be."

"Good point."

"No use in inventing a problem that doesn't exist," Chelsea said.

I made eye contact with her while nearby pigeons clapped their wings together before flying away. "Are you the best Chess player on your team?"

"You know it."

Freddie put his hands on his hips after making a beeline for us. "Should I be concerned?"

"Good to know you're developing a sense of humor," Chelsea said.

"What were you guys talking about?" Freddie asked.

"You do know that being bisexual doesn't mean I want to hump everything that moves, right?" I asked.

Freddie exploded into laughter. "I know. Chelsea was right with her initial comment. I'm just messing with you, because I know you two would never betray me like that."

Great. At least I had one less problem because of Freddie's comment. It didn't matter how much someone liked teasing. The fuzziest line between a joke and reality always lingered because of the power of suggestion. Nothing might've been going on with Chelsea and I, yet all she had to do was make one comment for Freddie to cut her out of his life for good. Humans were insecure creatures, and doubt therefore proved more powerful than a gun or knife.

"Damn straight," Chelsea said.

Freddie's grin expanded—as if that were even possible. "Although feel free to share what you guys were talking about."

Perhaps Freddie should've dropped out of school and went to the nearest police academy. A detective didn't just need good observational skills. A cop also needed determination. Watching old *Law and Order* reruns with my mother when I was younger meant inferring how some murder investigations wouldn't just be difficult in terms of pinpointing a suspect. They would also be horrific in terms of both the specific case details and what the truth uncovered. Because it didn't matter if television wasn't "real." The point was, a television show still revealed occasional wisdom by emulating an emotional truth despite being fiction.

"Sorry, Freddie, but gay guys aren't the only ones who need a straight girl best friend. Bisexual guys also need a straight girl best friend," Chelsea said.

Freddie gave us a mock frown. "Fine. Be that way. Anyway, what are you guys up to?"

"We were gonna do tequila shots back in my dorm room," Chelsea said. "Want to join?"

"She's joking," I interrupted. "We were just gonna

hang until dinner."

"Boring. Let's skip the dining hall tonight, and order a couple of pizzas. My treat," Freddie said.

Chelsea and I shook our heads at Freddie. No need to ponder Freddie's offer for too long. Pizza would always be a good choice.

"Although we should text Amanda and see if she wants to join us," Freddie said.

"She can't. She has a Biology test tomorrow," I said.

***

TUSEDAY, NOVEMBER 12, 2019

"Hi, Carson," Billy said after strutting into the classroom and grabbing the desk next to mine in the front row.

"You having a good day?" I asked.

Billy took off his backpack from his shoulders before shoving on the floor under his desk. "I am. What about you? Everything good?"

Smart guy. Because I could've only imagined how some people wouldn't have had the same tact—even though a few other chairs were occupied by fellow students—and might've asked directly about my rape.

"I can't complain," I said.

"That's good to hear.

"I'm just glad I'm not in science or math class."

"Same," Billy said.

A few more students stepped into the classroom before picking seats in back, which almost appeared bizarre. A short story class should've been something students look forward to, not dread—even if it still counted as a class. It wasn't like we had any tests or quizzes. Nope. Class just consisted of reading one short story each class and then three or four students sharing an in progress short story, revised short story, or new short story.

Footsteps echoed, and I looked up. A lady in high heels sauntered into the classroom, and now stood by the wooden desk in front of the whiteboard. But no legitimate reason for fear existed despite how formal attire—including what shoes someone wore—proved cringe worthy for some. Mrs. Roberts always had high heels even though a creative writing class would always be less formal than a math, science, or history class.

Mrs. Roberts rubbed her hands together after squealing. "Good afternoon, students!"

"Is it really a good afternoon, Mrs. Roberts?" piped one of the guys in the back of the classroom.

"Yes. It's a good afternoon because you know my one classroom rule. No being a buzzkill," Mrs. Roberts said.

Too bad the headmaster or other school official hadn't been near the door when Mrs. Roberts made her comment. They would've just loved her referring to a classroom matter in terms of whether or not said thing was a buzzkill. The headmaster and school administration had to at least pretend that the students didn't drink and party during their free time. Because they so should've advertised how they didn't care about the partying, drugs, or alcohol so long as they did it in secret in the school's brochure.

"Sorry," said the guy. "But I can't help wondering if you've taken too many 'happy' pills today, Mrs. Roberts."

Billy and I stole a glance with each other regardless of how some people might've thought Sal's comment was more than a little rude. There was no way somebody was naturally so happy, though, proving every single person in our class really must've wondered if Mrs. Roberts was taking pills—even if most wouldn't have vocalized the question.

"As I was saying, nothing can kill my mood. We're at the point in the semester when it'll be time for you guys to partner up, pick a story we haven't read, and do a brief presentation about why said story informs your writing craft," Mrs. Robert said. "Anyway, go ahead and pick your partners. That's not my job."

I scanned the room while desks scraped across the ground. However, I just remained seated. Mrs. Roberts might've insisted on this assignment falling under the group work category, but maybe, just maybe, I would be able to work alone. It wasn't like I could ask Billy. Seeming desperate would've only created another reason for staying up later than I should've each night.

A girl approached Billy. "Would you like to work together?" she asked.

"I appreciate the offer, but I want to work with Carson. Maybe next time, though," Billy said.

Not knowing whether I should've hugged Billy or slapped him was the question of the day. Billy did me a kindness, yet I couldn't forget about this comment's ambiguous subtext. He shouldn't have offered a next time if he wasn't serious. Life was too short for bullshit.

I couldn't chastise Billy too much, though. In this moment, he gave me something I needed without any questions, and only a fool would've ignored the beauty of simplicity.

Billy winked at me. "Should we work at your place or mine?"

NOW

WEDNESDAY, SEPTEMBER 23, 2020

Dean touched my shoulder. "No offense, but you don't look like you're having fun."

Being obvious didn't make Dean clever, yet I couldn't criticize him for his response while I sat at a table, staring at my pizza, in front of one of the glass dining hall windows. He was correct. There was no easy way to say that life would always be more complicated than it should've been. I was only 17 years old, and should've been concerned with school work, SAT prep, thinking about colleges, and partying; not about how my best friends were unreliable.

"Yeah," I mumbled.

His eyebrows shot up. "Mind if I join you?"

"Sure."

Dean sat down at my table while the scent of

warm cheese, tomatoes, and other herbs wafted through the air. Yet my taste buds weren't electrified when I bit into the pizza. Nope. No amount of decent food would make the empty feeling in my stomach okay. I wasn't a robot, and couldn't pretend I was fine.

Dean chuckled. "Good to know I'm not the only one who eats dinner before it's officially served."

Yup. Dean wasn't mistaken. Dinner could still be eaten at 4:30 P.M. despite how the official serving time was 5:00 P.M. The dining hall often put the food out early, and I would've been out of my mind not to consider eating early today. Running into Amanda, Freddie, and Chelsea just couldn't happen.

"I wanna apologize." Dean munched on a bite of his salad. "I never meant to come on so strong."

I inhaled a breath. "Don't worry about it because you didn't cross a line. I can tell the difference between you and a predator."

My comment was completely accurate. Sure. Dean's self-awareness might've been refreshing compared to most of our fellow classmates, yet he was a little too hard on himself. Pursuing something more with Dean might've only complicated my life as a result of me trying to unravel the truth about Billy's death. However, Dean never made me squirm like Jonathan did.

"Do you wanna talk about it?" he asked.

"Nope."

"That's cool."

"But I do have one question, and I don't want you to take it the wrong way. I'm just curious."

"Okay. Shoot."

"Why are you so drawn to me?" I asked.

Dean shrugged. "I don't know. I'm just looking for something different."

***

THURSDAY, SEPTEMBER 24, 2020

I scurried out one of the academic buildings while gray clouds remained shoved together in the sky.

No need for a heart attack, though. A difference existed between the numerous gray clouds and a tornado. Besides, the writer in me couldn't criticize dreary weather. Rainy weather was the type of setting that added atmosphere to a story, especially when writing a murder mystery. Whether other writers realized the truth or not, universal details weren't cliché. Inclement weather might've been a boring, but the story's unique details were what mattered. In my opinion, that was.

"We need to talk," Freddie said while he, Amanda, and Chelsea accosted me in front of a tree.

Shit. Life couldn't be simple for one fleeting moment. I so needed to have more drama. It wasn't as if I experienced enough drama to last several lifetimes. Nope. That wasn't the case, and I prayed the universe would make life as fucked up as possible.

I scoffed. "I have nothing to say."

"Then let us talk," Chelsea said.

My nails dug into my backpack straps harder— almost as if any distraction would make my life better. "Then you must be smoking something. You'd be out of your fucking mind if you thought we would ever chat."

Amanda played with a strand of her hair. "We feel really bad about what Jonathan did to you, and want to help."

Sorry, Amanda. Caring less about what you said or thought proved best. The time to help me was when I brought up my concerns about Billy's death not being suicide. My original thought remained true because I deserved to test my hypothesis—especially if I wasn't harming anyone by doing so.

"I didn't tell you about Jonathan for sympathy," I spat.

The bitchiness in my tone didn't make me cruel; adding attitude to my response made me practical. Standing by my principles was the least I could. It wasn't like I had anything else to lose.

Freddie's face drooped. "That's not what we're saying."

"This might shock you, but I don't need you guys," I said. "I don't wish bad on you in addition to not scheming against you, but I don't want to know you. I don't deserve to be gaslighted because you guys are supposed to give me the benefit of the doubt when nobody else will."

Chelsea swallowed the lump in her throat. "We're serious. Jonathan should pay for what he did to you, and we're gonna help."

I yelled at them. "Unless you can take back that night, I'm not interested. None of you will understand how it feels to lose complete control in a situation that isn't your fault."

Not budging with my friends was best. Maybe, just maybe, we could become friends again in a vague, distant future. But not today. Not when I had zero fucks to give. They weren't the ones who were held against a tree with a cold sensation washing over them as a result of Jonathan's icy hands.

"Please let us help," Freddie said.

"Not interested," I said.

Chelsea looked me in the eye. "You need a support system after everything you've been through."

Footsteps pounded against the ground while various students continued trickling by. "Is this a bad time?" asked a guy.

"No. It's a perfect time, Otto. They were just leaving," I said.

Amanda grunted at me. "Fine. But this conversation isn't over. No matter what differences we have, you can't push us away."

"Watch me," I said.

Amanda, Freddie, and Chelsea left without another word, and were soon out of sight. Yet Otto just continued standing in silence, which was almost enough of a reason to fret more. Keeping me in suspense was just what I wanted.

"What's up?" I asked.

Politeness didn't make me a hypocrite even though some people might've thought my visceral reaction should've matched the rage jerking through my body right now. Otto still belonged to Charity Now, and that meant he might be useful about getting to the bottom of Billy's death.

"I was wondering if you'd want to visit my dorm room at some point," Otto said.

"I don't understand. Are you trying to proposition me?"

"No. It's just that Billy's parents never moved his shit out of my room in addition to how the administration won't budge. So, I thought you might want a memento to remember him by."

"His stuff is still in your dorm room?" I asked.

"That's what I said."

"Sorry. I didn't mean to sound so stupid. I just can't believe his stuff wasn't cleared out."

"Me too. Anyway, what do you say?"

I nodded. "Sure. A memento would be great."

Yup. Otto's question was the easiest thing I ever answered. And my reasoning wasn't even because of the nights I still stared at my ceiling while Billy weighed on my mind. Going through Billy's stuff might provide with me a clue, and I therefore would've been stupid to waste the opportunity. Almost as if I was a drowning victim, and could either except help from a rescuer or die in stubbornness.

"Great," Otto said. "You can stop by whenever, just text me first to make sure I'm there. Hopefully, you still have my cellphone number from Geometry last year?”

“Yup, I do.”

***

FRIDAY, SEPTEMBER 25, 2020

“No offense, but I would’ve expected to win the lottery before you texted about hanging out,” Dean said.

Too much flattery would’ve been a mistake, yet I needed to take a moment and I appreciate what Dean said. He could’ve been bolder with his response. But he hadn’t. He just danced around my reluctance to be anything more than casual acquaintances.

I fidgeted in my chair while we sat in back of the local Starbucks in town. “That makes two of us.”

“Why’d you want to meet?” Dean slurped on his Iced Coffee before nibbling on a bite of the chocolate chip cookie we shared.

“I owe you an apology.”

Yeah. I hadn’t been injected with a mysterious virus that effected my cognitive function. I meant what I said, and Dean needed to know the truth. Well, at least a version of the truth. Spin always exited no matter how honest somebody might’ve been.

“For what?” Dean asked.

“I haven’t been honest with you about why I rebuffed your advances.”

“It’s fine. You don’t owe me any explanations,” he said.

“Yes, I do.” I sipped my Iced Caramel Macchiato, and the mixture of the bitter espresso flavor and sweet caramel flavors still jolted my tongue even though I hadn’t ordered the hot version of the beverage.

Dean shook his head. “You’re mistaken. You haven’t done anything wrong.”

“I’m gonna tell you about something that happened to me, and you've gotta promise you won't tell anyone. Not the headmaster, not a teacher, and definitely not your parents."

He crossed his fingers. "Sure. I'd never break your confidence."

Okay. Good to know Dean was capable of keeping a secret. Because overly moralistic people would always make disapproval radiate from my body. Doing the right thing might've been great in a perfect world, but one only needed to watch the news to realize life wasn't perfect.

I wailed. "The reason why I've been evasive isn't because of you. It's because of Jonathan."

"Huh?"

"Jonathan raped me at one of the Barn parties last year." I grabbed a napkin from the dispenser resting on the table, and wiped my eyes. Because it didn't matter if I told the story once or one-hundred times. Being violated would never be okay, and I needed to allow myself to feel whatever I felt.

His jaw lowered. "Are you kidding me?"

Criticizing Dean for the shock fluttering through his body would've been unfair. My comment might not have been news to me, but I wasn't an idiot, and appreciated how some people might've been more sensitive to issues than others. And that included how someone reacted to finding out about a rape. In my case, Dean's soap opera like reaction was best. Not being able to fathom such a despicable situation provided hope that Dean might've been a good person despite now being the president of Charity Now.

"I wish I was," I said.

"I didn't realize Jonathan isn't straight."

"People do depraved things regardless of their sexuality."

Dean guzzled down the rest of his beverage. "Of course. I didn't mean anything bad by comment. I just meant I never thought of Jonathan as someone that'd having sex with other men."

A grinding sound echoed—like the kind of noise someone expected from a tractor or vacuum cleaner. Yet I didn't have a tantrum about the loud sound. In this case, the nuisance was welcomed. A customer ordering a Frappuccino meant keeping winter and subsequent colder temperatures away. And that was more than worth celebrating. A shivering body would never be welcomed. Nothing good existed about the cold no matter how optimistic someone might've been.

"Anyway, now you know why I am the way I am," I said.

His elbows slid onto the table. "I apologize for putting you on the spot, but have you thought about reporting Jonathan?"

Dean might've framed his response with a kindness because of qualifying his statement, yet he should've known considered not saying what he just did. Reporting a rapist didn't mean life would be perfect. Nope. If anything, life would've become more complicated. I needed all of two seconds before figuring out the questions that would've been asked of me, such as: Did I flirt with him? Was I tipsy? Was I overreacting? Because the reality was, problems didn't have easy fixes.

I averted my gaze. "I just need to move on…"

"Why are you telling me this?"

"I like you, and want the opportunity to be more than friends. I just want it on my terms." I broke off a bit of the chocolate chip cookie, and ate it before my taste buds became electrified as a result of the mixture of the doughy, chocolate, buttery, and sweet flavors.

"Really?" he asked.

"Absolutely. Pardon the cliché, but I don't I need the truth to set me free."

Dean squeezed my hand. "I don't think you sound cliché at all. I think you sound genuine."

Shit. I didn't need to eat spicy food for the burning

sensation in my stomach. I wasn't an idiot, and could feel guilty about my comment. Life once again contained ambiguity. Being raped meant having reservations when dealing with new people, yet I still couldn't' forget about not wanting life to be more complicated as a result of blurring the lines between operation discover the truth about Billy's death and my interactions with Dean. My earlier opinion remained true. If any other situation, Dean and I would've been dating as a result of how he wasn't terrible to look at. Yet I had to be realistic. Going through Billy's stuff in Otto's dorm room meant priming Dean in case I needed to ask him more questions.

"Anyway," Dean continued. "How would you feel about going on a real date?"

"I'd like that."

"Great! However, don't look now, but you have a little something on your lips." Dean wet his finger, and wiped my upper lip.

A tingling sensation trickled through my body. Not being touched in a romantic way in a long time meant feeling the type of excitement that existed from waiting in line for hours to get an autograph from a favorite celebrity. Because I might as well have kissed Dean right here and now if he eye-fucked me.

"Thanks," I said after Dean pulled back.

"I hope that was okay?"

Respect would always be cherished, but Dean might've been spending too much time with me as a result of worrying. Being raped wasn't the same thing as never wanting to be touched again. Romance, love, intimacy, and sex weren't supposed to be terrible things. They were things that should've made my stomach do nonstop flips if said things were with the right person.

I raised my hand at him. "Stop. It was fine. I'll let you know if you offend me."

"Great. Anyway, what would you like to do for a first date?"

***

SATURDAY, SEPTMBER 26, 2020

Tears trickled down my face while I sat in the chair in front of Billy's wooden desk. No worrying necessary about someone seeing my vulnerability, though. Otto let me have my privacy to go through Billy's things because he was currently at the gym.

Flipping through Billy's diary, which was in the top desk drawer, was the first thing I did. But my body continued shaking. Sure. Nothing scandal worthy technically existed from his entries, yet I must have been drunk off my ass. The diary entries before Billy and I met were about his father accepting his sexuality, which was a big, fat fucking lie since he told me his father was super conservative.

***

SUNDAY SEPTMBER 27, 2020

I tapped my feet against the ground while I continued sitting on a bench on the south side of campus.

Not being in immediate physical danger didn't mean sweat couldn't tumble down my face while not even a public safety officer was around as a result of it only being eight o'clock in the morning, because it did. Meeting the person that I was about to chat with meant deserved credit as a result of me trying to be the better person.

"Sorry I'm late. I had to run an errand." Amanda handed me the Venti Starbucks cup before sitting down on the bench next to me.

"I only agreed to meet so you'd stop texting up a storm."

Yeah. I still wasn't smoking my clothing. Giving

someone what they wanted was easier than avoiding the person. Unless the situation involved sex. That scenario would've been different because I wouldn't give myself up so easily. Not after Jonathan.

"I don't care. The important thing is we're talking," she said.

"What's up?" I demanded.

Agreeing to meet with Amanda didn't guarantee politeness. It didn't matter if we had been friends for ages. Firmness would never go out of style since Amanda had a lot to make up for. I would've never treated her like she has treated me. Nope. Friendship would always be different than parenting someone, and that was a point she needed to comprehend ASAP. The idea was simple enough to understand because she didn't need a textbook to study the idea.

Amanda whimpered. "I implore you not to shut Chelsea, Freddie, and me out."

Maybe, just maybe, Amanda was destined for an Oscar. Her comment was the type of response someone would've expected in a more dramatic situation, yet she had no problem with making said remark during this conversation.

"And why should I do that? You're practically ready to declare me crazy because I don't think Billy committed suicide."

Amanda shook her head. "I don't care about that at the moment. I just want you to know I'm here for you. My cousin was raped, so I know it's not a joking matter. Not ever"

Perhaps I had a lot to learn about life. I never once considered how Amanda was a complicated person like me. Including how there must've been a bunch of stuff that I didn't know about her.

"I'm sorry to hear that, but I don't understand what you want from me?" I asked.

Amanda gripped my hand. "Just consider being

friends with Freddie, Chelsea, and me again."

***

"I can't believe you texted again so soon," Amanda said sometime later her, Chelsea, Freddie, and I sat a table in the dining hall.

Yeah. Amanda didn't need to get a grip on reality. Her, Chelsea, Freddie, and I were sharing a meal together. Even if someone should've questioned my sanity for meeting with them in light of everything that happened.

"Believe it." I cut off a piece of my chicken and I devoured the fried breadcrumbs in a matter of seconds.

Freddie snickered. "I wanna know what changed your mind."

No offense, but Freddie shouldn't have stated the obvious. I'd get to my point, and he, Chelsea, and Amanda just needed to give me time. I was the one who would've complain about someone else wasting my time.

Chelsea sipped her drink. "Me too."

"Did you really mean what you said about being there for me, Amanda?" I asked.

Amanda twisted a strand of hair around her fingers. "Absolutely."

"Okay. Well, here goes. Billy lied to me," I revealed.

Amanda cackled. "Are we supposed to be surprised?"

Freddie gave Amanda a dirty look. "Knock it off. Let's hear what Carson has to say before we judge him."

Thank goodness for Freddie, because he was correct. Amanda might not have been a serial killer, yet she should've watched what she said. My life wasn't a game, and my feelings deserved consideration. Because she could've typed her thoughts out in a text if she wanted to mock me.

"Billy's father was never conservative or homophobic," I said.

The comment resembled my rape in a small way, and I wasn't even talking about the possibility of Billy's comment hinting at a betrayal. The point was, the universe would never stop surprising me no matter how much contempt lingered in my body. Because I never once considered how Billy couldn't have been taken at face-value.

Chelsea shot me a confused look. "What's your point?"

"There was a lot about Billy that I didn't know," I said.

Amanda reached for my hand. "I'm sorry he was so dishonest. I know that must have been difficult for you."

No criticism necessary regardless of how obvious Amanda's comment was. At least she hadn't told me how to think or feel. Anything was an improvement from her acting like a nanny, and I wouldn't forget that point.

Chelsea giggled. "I don't mean to sound stupid, but I still don't get what your point is."

"Yes. The discovery had nothing to do with his death, but I'm not giving up. I didn't know everything about Billy, and would appreciate if you guys helped me."

Amanda, Freddie, and Chelsea exchanged a look with each other while my pulse echoed in my ears. They didn't have to tell me a family member died for my increased breathing. Every second that went by was another second I didn't know what their response would be. Asking them for help meant risking vulnerability, and they hopefully at least considered that point for one fleeting moment. Our friendship would've been for nothing if they weren't sensitive.

"I have no problem helping you if it means giving you closure," Amanda said.

"Me too," Freddie said.

"Freddie and Amanda are right. You deserve a fresh chapter in your life." Chelsea grabbed a French fry next to her hamburger, and dunked it in the ketchup she squirted onto her plate minutes earlier.

I smiled. "Thanks. You have no idea how much this means to me."

Yup. I was also capable of resembling a corny grandmother. Positive outcomes needed to be reinforced so they'd happen again.

"No problem. Besides, it's not like we could continue feuding for the rest of our lives," Amanda said. "Because you know I'd worry about you."

THEN

WEDNESDAY, NOVEMBER 13, 2019

"Thank goodness you don't have a roommate," Billy said.

We sat in wheelie chairs in front of my wooden desk while the blue waned from the sky outside. Although no shock existed from the sky almost being dark before five o'clock. This was fall, not summer.

I scrolled down on my laptop, which was on my desk. "Don't worry about it. Anyway, our project looks good."

"I never knew Roald Dahl wrote adult short stories."

Wow. Life once again offered more surprises than I realized because I knew something that Billy didn't, and that fact was worth calling every media outlet in the country. Billy might not have been a nerd, yet he didn't strike me as stupid. Guessing he might've known about more Roald Dahl (before today) therefore wouldn't have been unreasonable. But no. I had more control in this conversation, and a small amount of glee radiated from me because of that. I was almost never in control.

"They're better than his children books," I said.

"You're just full of surprises."

"I don't understand…"

"I never knew you were so smart."

Perhaps I should've been offended by Billy's comment. If I didn't know better, his remark implied I was dumb, and that was the last conclusion I wanted or needed. Just because I might not have been in same social strata as Billy, didn't meant I was useless. I wasn't. I just chose when to reveal myself. Like the one moment each week I participated in class. Because I wasn't like my fellow classmates who always raised their hands, craving a teacher's approval. No thanks. I wasn't in the blow job or asskissing business. My sense of worth had to come from myself. Someone's chattiness didn't mean that person was a better student. It only meant the person was a good bullshit artist. If a quiet student had an A average before class participation was factored in, but ended got a B while the person with a C+ average got a B+ when class participation was factored in, then that was bullshit.

"You have to be a reader if you want to be a writer," I said.

He snorted. "Okay…"

Yeah. No qualms existed about sounding corny. This conversation was when a silly statement contained a profound truth. Reading didn't just apply to classics—even a writer reading a book in the genre he or she wanted to write was enough. The point was, being well-read was comparable to someone in another field doing research as part of his or her job.

I arched my eyebrows. "Do you disagree?"

"Yes. But the only thing that matters is getting an

A on this presentation."

Smart guy. Some people wouldn't have been so graceful and might've caused an argument. Doing so wouldn't have helped either one of us since I couldn't imagine doing a class presentation with someone I got into a quarrel with—even a disagreement involving something insignificant.

"You mean A+," I said.

He elbowed me. "An A is the highest grade, smartass."

"I know. I was teasing."

"I just hope Mrs. Roberts won't be scared because of the short story we chose."

"'The Landlady' isn't a scary story."

"Speak for yourself," he said.

I drew in a breath. "Anyway, it was nice you worked with me instead of that other girl."

"No need to thank me. I know who the hotter person is."

Someone should've pushed me into a tub filled with cold water. Billy couldn't have called me hot. Because I had to be honest with myself despite my pulse roaring in my ears. What exactly was happening between Billy and I remained a mystery. I never once referred to Freddie, Amanda, or Chelsea as hot.

"Are we done?" I asked.

Billy closed my laptop before extending a hand, and parting a lock of my hair to the side. However, an increased pulse wasn't the only thought that popped into my mind. Billy's eyes once again remained glued to mine.

"Do you think that little of yourself that you'd wonder why I'd work with you?" Billy asked.

Yeah. Billy had a future as a psychic. He hadn't just had a gutsy thought, he actually verbalized it, and was correct.

I looked away. "Do you even have to ask?"

Shame shouldn't have been shooting through my

body, yet I couldn't help myself. Being a teenager meant imperfections.

He licked his lips. "You've got a lot to offer, and you better not forget it."

"I won't."

"Because you really are the hottest partner I've ever worked with on a school assignment." His lips brushed against mine, and my body tingled after the soft texture of his skin rubbed up against mine. His hands moved to my cheeks, and he even stuck his tongue in my mouth.

"Wow," I said after pulling back from him a couple of minutes later.

"Yeah. That was something."

Okay. Good to know we agreed about something. No explanation necessary how having different opinions about a kiss would've complicated life more. Ambiguity still only belonged in pop culture, as opposed to real life.

"So, would you like to go grab dinner in the dining hall?" I asked.

Shit. I should've known better than to ask a silly question—even if sharing a meal with someone was harmless most of the time. I couldn't do anything to make myself seem clingy or needy. I would've laughed if someone told about meeting someone off a dating app, and said person already talking about being in love before even having a first date.

He stood. "Sorry, but I have to go. Raincheck, though. Also, please don't forget to email the PowerPoint."

* * *

THURSDAY NOVEMBER 14, 2019

"I might've made a fool of myself," I said.

Chelsea cocked her head towards me while we continued sitting under a tree on the south side of campus while swaths of orange sunlight beamed from the sky. Although no students flocked by right now—almost as if they ran back to their dorm rooms the second their classes finished.

"You're gonna have to be more specific," she said.

"Never mind. Doesn't matter."

She plucked a loose eyelash. "Is it about Billy?"

Learning to be transparent was definitely a skill worth knowing. Not being perfect was one thing. Yet I couldn't have been so sloppy with how I projected myself that my feelings were clearer than a glass of water. It would've only been a matter of time before someone used my emotions against me.

"Good guess," I mumbled.

"Tell me whatever is you wanna tell me. You already know I won't judge you."

"We kissed again."

She smirked. "Perhaps you're a bigger sexual deviant than I realized."

Forget about reading people. Chelsea had a future writing an advice column in a newspaper or online. Not everyone would've had the guts to be so blunt, yet she hadn't even blinked when mentioning the sexual deviant part of her comment.

"Chelsea, please!" I exclaimed.

Yeah. Being best friends with someone wasn't mutually exclusive with having a racy conversation. There was blunt, and then there was Chelsea. Someone should've dared Chelsea to be so ballsy in front of a room packed full of adults.

"God. You're as bad as Freddie," she said. "Because if I had a dollar for every time that he said that, then you, me, Amanda, and him would be spend the rest of our lives in the South Pacific, drinking Mai-Tai's."

I laughed. "That wouldn't be so bad."

"My point is you need to worry less. Enjoy things for what they are. No offense, but you might be paying too much attention to things. Being consciousness is one thing.

However, not every little thing needs to be deconstructed."

Just because there weren't any students—or even teachers—wondering about nearby didn't mean this part of campus should've been labeled a ghost town. Several feral cats just darted across the grass in the distance before disappearing into the woods. And my body should've convulsed. It was only a month ago that I dreamed I was tied down to a bed while two cats kept licking the insides of my ears. Because to say the dream defined strange was an understatement.

"Do you even know how to use 'deconstructed' in a sentence?" I asked.

"Don't be fresh. I'm giving free advice."

"Enough about Billy. Tell me about how the Chess Club is going."

***

FRIDAY, NOVEMBER 15, 2019

My short story class might've not have been a science, math, or history class, yet my eyes remained on the ceiling while Billy and I stood in front of the desk while Mrs. Roberts was in one of the student desks. The projector with our PowerPoint also happened to be on in addition to how we had a printout of our presentation on, "The Landlady." However, the tightness in my throat hadn't vanished. If anything, ten elephants might've as well have sat on my throat. Because presentations were better than Christmas morning.

"How about you start the presentation, Carson?" Mrs. Roberts asked.

No disrespect to Mrs. Roberts, but it wouldn't have been the end of the world if a piano fell on her later today. This class wasn't fucking Kindergarten, and she didn't need to tell us how to do our own presentation. Dread didn't need to fill my body because of her putting me on the spot. Besides, the whole point of these presentations was for her to keep quiet and let students talk.

Maybe, just maybe, the idea of a piano falling on her was harsh. It wasn't like I wanted to kill her in cold blood. She just needed to learn some manners—almost as if she was a five-year-old that couldn't say please or thank you. So, yeah. Her getting stuck in traffic was an adequate punishment for being so incompetent.

Mrs. Roberts glared at me. "I'm waiting…"

Billy grimaced at her. "I wanted to speak first—that was how we planned the project."

I wasn't a religious person, but God bless Billy—even if he was the boy of a million contradictions. In this moment, he gave me something I needed, and I'd never forget that. Some people would've let me floundered while profuse amounts of sweat rolled down my back. However, Billy knew how to be a decent person.

"Fine," Mrs. Roberts said.

"Okay, thanks," Billy said before he started rambling.

The classroom erupted into cheers and clapping once Billy and I finished our presentation a few minutes. Although I couldn't tell if they were being polite or sincere as a result of the pitch from their excitement.

"You guys did a great job with your presentation because it's obvious you put a lot of time into. However, you get an A, Billy, and Carson you get a C," Mrs. Roberts said.

"Are you fucking kidding me?" Billy asked.

"I appreciate your enthusiasm, but this is still a classroom, so watch the language. But no. I have no choice with giving you a higher grade. Carson only spoke once during the presentation," Mrs. Roberts said.

Billy crossed his arms. "No disrespect, but that's not fair. He helped a lot with planning the presentation."

"Doesn't matter," Mrs. Roberts said. "Being a good student means participating in class."

"Then give me a C too," Billy said.

Defending me was one thing, yet Billy couldn't have demanded a C. The idea was just ludicrous. No reason existed why we both needed to get a good grade. Because someone might as well have gotten an A after all the time I put into analyzing, "The Landlady" and typing up the PowerPoint.

"Are you sure?" Mrs. Roberts asked.

"Fair's fair," Billy said.

Wow. Someone needed to throw Billy a parade like yesterday. Making a comment was one thing, yet he wouldn't back down. Because I had to be with myself even if I couldn't tell my next thought to anyone else. No guarantee existed that I would've done the same thing if roles were reversed, and Billy was the one who earned a bad grade.

"Fine. You both get a C." Mrs. Roberts turned on her iPhone for a second. "Anyway, class dismissed. Although I'd like to speak with you for a second, Carson. Saying your participation was disappointing would be kind."

Giving me a C shouldn't have been synonymous with having flushed cheeks. It didn't matter if she was an adult, and I was a child. She needed to act professional. Besides, the students were technically her boss as a result of how our tuition kind of paid her salary.

"I might even have a chat with the Dean of Students and your parents," Mrs. Roberts continued. "There's no point in being enrolled in this class if you won't contribute to our discussion. Even if withdrawing from the class would mean an F since it's so late in the semester."

Counting to twenty in my head had to make my clenched fists disappear, and my reasoning wasn't even from Mrs. Roberts retaliating against me. Having an emotional episode might make me seem unstable, and I couldn't have that. Life was already bad enough with how

I still went to the same school as Jonathan.

"In fact, your behavior is really astounding. I don't understand how students like you think it's okay to come to class and not participate. Now that I think of it, you haven't once raised your hand all semester," Mrs. Roberts said.

Screw what she said. Someone might as well have been paying her by the word. Yup. I never had a teacher who crammed so many points into a ramble.

Mrs. Roberts adjusted her glasses so they were no longer dangling by the edge of her nose. "In fact, I wish you hadn't even wasted my time by enrolling in this class."

Wow. One tilt of my head was what I needed for my dilated pupils. Everyone remained in their seats despite how Mrs. Roberts dismissed the class a couple of minutes ago.

Mrs. Roberts threw her hands up in the air. "Forget it. There's no point in talking with you after class. It's not like you'll say anything."

The image of Jonathan pinning me against the tree in the woods while he grunted and I wished God struck me dead with a bolt of lightning returned to my mind. Someone didn't have to rape me in order for the entire classroom to whirl around me like a tornado closing in, giving someone no room for escape. The point was, I shouldn't have been in a position where someone abused me—whether the abuse was physical or emotional. And that was why enough was enough, and something had to be said. Being a teenager didn't mean doing whatever an adult said.

I screamed at her. "You should be fucking ashamed of yourself, Mrs. Roberts. You're nothing but a nasty, bitter, fucking old bitch. Not everyone is good at public speaking. Anyway, feel free to go to Hell."

I ran out of the classroom without another word before going into the nearest bathroom and staring into the bathroom mirror.

Tears trickled down my cheeks while I punched the bathroom mirror. Just because I stopped myself from having a complete meltdown, didn't mean suppressing my emotions when I was alone. I wouldn't. I couldn't. I was only human in addition to understanding how my emotional state would've only become more volatile if I tricked myself into believing I was okay when I wasn't.

The door creaked, yet I didn't turn around. A quick look in the bathroom mirror was all I needed to know who joined me.

"I don't mean to intrude, but you forgot your backpack." Billy shuffled over to me, and tossed my backpack at me.

Perhaps Chelsea was correct, and I needed to worry less about Billy's evasive personality. People were allowed flaws in addition to how him bringing my backpack to me proved he had to have been a little decent. Everyone else probably wouldn't have given a rat's ass about whether I had my backpack.

"Thanks," I whispered before strapping my backpack to my back.

"I'm so sorry about Mrs. Roberts; you didn't deserve that."

"No shit."

"I also want you to know I'm not angry. It's okay if you aren't good at public speaking."

Wow. Billy was hitting touchy point after touchy point. Because I wouldn't have been able to keep lingering on the subject if I were him. Nope. Doing so would've ensued possible awkwardness from not knowing how to react if someone became riled up. Empathy and showing compassion during a difficult situation were two different things.

"Good to know." I yanked the right faucet knob, and water gushed out of the sink in a matter of seconds. Then, I threw some water on my face, and turned the sink off.

"You were brave," Billy said.

Thank goodness for Billy. Someone needed to keep the compliments coming because ego boosts were okay in small doses. It wasn't like I expected everyone to bow down before me. I just needed something to hold on to, anything that hinted life would be okay and didn't have to be concerned with Mrs. Roberts retaliating against me.

"It's kind of you to humor me, but you don't have to," I said.

Yup. Getting ego boosts and having modesty were sometimes interconnected. I just didn't think it was true for someone to say so many nice things about me in such a short period of time. Nope. Real life was messier than an episode of television, proving people often didn't erase their pain. They simply learned to live with it, which in my case meant dealing with what Jonathan did to me.

"I'm serious. Most people wouldn't have said anything to Mrs. Roberts."

"Someone had to shut her up."

Billy rubbed a tear from my eyelid. "You're too pretty to cry."

There was no way he gave me another compliment; life didn't work like that. Even one good event occurring meant the universe taking away two things in exchange.

"Don't you mean handsome?" I asked.

"Same difference."

No disrespect, but Billy provided more amusement than he might've realized. Anything was better than dwelling on what my next interaction with Mrs. Roberts since I so needed another confrontation.

Billy cleared his throat. "I'll back you up if Mrs. Roberts gives you a difficult time."

"You'd do that for me?"

"I might need someone to help me someday," he said.

Scrunched eyebrows would've only wasted time.

Whether I admitted the truth to myself or anyone else, Billy would always be an enigma. He just couldn't make a simple statement. Hinting at needing help was the type of comment one made in a television show or movie when leading a double life.

However, Billy's lips pressing against mine meant silencing all the concerns racing through my mind. AT least for one fleeting second. Billy's kiss revealed vulnerability, though. He was still closeted, and it only took one person to walk into the bathroom to discover us making out.

NOW

MONDAY, SEPTEMBER 28, 2020

"I can't believe we're drinking on a school night," I said before taking a swig of my Margarita while Dean and I stood by a pool table.

Dean chuckled. "It's okay to sometimes take risks."

Some people might've had rage fester in their body because of an offhanded comment, but not me—at least not right now. I'd never make it in life if I got offended by every little remark. A difference existed between having an opinion and verbalizing said opinion. It wasn't like all my thoughts were priceless.

"Forgive me. I've just never played pool before," I said.

Yup. I wasn't dreaming. Dean and I were in the pool hall a mile from campus. Although we should've found another place that didn't card. Squinting was inevitable because of the dim overhead lighting. In fact, the lighting was so dismal that people would've bumped into each other if the place was any darker. And I couldn't forget about the acrid scent lingering the air. Because I could've sworn it smelled like a mix of piss and stale beer. That concoction was the only smell that would've stung my nostrils—almost as if the stench was worse than cigarette smoke.

Dean winked. "No need to be bashful because I'd be happy to teach you how to play pool if you're still interested. However, I'm fine with just talking."

Taking a breath meant time to think. Learning new things wasn't always fun, yet teaching me how to play pool entailed boosting his ego. And that was what I needed if I wanted to stay in Dean's orbit.

"Let me have one more sip of my Margarita first," I said.

"Sure."

I slurped more of my cocktail, but I might as well have been drinking hydrochloric acid. Putting salt on the rim of my glass was bad enough, but the fact that the acidic flavor still lingered on my tongue after a good fifteen seconds meant the bartender used too much lime juice.

Whatever. The important thing was Dean agreed to pay for our date. Because I would've needed to visit a doctor if I thought turning down free booze was okay.

I shuffled toward a few feet after putting my drink down on a nearby table. I then bent over and Dean stood behind me—almost as if we were about to have sex against the pool table.

Yup. The sweet aroma of whatever aftershave Dean used prickled my skin as a result of how he was almost on top of me. Dean grabbed the pool stick, and I gripped both hands against his, ignoring the cold texture jolting my skin before he placed his hands on top mine. My blood pumped through my body faster. I shouldn't have enjoyed being so close to Dean, yet I couldn't help myself. Tricking myself into acting like a robot didn't mean erasing my humanity.

His lips grazed my right ear. "I want you to aim the stick to the ball that's left of you. But the key is using enough force to get the ball in the hole at the opposite end of the table, yet not too much force that the ball just thuds against the table."

Someone should've slapped me in the face. Suppressing my laughter to the point a metallic taste almost filled my mouth from biting my lip too hard meant I couldn't hold out much longer. Billy would've compared Dean's guidance to sex because that was something that needed to go at the right pace.

"What are you waiting for?" he asked.

"I'm visualizing." I held the pool stick tighter, and Dean did the same. The stick moved forward in one swift motion, and the ball thumped into the hole.

"Wow. I'm not a terrible teacher," Dean said after I placed the pool stick down on the table and shifted my weight to face him.

Maybe, just maybe, Dean might've already spent too much time with me. A worrying statement was something I would've said.

"Maybe you need more confidence," I said.

"Fancy seeing you two here," called out a voice.

Yup. Only one voice would've made my back hairs stand up. I didn't have to run into a snake for my chest to expand and contract faster while each subsequent breath required more effort. Running into Jonathan sufficed. Besides, for all I knew, Jonathan could've been a snake.

"What are you doing here?" Dean asked.

"I felt like grabbing a drink. A person can only drink in a dorm room for so long before getting bored," Jonathan said.

Dean folded his arms. "You should go. We're on a date."

Jonathan cackled. "I'm sorry. Don't let me interrupt. If memory serves, Carson knows all about having a good time."

That sick fuck. Jonathan couldn't have said what he just did. Not when he raped me last year. He might've been a lot of things, but he wasn't stupid. Especially after Billy's warning last year.

Dean squeezed my shoulder before lunging forward. "You should go, Jonathan. We might be in the same club, but I don't have to tolerate you. I know a lot more than you realize. Like what happens at our parties, and how it wouldn't be good if certain details got out."

"Fine," Jonathan mumbled. "I'll leave you guys alone."

I shook my head after one glance at the window. For a split-second, Billy stood on the sidewalk outside, yet that was impossible. He was dead, and my mind must've been playing tricks on me from the stress of running into my rapist. Besides, Billy wasn't there when I opened my eyes.

"That's more like it," Dean said.

Forget about how I might've seen Billy. I had to dwell on Dean's comment since the writer in me almost squealed. The truth was in what Dean didn't say. He didn't have to say he knew Jonathan raped me to articulate his point. Jonathan still flinched, and that fact was all that mattered.

"Enjoy the rest of your evening." Jonathan darted towards the front door without another word. In fact, the placard chimed against the door for a good ten seconds since Jonathan slammed the door so loudly.

"I hope my comment didn't offend you. Jonathan just had to know he wasn't welcomed here," Dean said.

"Relax. You didn't offend me."

"I know you must think I'm another spoiled teen who parties too much, but I'm thankful for the opportunity to prove myself."

Yeah. He definitely spent too much time with me. Contemplating an issue was one thing, yet Dean blurted out something without any consideration about how his comment might've been awkward. It wasn't like he was required to tell me everything on his mind.

"You should get another Gin and Tonic," I said.

"The only thing I wanna do is kiss you, but I won't. However, I want you to also know doing the right thing is important to me, which is part of why I had to say something to Jonathan."

Dean's comment told me everything I needed to know. And that was why I tugged at his hand and kissed him. In this moment, he wasn't the guy who might've known something about Billy's death. He was the guy who wanted to be a good person, and that fact was enough for now. Expecting complete perfection would've only entailed disappointment since perfection only existed as an abstract concept, not a reality.

***

TUESDAY SEPTEMBER 29, 2020

"No offense, Carson, but you look too good for someone who went out partying last night," Freddie said.

Gray clouds remained smooshed together in the sky while not even one stray strand of sunlight poked through while Freddie, Amanda, Chelsea, and I stood a few hundred feet away from one of the academic buildings.

"I only had three Margaritas," I said.

Chelsea yanked her backpack straps up her shoulders more. "I'm kind of disappointed you didn't have more. But you can make it up to me this weekend."

"Please tell me kissing Dean wasn't about feeling obligated. Because I have no problem chopping off Jonathan's dick," Amanda said.

The wind whistled, pushing a loose sheet of notebook into the distance and out of sight.

Now wasn't the time to think about how a single piece of notebook paper would've made for a beautiful metaphor for loneliness if I wanted to write a poem. All my energy had to be focused on being calm. Getting worked up wouldn't accomplish anything, and that was why I counted to twenty in my head.

Freddie winced. "No need to be so graphic."

"I can't help it. You know my policy about assholes," Amanda replied while a few students trekked by.

I rolled my eyes at Amanda. "Why can't I both like Dean and want closure about Billy?"

Amanda swallowed the lump in her throat. "You're right. And that's the last time I'll argue with you. I support you, and nothing will change that fact."

"Do you understand?" screamed someone. "You've made a big mistake, and you and your friends are going to pay for it."

Good to know a fight worthy of cable TV was unfolding in front of the academic building to the left of us. However, the fact that the fight included Dean filled my body with joy. I so wanted to think of him in a negative context. Doing so would've pushed me towards clarity about what Billy meant to me.

"Calm down," Dean said.

The redhead screamed again. "Don't tell me how to act. My boyfriend is dead because of you, and you and your sick cult won't get away with it."

"I'm gonna see what the problem is," I said before walking away from my friends.

Involving myself in someone else's drama was never ideal, but I stopped doing the easy thing ages ago. Yup. A little drama offered intrigue. Almost as I was watching a car crash right before it happened.

"Everything okay?" I asked.

She made a fist. "Don't ask a dumbass question. My boyfriend is still dead."

Dean's jaw lowered. "I'm sorry about Henry, but I don't know what you want me to do. Anyway, our date was great last night, but I have a tutoring session now. However, maybe you can talk some sense into Lexi."

He gave me a quick kiss on the cheek before scurrying away, leaving Lexi and I to ourselves. However, Lexi didn't say anything. Instead, she continued whaling. As if someone told her that her entire daily and childhood dog on the same day. No shade, but I never heard someone sob so loudly before.

"We can go somewhere private to chat if you want," I said.

"A conversation won't bring Henry back, nothing will. But you must know all about that since Billy is dead."

Good gracious. Whether I always realized the fact or not, life always came back to Billy. And I wasn't talking about playing amateur detective. I was referring to the quieter moments that nobody labeled. Like last night in the pool hall. Dean's behavior was reminiscent of Billy because he also stood up to Jonathan, yet now wasn't the time to speculate if a certain type of guy attracted me. Lexi had walked away without me even noticing while all I had was some clue. A dead boyfriend was something specific and I'd probably be staring off into space for the rest of the day while wondering her point. Henry's death was an accident as far as I knew. Apparently, he took one too many bumps of cocaine at a party last spring. Although that hardly seemed like something to scream bloody murder about. It wasn't like Henry couldn't swim and someone forced him to go in the deep end of a pool.

***

WEDENDSAY, SEPTEMBER 30, 2020

I tapped someone's shoulder while surveying the premade breakfast sandwiches in the dining hall.

The girl spun around, and her lips curled. Although Lexi should've at least pretended to care about the frown lines on her face. Because Grandma would've mentioned Lexi needing Botox with the next five to ten years if the constipated expression didn't disappear from her face like yesterday.

"What do you want?" she asked.

"I wanna talk, and I promise I won't judge."

"I have nothing to say…"

I pressed my hands together. "I'm just looking to understand why you're so angry. Dying of a cocaine overdose is a tragedy, not cause for a witch hunt."

"Henry never did cocaine. He was only a social drinker."

"Maybe someone pressured him to do cocaine. No disrespect or anything…"

Qualifying my statement had to be done despite how I would've been the person with no more fucks to give in an alternate universe. Whether I accepted the truth or not, Lexi and I had a bond. I might not have known all the thoughts swirling in her head, but losing the love of your life was something a person never forgot. Not now. Not in ever.

"I have no doubt someone pressured him. But it had nothing to do with cocaine," Lexi said.

"Can you be more specific?"

"Henry was a new spring recruit to Charity Now when he died."

"I'm still not getting your point."

"What more do I have to say?" Lexi asked. "Or are you just that stupid? Charity Now hazed their newbies."

Criticizing Lexi for slandering Charity Now would've been unfair. I hadn't known everything about the club when I "dated" Billy, yet he mentioned something in passing about hazing. And I hadn't questioned him. Being president of the club didn't mean he controlled everything since Billy was only one person.

"Or maybe I should mention how I was at the party where Henry died. And how some of the guys promised to stop hazing him if he jumped off the banister." Lexi took her sleeve, and wiped her right eyes.

Yup. Lexi hadn't misspoken. The Barn had a stairwell—that led to a big room upstairs—at the opposite end of where the snack and beverage table usually was.

"Did you bring your concerns to the school administration?" I asked.

"Yeah. And I even got Henry's parents to threaten a lawsuit."

Perhaps Lexi had more guts than I gave her credit for. Most people did what adults told them to do, and therefore couldn't have dreamed about being so blunt even during their most rebellious moment.

"What happened? How come his death was chalked up to a cocaine overdose?" I asked.

She looked away. "The parents of each Charity Now member have donated a lot of money to the school."

"Oh…"

Having a stupid expression once again couldn't be helped. I could never wrap my head around how money always controlled life. People should've known better than to let material items dictate what happened in life, yet they didn't. A plane ride to Washington D.C. wasn't required to understand corruption because politicians weren't the only people capable of greed.

"The kicker is the school gave me ten million dollars, but I had to sign a non-disclosure agreement," she said.

A few more footsteps pounded against the ground, and I cringed. Expecting to be the only people might've been a naïve thought, yet I couldn't help myself. Especially in light of what I already knew about Lexi's emotional state. Having witnesses to such a high stakes conversation meant someone might've been able to overhear the intimate details of what Lexi told me. And that couldn't happen. Not because I thought life was perfect, but because it wasn't perfect. It wouldn't have killed the universe to just let one thing go right me for once. I just dreamed of having to explain this conversation to other people.

"How did you get the money?" I asked.

Being the guy who picked up every little detail of a story would never change. If Lexi expected me to believe her, then she had to be honest with me. Not 95 percent honest or 99 percent honest—100 percent honesty.

"I'm not rich like almost everyone at this school, and Henry's parents thought I should have the money since I was in love with him," she said.

"Why are you telling me this if it means possibly getting into trouble?" I asked.

Her laughter pierced the air. In fact, she laughed loud enough that she would've convinced anyone that she was a witch from a fairytale who succeeded with casting some wicked curse. "It's not like the school will know I broke the agreement. You also deserve to know what you're getting yourself into if you wanna date Dean."

"Do you know who specifically is responsible for the hazing incident?"

"No. I wasn't paying enough attention."

***

THURSDAY, OCTOBER 1, 2020

"We need to talk, Otto," I said while standing in front of his dorm room after my last class finished for the day.

"Sure. What's up? Would you like another souvenir of Billy?"

A girl sporting a tangerine scented perfume scurried by, and I remained silent. Yup. I had to act like I was in a spy movie. Nobody could detect what we were up to. Nope. It just wasn't an option.

"You might want to have this conversation in private," I said.

"I'd rather talk here."

Interesting. Life still couldn't be easy no matter how much I wished the opposite were true. It wasn't like I'd slit Otto's throat the second we stepped inside his room. Because he really had no reason to fear me.

"Fine. Have it your way," I said. "But just remember I tried to be accommodating."

"What the hell is that supposed to mean?"

"I know about what happened to Henry."

"His death was a tragedy," Otto said without blinking.

There was cold and then there was Antarctica cold.

Showing emotion wouldn't have killed Otto. Anything was better than being left with a negative impression of him. Because the cliché of teenagers being careless couldn't have been true. Said fact meant being at Grand Prepatory would've therefore wasted my time since I didn't deserve

"I know a lot of you hazed the newbies," I blurted.

"I'd be very careful about what you're implying."

Perhaps Otto might've been capable of winning an Oscar. Making a thinly veiled threat wasn't something an average person was capable of. Nope. Most people suppressed their feelings when given a choice between being honest and avoiding confrontation.

"Your club is the reason Henry is dead," I said.

"You know what? I'm sick of the drama," Otto said, raising his voice. "First Henry dies last spring, and then Billy. Because it's a miracle our club hasn't been shut down yet."

"What are you talking about?" I demanded.

Otto sighed. "I might as well tell you because I'm tired of keeping it to myself. The stress just isn't worth, and I would quit the club if it weren't for how doing charity work looks great for colleges."

"I don't understand…"

"I lied to you. The senior members of Charity Now and I didn't just talk to Billy in the woods before he died. We were with him by the cliff."

Most people wouldn't have picked up on every little detail, yet I had no qualms about counting myself as someone who didn't fit said label. It didn't matter how many times Otto talked his way out what he just said. He mentioned died, not suicide.

"Except he didn't kill himself. Jonathan pushed him off the cliff and into the ocean," Otto revealed.

"Why?"

"Billy wasn't the perfect kid he made himself out to be. Although you don't need any explanation."

"Elaborate."

Otto gripped a chunk of his hair—almost as if anything was better than proceeding with whatever revelation he was about to drop. "We wanted to stop the hazing at the beginning of the school year, yet Billy didn't. So, we staged a coup, and Dean became president of the club. But Billy wasn't having it, and threatened to tell the school administration we were going to continue hazing newbies if we didn't let him back in the club."

"And why should I believe you?" I asked.

"I have nothing to gain by being honest."

"How did you even make it look like a suicide?"

"They made me go back to our dorm room and grab his sweater and paper with his handwriting, so we could forge a note using his stationary," Otto said.

Having a theory and a hunch becoming true were two different issues. I would've been lying if I didn't mention how a part of me thought I'd never get closure about Billy's death. However, any shock shooting through my body needed vanquishing. The universe was still the universe, and that entailed the most surprising revelations happened during the quietest moments. Like my current conversation with Otto.

"But his body never turned up?" I asked.

"It probably washed out to sea."

I grimaced at him. "You can't tell anyone about this conversation—especially not Dean."

"How stupid do you think I am?"

***

FRIDAY, OCTOBER 2, 2020

Gray once again tinged the cloudy sky while the wind cut across through ocean and salt wafted through the air. Hell, my teeth even chattered from the dampness permeating the air.

I couldn't complain about not having ideal conditions, though. Freddie and I just got out of the rowboat, and now stood on the sandbar bellow the cliff where Jonathan pushed him off, which meant it was now time for our mission.

"My brain hasn't recovered from what you told me," Freddie said.

"I'm glad you still have access to the rowing team's boats during the off season."

"Chelsea would've been annoyed if I didn't help you. Although I don't understand what we're looking for."

"It's not that I expect to find something. But it'd be nice if we did."

"Would you really go to the school administration?" he asked.

I shrugged. "I don't know. Maybe. But let's see what we find. Because there's no point in getting ahead of ourselves."

Yeah. Idealism didn't mean stupidity. A difference existed between wanting proof and finding proof.

"What are you gonna do about Dean?" Freddie asked.

Great question. As if I didn't have enough to think about. Nope. The universe did me a favor by creating more problems. Because my genuine moment with kissing Dean at the pool hall didn't qualify as a serious problem.

"I don't know," I said.

"Are you disappointed he witnessed Billy's death?"

"He stood up to Jonathan…"

"That's true," Freddie said before we started walking through the rocks, which varied from the size of my foot to bigger than my body.

My silence wasn't about Freddie needing to come up with more than a two-word response. Both of our gazes remained fixated on the end of the sandbar that hugged the cliff. A rock the size of my stomach was drenched in red. Like the kind of stain that one expected from someone losing some blood after being pushed and banging his head against a rock.

"Ouch," Freddie said. "Hitting your head on a rock is a terrible way to go."

"Let's not even think about it."

"What are you gonna do now that you've got proof?"

"Get evidence." I pulled my iPhone out of my pocket before pulling up the camera app and focusing on the bloody rock. A clicking sound then echoed a couple of times before I emailed the two photos to myself.

"There's another point we haven't really addressed. How do you feel about Billy not being the person you thought he was?"

"He didn't deserve to die."

"Fine. But this discovery proves he's always been the person you feared he was."

My iPhone fell and collapsed onto the sand while I let out several screams. "Fine. Do you want me to admit I was in love with an asshole?"

* * *

MONDAY, OCTOBER 5 2020

A baby blue color stained the cloudless sky while several birds screeched through the air while I shuffled out of one of the academic buildings on the north side of campus, clipping through the crowd of students.

Except Mondays were never meant to be simple. Dean just approached me, and I only had a split-second left to brace myself for our conversation.

"Hey," he said.

"Dean…"

Yeah. Even I was sometimes guilty of using a one-liner. Dean and I hadn't spoken since I found out the truth about Billy, and feigning politeness ensured not having a meltdown. Because my memory wasn't too shot for me to forget about my emotional moment with Mrs. Roberts last year.

"Something wrong?" Dean asked.

"I know what happened to Billy."

He pulled me to the side so we got out of the way of the students who continued pouring out of the academic buildings. "How did you uncover the truth?"

"It doesn't matter. I know everything."

"It's not like I pushed him off the cliff."

Interesting response. Dean could've denied the truth, and I'd have to figure out if I should've been terrified or relieved that Billy wasn't lying to me. Dishonesty was the easier option, yet hadn't chosen it.

"That's not the point," I said.

"Where does that leave us?"

"I don't know. But it's probably best if we don't talk for now." I bumped my shoulder against his before strolling away.

The Dean/Billy issue was one of those times when the, "I don't know" response was best. I still never once anticipated getting closure with Billy's death, meaning doing nothing was the only thing I was certain of. Only a child would've rushed into a situation without thinking about consequences. Because that was the exact opposite of what I should've done if I wanted to simplify my life.

THEN

SATURDAY, NOVEMBER 16, 2019

"I hope you don't think I'm elitist because I like Post-modern cinema." I shut my laptop while our backs were pressed against my gray dorm room wall while we sat on my bed.

Billy snickered. "No offense, but you've gotta stop worrying about what people think about you. I don't, and look how perfect I am."

Pouting would've only wasted time. Billy was right. Confidence didn't entail arrogance. Everyone deserved to feel good about themselves. If I didn't ever feel good about myself, then I'd never convince anyone else I was worth anything.

"I didn't offend you, did I?" he asked.

How considerate of him to be concerned about offending me. Backtracking from a statement was something

I'd have done if the situations were reversed. If drama could be avoided, then that was a good thing.

"Nope. I'm just glad you enjoyed the movie," I said.

"Even if I still don't understand what Postmodernism means?"

"Don't worry. It's not for everyone."

Billy adjusted his shirt collar. "Are you saying I'm dumb?"

Okay. Billy had to stop hanging out with me like yesterday. My quirky tendencies couldn't have rubbed off on him. Not when we hadn't even known each other for a month yet.

I wiggled my eyebrows. "Don't be ridiculous. I just meant some art isn't meant to be enjoyed by everyone."

"Fair enough. But I was teasing." He grabbed a handful of sour cream and onion chips from the bag on top of my bed comforter. And he scarfed down the chips in a matter of seconds. Almost as if he was a famine victim who hadn't had a proper meal in ages.

"I'll never be able to read social cues," I said.

"Don't say that. The right teacher could do wonders for you. Anyway, are you nervous for class on Tuesday?"

Billy just had to mention Mrs. Roberts. I so wanted to obsess what our next class would be like. In fact, this conversation was the best day of life. Yup. No other day compared to the sweat seeping through my pores at the possibility of Mrs. Roberts tattling to the school administration.

"Don't even mention it because I can't think about what will happen," I said.

Billy smirked. "Don't be so worried. Problems sometimes take care of themselves."

"Meaning?"

Demanding clarification didn't make me a buzzkill. I challenged anyone not to tremble for a few seconds after enduring with a depraved teacher. Feelings weren't magic, and couldn't be controlled by snapping my fingers.

"I'm sure everything will be fine," Billy said.

"I hope so." Scoffing at the guy I was kind of dating didn't reveal a lapse in judgment. There were no more chips in the bag, and it wasn't like I had more snacks tucked away in one of my drawers. Nope. I was saving my grocery store trip to when I went home over Thanksgiving. If something could be procrastinated, then I'd find a way to avoid doing said task—at least the unpleasant tasks.

Billy bit his lip. "Sorry! I didn't mean to finish your chips."

"No worries."

Yeah. Even I was sometimes capable of filtering. Nothing good would come from starting trouble over a small issue. It wasn't like doing so would bring me joy.

"Anyway, I have a confession to make" he said.

"Don't tell me you killed someone? I'll put up with a lot, but I draw the line at murder."

He nudged me. "Don't be morbid. I was talking about you."

Yup. Billy shouldn't have expected anything else besides my usual unique personality. It wasn't like I actually thought he was capable of killing someone. Nope. Only Jonathan had that honor. And no. Jumping from rape to murder wasn't illogical. He was already halfway to killing someone. Raping me meant murdering my soul, because I'd never get that night in the woods back.

"Have you forgotten who you're talking to?" I asked. "I mean, you could at least clue me in."

Billy ruffled my hair, yet ambiguity once again confronted me. Two interpretations existed about him messing up my hairdo beyond ruining my style being a dick move because of all the time styling my hair took each morning. Billy touching me might've been another flirty gesture or it might've just resembled a parent patting their child on the head. And I so wanted the latter option to be true. "I was hoping to take things to the next level," he said.

"Excuse me?"

He wrinkled his nose. "You're hot, and any guy or girl would be lucky to have you."

"Are you saying you want to have sex?" I asked.

"Yup."

"I'm sorry, but I don't know how to respond," I stammered.

"I understand if you aren't ready..."

Someone must have given me a pot brownie when I wasn't looking. That explanation was the only reason for why Billy wanted to sleep with me. Having "fun in life was one thing, but I was only seventeen, and thus had plenty of opportunity to explore sex. Like in college when I never had to see Jonathan again. Unless the universe intended on us going to the same university—although that would've been too cruel even for a universe that prided itself in a sick sense of humor.

I blinked. "You really wanna have sex with me?"

"Is it that hard to believe that someone finds you hot?"

"No. It isn't a self-esteem problem. I just didn't know giving into desires was so easy."

He pressed his lips against my ear. "All you have to do is say the word, and you can have everything you want."

"Okay. Let's do this."

"Are you sure? Now would be the time to change your mind."

Giving me ample opportunity to change my mind might've won him points for sensitivity. But I wasn't some celibate monk, and deserved not to be so scarred for the rest of my life that I never enjoyed sex again. Because that would've been tragic.

"Nope. I've made my decision, and it's final. If you

want this, I want this," I said. "Although we have some technical things to figure out."

A couple of birds outside my dorm room cawed while black now stained the late-afternoon sky. Rambling about how *The Birds* was my least favorite movie could wait. Debating whether birds, snakes, or alligators were worse wasn't sexy. If anything, contemplating predatory animals would've made me hide under the covers for the rest of my life, and I couldn't have that. Nope. Surviving Jonathan raping me proved I could get through anything. I just had to want said thing bad enough.

"I'm pretty confident we can solve any problem." Billy pulled me towards him with one swift grip before kissing me. His fingers traveled from my cheeks to my stomach in a matter of seconds, and he lifted my shirt off my body. It landed on the floor, but I also wouldn't contemplate future cleaning by picking up our trail of clothes which would eventually be on the floor. Nope. Getting a redo with losing my virginity was the only thing that mattered in this moment.

* * *

SUNDAY, NOVEMBER 18, 2019

Sunlight peeked through my dorm room curtains. I yawned, then rubbed my eyes before cocking my head. My clothes were the only ones on the floor in addition to how Billy didn't occupy my bed.

Damn. Billy couldn't even stay the night, proving I might've gotten more than I bargained when I slept with Billy.

Whatever. At least sleeping with Billy didn't cause me to curl up in a ball on the floor, and Jonathan could be forgotten about.

Going out to breakfast wouldn't have been terrible, though. Doing so would've given Billy and I another opportunity to spend more time together. But getting my way would've been too simple for the universe, and Billy once again had to leave me wanting more.

* * *

MONDAY, NOVEMBER 18, 2019

"Hi, buddy! How are you? No offense, but we were worried when you didn't respond to any of our texts," Freddie said after he, Chelsea, and Amanda approached me as I stood in front of one of the academic buildings.

"I'm fine," I said.

Chelsea elevated her eyebrows. "Try again. We aren't that stupid."

"Who said anything about being stupid?" Amanda asked.

Amanda was a lot of things, but she could also benefit from understanding social cues. Not everything had to have a literal meaning. Like when I said I could kill Billy for not staying the night. It wasn't like I'd actually kill him. Nope. He wasn't worth going to jail over.

"Fine," I interrupted. "You wanna know the truth? I slept with Billy Saturday night, but he was gone when I woke up in the morning."

Amanda rolled her eyes. "No surprise there. Even I could've told you he'd ditch you the second you fell asleep."

"At least I'm no longer a virgin," I said.

Freddie glanced at me. "Are you sure that you're okay?"

"Yeah, I am fine," I said. "But I'm sorry if I offended you guys by blowing you off. That wasn't my intention."

"No worries," Freddie said.

Chelsea's pendant bounced against her after she stopped clutching it. "Have you thought about what you're going to say the next time you see Billy?"

"No. I'm just trying to make it through today," I said.

A group of students dashed by us, and someone should've clapped for purple haired girl. That wasn't a hair color I saw often in addition to how I couldn't forget about the twisted irony. Spotting someone with an unusual hair color revealed Billy was right. The girl's head was held high, proving she must've had confidence.

Freddie exhaled a breath. "I'm not trying to tell you how to live your life, but knowing what to say might comfort you."

"Like what would you do if Billy stares at you intensely?" Amanda asked.

Wow. For once, Chelsea wasn't the one making a ballsy comment. Because what Amanda said was the type of thing she would have said.

"Amanda, please!" Freddie said.

"I'm being honest. It's important not to let people control you, Carson. People like Billy thrive off you wanting them," Amanda said.

***

TUESDAY, NOVEMBER 19, 2019

Arriving early to my short story class might've entailed spending extra time in said classroom, yet I didn't have a choice in coming early. Preparing myself for Billy and Mrs. Roberts was the only thing worth doing. Billy wasn't right about most things, but I couldn't waffle. If I wanted something, then I deserved to fight for it. Even if intellectualizing an idea and following through with said idea were two different things.

"Good morning," Billy said after sitting down in the desk next to mine in the front row.

"Morning," I mumbled.

"That's all you have to say?"

"I'm not the one who left someone in an empty bed."

Billy snorted—almost as if he sounded like a pig. "Don't be so dramatic. I had things to do, and didn't want to hurt your feelings by not spending the day with you."

"Whatever. It was fun, and that's what matters."

Yup. Even I was sometimes capable of resembling a five-year-old throwing a tantrum. It must've killed Billy that I wasn't mesmerized by him. And that was exactly what he needed to feel. Only then would we be on equal ground. He shouldn't have had all the power in our dynamic. Nope. My feelings deserved acknowledgment, and maybe standoffish treatment would make him regretful— that was if he was capable of real feelings.

"We both know it was more than fun," Billy said.

"I don't know what you want me to say."

He licked his lips. "How about asking when it can happen again?"

Not staying the night was one thing, yet Billy brought any criticism on himself. He wasn't good enough to make me get on my hands and knees and beg for another tryst. Nope. I had more self-respect than that.

"You wish," I touted.

"Just you see. Your mood is about to improve. Give it five, maybe ten minutes tops, and then you'll be smiling."

"I don't follow you."

"That's okay. Because you'll like this surprise," Billy said.

A man with a Polo shirt, khaki shorts, and flip flops ran into the classroom several minutes later while the various student conversations echoed. Except he stepped too far to the left, and dropped his leather briefcase against the ground when he was only a matter of inches from the teacher desk in front of the classroom. Yet he didn't flinch. Instead, the man picked up his briefcase before it thudded onto the desk when he placed it a moment later.

He turned around. "Good morning, class. My name is Mr. Baker."

"Where's Mrs. Roberts?" asked a student.

"She's been suspended for the rest of the school year. Anyway, enough about her. The only thing that matters is I'm your teacher now," Mr. Baker said.

Billy laughed, yet tried hiding it in a cough. Then, I glanced at Billy. The grin on his face expanded—as if he was the Cheshire Cat from *Alice and Wonderland*.

NOW

THURSDAY, OCTOBER 8, 2020

"Don't take this the wrong way, but you seemed like you never wanted to see me again." Dean took a bite of his croissant before sipping his coffee while we sat on a bench near one of the academic buildings.

A few students trekked by as Dean and I sat in silence for a beat. Yup. Awkward moments from youth weren't just anecdotes people shared at cocktail parties in their late thirties. They actually happened.

I forced a laugh. "Don't be so dramatic. Anyway, no point in dancing around the issue."

"Meaning?"

"I'm not going to snitch on Charity Now to the school administration or the police." Only holding my Caramel Macchiato as opposed to drinking it wasn't about making life more complicated by not accepting a kindness. I just had to shake my head because of Dean doing something nice for me. Billy would've never been so kind to me—or if he had, I would've paid for it later by him behaving like an asshole. "I'm not an idiot. Billy wasn't a nice person."

Yeah. I wasn't dreaming or under the influence of drugs. My response was correct. A person could only hold onto something for so long. Having my whole life ahead of me meant I was way too young to be the deranged lunatic who couldn't let go of anything. It wasn't like obsessing about Billy's death would undo his death. Nope. This was real life, and bad things happened all the time whether people wanted them to or not.

"Then why did you want to find out the truth?" Dean asked.

I shrugged. "Distracting myself with a frivolous task was easier than letting go."

"Wow. You're pretty self-aware."

No need for Dean to praise me. Being a writer didn't just mean observing other people. It meant understanding myself—even if I almost couldn't admit said flaw.

"It's the truth," I said.

"Relax. I believe you. Although I need to ask a question. What the hell did you see in Billy?"

Perhaps Dean had a future as a detective. There was just no stopping him with all his questions. Wanting one answer would've been understandable, but a second question pushed the limit. I didn't have to account for myself to him. However, something cathartic existed about this conversation. This moment with Dean was the first time since Billy's death that I was having an honest moment with anyone. And that fact was worth appreciating because a person could only be duplicitous.

"Billy knew how to make me feel special when he wanted even if he didn't give a shit about me," I said.

"Yeah. He was like that with everyone." Dean finished his croissant before wiping the crumbs off his coat and throwing the pastry bag into the garbage in front of him. "Don't get too upset about falling for him."

"It's also not surprising that Jonathan killed him in light of his past with Billy."

"Agreed. But I need to ask you another question."

Great. Asking two questions wasn't enough, and he had to demand another answer. Because I didn't have to be psychic to guess where the conversation was heading. Like when people got an achy sensation in their joints before a change in barometric pressure. Besides, I'd watched enough movies and television shows to figure out what happened when a con was the main romantic trope.

"Okay," I said.

Yup. New contradictions occurred everyday about me. Giving into Dean's demand simplified my life since he probably wouldn't stop hounding me if he really wanted to answer. And I therefore had no choice in ignoring the churning sensation in my stomach.

"Were you using me or did you actually like me?" he asked.

"Dean, please!"

"I want an answer."

I stood. "The truth is in the middle."

"This isn't a multiple-choice test where you can circle the letter that says both is the correct answer."

Dean had a lot to learn about life. I didn't have to be a philosopher to understand the truth really was sometimes in the middle. It wasn't like Dean was unattractive since my earlier comment about how I would've dated him in any other situation remained true. And that reasoning was why the uneasy sensation in my stomach still hadn't finished. Dean was still a real person, and I couldn't forget that fact.

"You wanted honesty, so that's what you got. Because, yeah. I intentionally spilled the water on you. But that doesn't mean everything was a lie. Our pool hall date was fun."

"What are we supposed to do?"

"I want to know why you aren't angrier with me?" I interrupted.

Maybe, just maybe, I was a lawyer in another life. That was the type of profession where someone dodged numerous questions by asking another question. Because anything was better than deciding what Dean meant to me.

"Billy shouldn't have died despite his lack of morality in addition to know how I'm not perfect," Dean said. "I never hazed anyone myself, but I was at that party when Henry died. Anyway, you didn't answer my question. We need to figure out what to do about us."

Shit. Dean couldn't let labeling us go. Because that would've been easier than prolonging the issue. The world wouldn't end if Dean and I no longer associated with each other. It wasn't like some law existed that said we had to be friends.

"There's nothing to figure out. We don't have to be anything," I said.

Dean tossed his coffee cup into the garbage can before standing, and reaching for my hands. "You don't mean that."

"We don't owe each other anything," I said, still not shoving Dean's hands away.

"Why do you have to be so difficult? I'm trying to give you a second chance."

"I never said you owed me." I paused for a beat. "My turn to ask a question. Why are you so desperate?"

Just because cruelty complicated life didn't mean I couldn't put someone on the spot. I deserved an answer since Dean treated me like a life jacket despite how romance wasn't enough for a perfect life.

"I'm tired of my shallow life. Yeah. I might go to parties and get good grades, but I want more out of life," he said.

"Have you tried dating apps?" I asked.

"I want an opportunity to get to know you."

"I'm sorry, but I need time to myself."

The nearest psychiatrist or psychologist should've thrown me a parade. Taking time for myself was the most emotional healthy thing to do because I could never get someone to care about me unless I healed.

Dean chuckled. "You're gonna have to try harder than that if you wanna push me away."

***

FRIDAY, OCTOBER 9, 2020

"Something wrong with your food, Carson?" Freddie asked while we sat at a table in back of the dining hall while a mixture of orange, pink, and purple swirled together in the afternoon sky.

I would've even snapped a photo of the sunset on any other day since the detail would make for a nice setting detail in a story. But not today. Staring at my pizza without having one bite was task enough—even though the warmth of the cheese, tomato, and other herbs wafted through the air.

I shoved my plate to the side. "Not hungry."

"No worries. At least you texted me back first about grabbing a bite to eat. Because that's more than I can about Chelsea and Amanda."

"I'm sure they would've come if they could."

"Yeah. You're probably right. Anyway, I want to know why you like you just got told you have to go to summer school."

I waved my hand through the air. "I'd rather hear about you. I mean, I'm rambling about my problems."

Yup. Even I sometimes realized when I blabbered for too long. Because the conclusion had nothing to do with a self-esteem crisis. It was the truth. Being best friends with Chelsea, Amanda, and Freddie meant taking an interest in their lives.

He smirked. "I'm your best friend, which means it's my job to listen."

"I know, but I don't want you to think I'm selfish."

"We would never think that. You also are being too hard on yourself. Anyone would need extra support after everything you've been through."

Perhaps the truth was once again somewhere in the middle. Being more interested in what my friends were up to wasn't mutually exclusive with being tough on myself. My age meant I was at the one point in life when a little selfishness was okay. It wasn't like I wanted to be like Gatsby, live in a mansion, and always throw lavish parties that people anticipated more than having a day off from work.

"Dean knows everything," I blurted.

"Wow. You really don't know how to be subtle."

"There's more."

He furrowed his eyebrows. "Do I even wanna know?"

Only Freddie could get away with that comment. Because I would've gone apeshit if anyone else joked with me like he just did. Life wasn't that tragic; it was just quirkier than the average teenager realized.

"Dean wants to get to know the real me. Almost as if being honest showed my vulnerability," I said.

"And how did you handle it?" he asked.

"I conceded the truth was somewhere in the middle, but that was it. I need time to myself regardless of how Dean believes I'm pushing him away."

"Okay," Freddie said. "But have you ever considered Dean might be right? And please don't be mad at me for making that comment. It's only the two of us right now, and I'd never put you on the spot like that if Amanda and Chelsea were here."

It didn't matter if I was five years old or fifty-five

years old. Looking away was sometimes the best option—
even if there wasn't anything to focus on since Freddie and
I were the only students in the dining hall right now.

Freddie patted my hand. "It's fine. You don't have
to answer my question now. Although you might want to
answer it for yourself at some point."

"Fair enough, but let's talk about you now. I want
to know what's new besides getting too much homework."

"I have a big debate with a local school next
week."

Holy shit. Forget about going to a party tonight. I
needed to go the pharmacy in town and get some vitamins
to help my memory. I couldn't have been so wrapped in
my own life that I forgot Freddie was on the debate team.

"Are you dreading the debate?" I asked.

"Nope. We've been preparing, and we're gonna
nail it."

"I don't mean to sound corny, but you and Chelsea complement each other with you being on the debate
team and her being on the chess team."

"Thanks. I never thought about that, but you're
right."

***

MONDAY, OCTOBER 12, 2020

I pushed my way through the crowd of students in the lob-
by of one of the academic buildings only to have a woman
accost when I wasn't even twenty feet away from the door.
A gust of wind also roared too, making my hair bounce.

The lady continued screaming. "You have a lot of
nerve to still be enrolled here after what you and Billy did
to me."

Shit. Dealing what Dean meant to me wasn't a big
enough problem. Nope. I also had to run into Mrs. Roberts. Because I couldn't forget about that day when her

replacement walked into my short story class, and Billy just kept smirking.

"How are you even back?" I asked.

"My suspension was only till the end of the school year."

"Whatever. I have nothing to say to you."

My response wasn't curt or rude—it was honest. Chatting with Mrs. Roberts wouldn't improve my mood, and I therefore needed to flee this conversation ASAP. A good chance also existed that I'd say something even harsher, which was all the more reason to leave. Yet I couldn't move my legs despite my brain knowing better. And I wasn't even referring to getting a rush from a dramatic situation. Mrs. Roberts deserved to suffer after how she treated me last year. It wasn't like I pushed her into a fireplace and have the scent of burning flesh waft through the air. She just deserved to feel shitty about herself. Adults, including teachers, weren't perfect and needed to know children and teens deserved respect. Because they'd never be respected if they didn't offer it in return.

Mrs. Roberts clutched her pearl necklace. "Excuse me?"

"You deserved your suspension. Having standards is one thing, yet you should be fucking ashamed for yourself. My lack of participation has nothing to do with whether or not I'm a good student."

"Yeah, it does."

"What was your goal with confronting me today?"

Yup. Time for Mrs. Roberts to be more succinct. Defending myself and letting her have it was one thing, yet I didn't have unlimited time to waste. Unless that was her goal in the first place. Because that fact wouldn't have surprised me. A lot of people were good at pissing away other people's time. Although said people probably would've been the first ones to throw a tantrum if roles were reversed. Life was always filled with hypocrisy at every turn. Almost like a parent who indulged fast food cravings telling his or her child to only eat fruits and vegetables.

"I just wanted to make you feel bad about how I lost my only source of income for seven months," she said.

Ouch. Perhaps Mrs. Roberts and I had more in common than I wanted to admit it. Our opinions didn't have to be the same in order to share a similarity. The fact was, we both wanted to make each other feel bad about our behavior.

I cackled. "It's not my job to care about your problems. But here's some free advice. If you want your students to like you, then don't be a bitch."

"I should report you for being so disrespectful," Mrs. Roberts said.

"Go ahead. I fucking dare you. But I'd take a moment to consider your behavior first."

"And what the hell is that supposed to mean?"

No offense to Mrs. Roberts but she was dumber than she seemed. Check that. No qualifier necessary—not after how she treated me. Anyway, my point was, being an adult meant she should've at least pretended to use her brain cells, including with figuring out how starting trouble wouldn't have been smart in light of her suspension last year. And the circumstances surrounding her complaining didn't matter. Even I wasn't oblivious to how I disrespected her more than once. She just shouldn't have attracted any attention from the school administration unless said attention involved getting a paper or book published. If less than a year passed since her suspension, then that meant the incident might've still been fresh in their minds.

"Never mind. Anyway, what exactly did Billy do to you?" I asked.

Confession time. I wasn't being dumb for the sake of being dumb. Billy never confessed what he did despite his telling look that day in class. And I wouldn't criticize myself for not being more demanding. Some facts weren't worth knowing—at least back when the original incident happened. I might've tricked myself into believing I was okay after being raped, yet that didn't mean I was fine since I could only handle so many facts. After all, I didn't need a PhD to understand how Billy loved making trouble. Because it wasn't just the fact that he had a look on his face when our short story class met Mrs. Roberts's replacement. It was the intensity of the look that mattered. The expression just hadn't resembled the Cheshire Cat from *Alice and Wonderland*. The look conjured up the idea of a child saying, "fuck you" to his or her parent when eating dessert before dinner when told not to.

"If you really wanna know, then I'll tell you. Perhaps learning the truth will shatter your precious of image of Billy," she said.

"Just get to the point."

"Billy went to the headmaster and accused me of both flirting with him and propositioning him for sex."

"And they just took his word for it?" I asked.

"The school has a zero tolerance for any type of sexual misconduct—whether the accused is a student or professor. Anyway, I have to go, because you've ruined enough of my morning." Mrs. Roberts strutted away while her high heels stabbed the pavement and a few more students trickled out of the academic building behind me.

I laughed. Mrs. Roberts heckled me, yet she believed I ruined her morning? Yeah. The woman needed serious help. Although what said help entailed wasn't for me to decide; I wasn't a professional. Besides, it wasn't like I cared enough to tell her she needed counseling.

***

TUESDAY, OCTOBER 13, 2020

Getting a text from my dead "boyfriend" wasn't the type of event that rolled off my tongue.

However, I couldn't ignore the message instructing me to meet in front of the chapel on the east side of campus—even if a steady drizzle now pounded against the crowd while the wind shot through the air. Because I had to see why someone would send me a message from Billy's phone. Although I didn't just have to worry about the rain and wind. Purple tinged lightning just zig-zagged across the sky, which was followed by several claps of thunder.

I cursed after checking the time on my iPhone. I wouldn't make it back to the dining hall before my first class, and the growling from my stomach wasn't exactly helping. Because it would only continue.

Shit. Someone must've been playing a joke on me since nobody approached the chapel yet.

Someone cackled. "You're finally getting what you deserve. Because you have no idea how much trouble you caused me."

Whirling around didn't even matter since a wooden baseball bat clocked me in the head the second I shifted my weight. I then clunked against the ground.

***

THURSDAY, OCTOBER 15, 2020

Footsteps echoed from the hallway and the shuffling of feet against the ground grew louder while I stretched and yawned.

I screamed after opening my eyes because of how I was in a gurney. One sniff of my surroundings was also all that I needed for how a python might as well have been wrapped around my torso, crushing me. Whether I realized the truth or not, the air wreaked of disinfectant.

Although I should've focused on the lock clinking and how someone sporting blue scrubs, a matching mask, and booties just shuffled into the room. The lights being off didn't help the blood traveling through my veins faster either. If I didn't know better, I would've guessed the person standing in front of me was about to kill me. Because that would've definitely happened if my life was a horror movie.

The person yanked the mask off, and my eyes almost popped out of their sockets. The guy standing in front of me couldn't have been real.

"I had to see you despite the risk," Billy said.

"I don't understand. What happened?"

"You're in the school's infirmary because you had an accident."

"The last thing I remember is getting a text from your cellphone saying to meet in front of the chapel."

Billy winked. "I'm disappointed. I thought I taught you better."

Now wasn't the time for sassiness no matter how much Billy's attitude was justified. Billy should've known I had no problem indulging some scenario where he was the one who texted me. I could pretend hope existed he was alive for one fleeting moment.

"Am I dreaming?" I asked.

Yeah. My question had to be stated. Discovering everything I did about Billy's death meant not even trusting my intuition. One minute Billy cared about me, and the next he didn't. One minute he was alive, and the next he wasn't. Because I could sit in bed all day listing his contradictions.

He sucked on his teeth. "You didn't just ask that question."

"Please tell me what's going on."

"You've been in and out of it for the past two days as a result of the painkillers they gave you," Billy replied.

Interesting. The painkillers might've meant I wasn't in my right mind. Although another possibility existed. My groggy state from almost being unable to keep my eyes open didn't mean Billy wasn't really standing here before me. My interest in writing meant clichés were just boring, not that they weren't true. Real life could be stranger than fiction. One only needed to watch the news to understand that fact.

"I was injured that bad?" I asked.

He gripped his scrub top harder—almost as if a small pathetic gesture was the only thing that would keep him from overreacting. "I'm afraid so."

"How'd you find out about the accident?" I asked.

"It was on the news, but that doesn't matter. I'm here now."

I touched my right eyelid and massaged it several times. "I know Jonathan killed you."

"We don't have time to discuss that. The important thing is getting to see you one last time."

Wow. His absence from my life didn't do anything to make him a better person. Because anyone else might've thrown him out of the room for refusing to be anything other than evasive.

"I also know about the hazing," I said.

"Stop ruining our time with serious talk."

"I can't help it if I don't like your dualities."

Billy didn't respond. Instead, he leaned in and kissed me. And I didn't even complain when a cold sensation jolted my cheeks from his hands pressing against them. The small amount of euphoria from a pipedream coming true needed to be prolonged as long as possible. I couldn't forget about the universe, and how something would happen in five minutes that changed my perception of my current moment with Billy.

"I should've known kissing you would shut you up," Billy said after pulling back from me a moment later.

"I want a real answer, Billy. Was it all a lie with us?"

Billy fanned himself with his mask, which still remained in his right hand. "You really should open the window. I'm gonna suffocate from how stuffy it is."

* * *

The wind rattled against the infirmary's brick exterior, and I whipped my head back and forth. There was just no other way to react. The window was open despite how it had been shut earlier. A mixture of an earthly and sweet-scented deodorant also filled the air. Like the kind of deodorant Billy wore.

Yeah. I might not have been certain of much, but one thing I didn't doubt was Billy's visit being real. That was the only explanation for his kiss being so tangible.

THEN

MONDAY, DECEMBER 2, 2019

"It's so great to be back at school." Amanda broke off a piece of her veal before dunking it in sauce and devouring the morsel in a matter of seconds.

Freddie snickered. "Do you ever get tired of school?"

Enjoying school was one thing, yet Amanda couldn't have been more enthusiastic about school if her life depended on it as a result of the inflection in her voice. And that was why I had no choice in agreeing with Freddie. It wasn't like he wanted to be mean. He just pointed out an obvious fact.

"You should eat your food before it gets cold, Carson." Chelsea reached for a napkin and blew her nose. "You need to keep your strength up if you expect to satisfy Billy's sex drive."

"Chelsea, please!" Freddie exclaimed. "We talked about having more discretion. Just because you have a thought, doesn't mean the rest of the world need to know."

Arguing wouldn't have accomplished anything since I could tell the difference between Chelsea and someone who wanted to be cruel in addition to how sitting at a table in the back of the dining hall meant nobody heard Chelsea's remark. However, Freddie was right. If I filtered my thoughts, then Chelsea could. It wasn't like she needed a high school diploma to know what was acceptable conversation.

I pouted. "It's not like Billy and I are talking."

"Shit! I forgot you have your short story class with him tomorrow." Freddie guzzled the rest of his Gatorade.

Yup. Mrs. Roberts leaving school didn't mean my short story class would be perfect. It wouldn't. Not when I hadn't discovered a solution to the Billy problem. Because I could either continue seeing him despite his enigma personality or I could find somebody new to pursue. Damn. I should've been more rationale. The smart thing to do would've been to pursue someone else. Yet that was the easier option and people often bombard children and teens with how the easiest option wasn't always the right option. Shit. If only problems were solved by flipping a coin. At least then I would've had less of a reason for my fluttering heart. I couldn't get that enraged if the only reason something happened was due to randomness.

"I know," I spat.

Chelsea flipped her hair over her shoulders. "You really should have the veal because I wouldn't lie to you if it was shit."

"She's right," Amanda said.

"I love it when you say that." Chelsea nibbled on her last piece of veal before grabbing another napkin and wiping the pale, brown sauce from her lips.

"Maybe I'm the stupid one. I should've known better than to sleep with him," I said.

Forget about whether I should've pursued Billy. Punishing myself was the easiest option. In a perfect world, I would've been interested in a straightforward guy or girl. Some mystery might've made life more exciting, but I didn't need a dynamic where I always asked myself what the hell was going on. That was no way to live since it was only a matter of time before my head exploded.

Amanda tapped my hand. "Everyone makes mistakes."

Chelsea giggled at the suggestion. "Sometimes more than once."

No shock necessary regarding Chelsea. Anyone could've guessed how she was the type of person to make that comment. This was the same person who talked about sex all the time.

"My point is that you shouldn't be too hard on yourself. You just need to make sure you learned something from said mistake," Amanda said.

"That's true." Taking a bite of veal wouldn't make my life perfect. But no reason existed for my stomach's loud noises. Not eating would also ruin my brain power since I wouldn't make any good decisions from my lack of concentration. If nothing else, I succeeded with creating minor amusement as a result of my teeth crunching down so loudly on the veal. Yup. The dining hall just didn't serve veal. They also coated it in a thick layer of breadcrumbs, which gave the meat a certain flavor that I couldn't resist.

"Did you guys have a good Thanksgiving?" Chelsea asked.

Amanda nodded. "It was okay."

"Same," Freddie said.

"I wish the vacation lasted longer," Chelsea said.

Kudos to her for saying what almost everyone other student on campus must've thought. Being trapped in school for the rest of my life would've been the ultimate nightmare. An education was only one facet of a person's life, and thus wouldn't matter ten or fifteen years from now. It wasn't like I needed an extensive education to be a writer. I just needed to be well-read and craft a beautiful sentence or two.

"We'll be done with the semester before you know it." Amanda took a bite of her pasta.

"That day can't come soon enough," Chelsea said.

My face drooped. "I don't mean to sound like a pathetic person. But what the fuck am I supposed to do about Billy?"

Yeah. I brought the subject back to Mr. Trouble-maker. Talking about an issue till I couldn't breathe might've seemed superfluous, yet I had to have a plan when I marched into class tomorrow. Not knowing what I wanted was when the trouble started because that allowed for manipulation.

Freddie looked me in the eye. "If you really wanna pursue him, then you'll have to accept his flaws."

Great point. Except intellectualizing an idea and following through with said idea were two different things. Marriage wasn't required for respect, yet Billy could've spent the night in my dorm room. Doing so wouldn't have killed him as opposed to making him drink an entire tub of hydrochloric acid.

* * *

Someone knocked on my door a couple of hours later while I sat by my desk watching TV. But I didn't get off my ass and answer the door. Nope. No thanks. Television was the one part of the day I could relax.

The noise returned.

Shit. I had no choice but to an answer my door. Although I deserved to be proud of myself. My heart didn't beat faster while I wobbled to the door. Nothing good came of inventing problems that didn't exist since I hadn't done anything wrong.

My jaw sank when I opened the door. "What are

you doing here, Billy?"

"I wanted to give you this." He handed me the roses. "I remember you said roses were your favorite flower when we did the project."

"You didn't have to do this," I said.

"Yeah, I did. You're clearly mad at me, and I intend on making it up to you."

"There's nothing to make up—we just had sex. We aren't friends or anything."

Yeah. Even I sometimes uttered an ambiguous sentence. Whether I liked the fact or not, only uncertainty existed these days. It wasn't like Billy would change into a different person no matter how much I might've wished the opposite was true.

I shoved the bouquet against his chest. "You can have them back. I don't want them."

Returning a gift might not have been the most thoughtful gesture. But I didn't owe Billy anything. Besides, if he wanted to fix things between us, then he would have to work for them. Otherwise he'd never become a better person.

"That's fine. The bouquet didn't even cost me anything," Billy said.

"What the hell are you talking about? It's not like they're raining down from the sky."

"My friend gave me the bouquet because he was going to give them to his girlfriend, but she dumped him before he could give them to her."

Causing a scene wouldn't win me any awards for stability, yet I didn't have a choice when I smacked the bouquet against Billy's chest. Wanting to be genuine couldn't be faulted. However, a friend giving the roses to Billy proved once again he was sort of a jackass. A real man would've bought a gift himself if he wanted to make amends.

Billy smirked. "No offense, but you're gullible."

"What the hell?"

"I went to the florist in town this afternoon. When I want something, I get it."

"You've gotta be joking," I said.

"Besides, my friends don't have good taste."

I put my hands on my hips. "How do I know which version is true?"

Screw my question's complexity since some people—like Amanda—might've thought getting a straight answer from Billy was impossible. My curiosity had to be satisfied if it was the last thing I did. Only then could I figure out how to handle Billy.

"I wouldn't lie about something simple," Billy said.

"Okay. Fine. Thanks for the flowers."

He beamed his eyes. "Are you gonna invite me in?"

Kudos to Billy for his tenacity. He might have been a lot of things, but I couldn't accuse him of giving up. And for all I knew, his life might've depended on talking to me right now since some people might not have been so push.

"We don't have anything to discuss," I said. "I've had a long day, and just plan on watching a little television."

"That doesn't sound fun," he said.

"Not everything in life is supposed to be fun. Anyway, I meant what I said. The gift is nice, but please have a good evening."

Billy whimpered. "What do you want me to do? Get on my hands and knees and beg for forgiveness since I didn't stay the night with you?"

"You still haven't told me what you want?" I demanded.

He took a quick glance around the hallway. Nobody was shuffling by, so he pulled me in for a kiss while the bouquet dropped to the ground.

I walked backwards into my dorm room while Billy closed the door before gripping my face.

Pushing him away would've only meant acting like a four-year-old, though, and I couldn't have that. Billy's character might have been more than questionable, but complaining wouldn't help if he was giving me what I wanted. Because even I still needed to get laid.

***

WEDENSDAY, DECEMBER 4, 2019

Billy sat up in my bed before grabbing his boxers, pants, and shirt, which happened to be on my pillow while stars lit up the night sky. He then slid into to his plaid boxers in a matter of seconds before shifting his weight.

I grimaced. Somehow, I hadn't noticed the red scars on his lower back before.

"Something wrong?" Billy asked.

"What happened to your back?"

"You wouldn't believe me. Nobody would." Billy slid into his clothes in a matter of seconds.

"You don't know that." I remained silent for a sec. "This might be a dirty thing to say, but I care about you."

"It's not a questioning of doubting you."

"Then what?" I demanded.

"Some things are better left unsaid."

"I'm not sure about that…"

Billy bit his lip. "Leave it alone, Carson."

"Fine. There's something else we should disuss." I gave him a dirty look, though. Staying the night every time we slept together might've been unrealistic, yet he also didn't have run as soon as he finished.

"Sorry, but I've gotta leave. I have an 8:00 A.M. class," Billy said.

"Whatever. I'm sure I could find another girl or guy to hook up so I don't have to spend the night alone."

My remark didn't make me a dick. It was about winning this power play with Billy—even if most people would've criticized me for that not being the healthiest attitude. I deserved respect, and harshness was how I achieved said desire. It wasn't like I had a voodoo doll of Billy that I poked whenever he disappointed me.

Billy cupped my chin. "Don't be like that."

"I was making a joke."

"It wasn't funny. Anyway, consider yourself lucky. You're the only person I've slept with more than twice."

"I still can't believe we've slept together four times now," I said.

I wasn't exaggerating. Billy and I slept together on Monday and Tuesday in addition to today. And that fact wasn't exactly a bad thing. Yes. More to life existed than sex, yet a euphoria still rushed through my body from Billy giving me something—even if something was only ten minutes of pleasure.

"Believe it. We're both two teenage guys," he said. "Although if it makes you feel better you and your friends can come to Charity Now's Christmas party this Friday."

"You're just telling me about this now?" I asked.

Only having sex as opposed to going on dates didn't mean I had to erase my personality. Billy and I were kind of friends before the first time we slept together, so he could've been a little more courteous. It wasn't like I had nothing better to than hope Billy included me in his life.

He frowned. "Calm down. The important thing is you know about the event."

"Is the party at the Barn?"

"No. It's in the Rec Center gym since the event is school related. Although that's kind of a bummer because there won't be any booze. Don't worry, though. We'll have an after party at the Barn around midnight."

"I'll think about it."

"Come on! You know you wanna go."

Whether Billy considered his comment or not, his remark meant being on dangerous ground. I didn't care if the Queen of England stood before me. Nobody told me what to think.

"Can I go as your date?" I asked.

"You know how I feel about coming out of the closet, Carson. Anyway, the only requirement is to either bring twenty dollars—cash or check—or a gently used item of clothing."

"Do the guys in Charity Now really have nothing better to do than to berate you for being whatever your sexuality is? They can't be that homophobic," I said.

Not outing Billy didn't preclude me from discussing his sexuality with him—I wouldn't ever out someone. However, I couldn't let go of how I deserved an epic romance. Unless sleeping with Billy was the universe playing a joke on me, meaning I had him without technically having him since he might not ever commit to me.

"It really would be so great if you attended the function. But I'm not going to force you to do something you don't want to do. Although remember your contribution if you come since we can't disappoint the homeless youth shelter." Billy kissed me before I could blink. Then, he darted towards my door, and I didn't even curse when the door's slamming echoed. In Billy's case, closing the door too loudly had nothing to do with being angry. He just wasn't the type of person who thought about the right way to close a door.

* * *

THURSDAY, DECEMBER 5, 2019

"Thank you for the Caramel Macchiato," Amanda said.

The cashier standing behind the coffee cart handed me the change before I shoved it inside my wallet and Amanda and I resumed walking.

"No problem. It's the least I can do when asking for advice," I said.

"Being your best friend means you don't have to

thank me for anything."

Sure. Her comment might have been true, but I wasn't clueless. Some people might not have had the patience to do with my quirks.

"So, what do you think I should do?" I asked.

Yeah. Even I sometimes was capable of getting to the point. Nothing good came from prolonging my question. Knowing the answer sooner rather than later would help because then I'd be able to decide what to do.

"I have a suggestion, but you aren't going to like it," she said.

"Don't tell me I should cut Billy out of my life?"

"The opposite. You should attend the fundraiser, and I'll be your date. It's the perfect place to stage a kiss," Amanda said.

I must not have heard her correctly. Friends didn't go around kissing their friends no matter how long they knew each other. Doing so wasn't normal behavior no matter how optimistic someone was.

I halted. "You wanna kiss me?"

"It might not push him out of the closet, but us making out is the type of thing that'll mess with his ego."

I didn't know whether I should've been concerned with Amanda's dark turn or applaud her remark. Coming up with a convoluted suggestion illustrated how she realized most things in life weren't binary. But she was still my best friend, and I couldn't let her personality become too twisted. Besides, she would've been the first person to criticize me for inventing an indecent proposal.

"Are you sure you just don't want revenge for how you're little one night stand with him didn't work out?" I asked.

"That too. But I was serious when I told you never to bring up my tryst with Billy again, because you're the only one who knows."

"Fine. I'm in. But you'll have to bring twenty dollars or a gently used item of clothing."

Our agreement didn't make me childish. Billy just needed to care about me more—even in a small way. Because I couldn't only be someone who gave him pleasure no matter how willing a participant I might've been in our hookups. I was still a person, and Billy couldn't forget that fact anytime soon.

"That won't be a problem," she said.

***

FRIDAY, DECEMBER 5, 2019

Amanda and I strutted into the Rec Center gymnasium with our arms linked together. But at least I didn't bet her any money about whether or not her plan would work. And I wasn't even referring to how being wrong sucked. I was referring to how Billy would've been the human equivalent to a deer caught in car headlights while he stood by the beverage and snack table a few yards away from the gym's entrance.

"Here you go," Amanda said, handing Billy our combined donation.

"Thank you," Billy said.

"Don't mention it. We're here to help," I said.

"Can I get you two a beverage or a snack?"

"I'm sorry, but there's something I have to do before we think about refreshments or food." Amanda kissed me, yet nobody from the various scattered locations in the gym stared at us. That was the thing about people. Most of the time, they didn't give a flying fuck about anyone else's drama.

"You two are dating?" Billy asked after Amanda and I detached from our embrace.

Amanda pushed her headband further up her head when it started to slip. "Yeah. I'd call it dating. I mean, we just became exclusive today, but that still counts, right?"

"Absolutely," Billy mumbled.

Punishing myself for how I should've been a better person could wait till later. Whether I thanked Amanda or not, Billy's hesitation proved I might've had to consult her more often when dealing with Billy. And that was exactly what I needed since dysfunctional games was sometimes the only way to get someone to respond.

* * *

Billy and I were in my bed sometime later with the bed comforter wrapped around us. Although a room full of nervous students about ready to take the SAT's had nothing on the silence right now. Just because Billy and I slept together for a fifth time didn't mean we had to speak.

He grunted. "I'm not as stupid as you think. Kissing Amanda was obviously a planned stunt."

Shit. Amanda's plan might've looked good on paper, yet I couldn't forget how I was still dealing with Billy. He might've been a lot of things, but I couldn't accuse him of being stupid. Not when he sometimes knew the right thing to say so I wouldn't cut him out of my life for good.

"I thought you didn't have feelings?" I asked.

"Very funny."

"Don't tell me you're actually bothered by me dating someone else?"

"Fine. You win," Billy said. "If you want more than sex, I'll take you out on a real date. But it has to be somewhere off campus where nobody will see us."

Getting what I wanted didn't always mean happiness filled my insides. If anything, the empty feeling in my stomach expanded. Relationships weren't supposed to be about power plays, yet I coerced more out of Billy than he wanted to give. And for that, I would absolutely stare at my dorm room ceiling a little longer tonight. Amanda could concoct one indecent proposal or ten indecent proposals. However, no amount of games changed Billy's character. Nothing would. Billy had to change for himself if he wanted to be a better person.

NOW

SATURDAY, OCTOBER 17, 2020

"It's bullshit that the doctor wouldn't let you get visitors till today." Amanda slouched while sitting in a chair in front of my gurney next to Freddie and Chelsea.

Freddie inhaled several deep breaths. "You need to relax, Amanda. Carson is okay, and that's what counts."

Chelsea picked at her nail. "No offense, but I would've brought you back to life just to kill you myself if you died."

"Really?" Freddie asked. "I don't think I need to tell you how that defines melodramatic behavior."

"I don't care. None of us can die. We're all going to live together in a mansion and drink gin till we're in our nineties," Chelsea said.

Yeah. Chelsea had more in common with me than

she realized. Making an idealistic statement was something I would've done on an ordinary Monday afternoon. However, I wouldn't fault her for her naiveté today. Getting smacked in the head made someone dream of living long life and partying. Fun sure beat death.

Sweat rolled down my face, and I shook my shirt in hopes of cooling off, yet the room might as well have been closing in on me. There was just no changing how an infirmary reinforced claustrophobia. Because I shouldn't have been stuck in this bed; I should've been focused on what I'd binge on *Netflix* tonight or what party I wanted to go too.

Amanda bit her lip. "Something wrong?"

"It's stuffy in here, so could one of you please open the window?" I asked.

"Of course." Amanda rose with fighting it out with Chelsea and Freddie about had to get up an open the window.

Cold air traveled into the room in a matter of seconds, yet I didn't sigh in relief. Not much sweat clung to my skin or hospital gown, but I couldn't forget about what happened the other day. My window had been opened after Billy left, begging the question of his visit being real. Although whether I could tell my friends about my concern was another matter altogether. Five seconds were all that I needed to contemplate whether I thought Billy visited me was only because of my pain killers or the event actually happened.

"Still too warm?" Amanda asked.

"Something else has been bothering me beside the temperature," I said.

Chelsea giggled. "You should tell us what's on your mind so you won't have to suffer alone."

Good gracious. There was no escaping the truth now. Not after Chelsea insisted I come clean. It wasn't like they could un-learn what I said.

Maybe, just maybe, I should've given my friends

more credit. They hadn't ditched me after my Billy theory, so there might have been hope for them thinking I wasn't out of my mind. Besides, I would never know how they'd react unless I gave them an opportunity to prove themselves.

"She's right," Freddie said.

"I don't think Billy is dead," I said.

"What are you talking about?" Amanda asked. "You know he's dead. You unraveled the phony suicide conspiracy."

Freddie gave Amanda a venomous look. "Take it easy. Maybe he has memory loss he isn't aware of."

"I remember everything except who hit me," I said. "Anyway, I'm talking about how Billy wasn't murdered. He visited me the other night."

"Why do you feel this way?" Chelsea asked.

Perhaps Chelsea had a future as a therapist. Only someone in the mental health profession would've been guaranteed not to judge a ludicrous comment.

"The window was open when I woke up, yet I know it was closed when I went to bed," I said. "I really am telling you the truth; I swear it. I'm the one who didn't snitch on Dean and company."

Freddie glanced at Chelsea and then Amanda, and then back at Chelsea. "Maybe we should tell him about Friday night."

"That can wait. We don't want anything to jeopardize his recovery. It's a miracle his attacker didn't hit him harder, because his skull would've been crushed," Amanda said.

Chelsea sighed at her. "I'm sorry, but Freddie's right. The truth can't wait when the stakes are so high."

"What do you mean?" I asked.

"Jonathan fell off the astronomy tower Friday night," Chelsea revealed.

My rapist couldn't have been dead. The universe didn't work like that. Killing off Jonathan would've been too easy. Although I wouldn't deny the relief flooding my body right now. Wishing bad on someone had nothing to do with my opinion. Some actions were unforgivable, and that included rape. Besides, I hadn't killed him, which meant my hands were clean.

"The official ruling is that his death was an accident," Freddie said. "But there have been whispers about how some students might've seen someone in a black hoodie push Jonathan off the astronomy tower."

"What does this have to do with me seeing Billy?" I asked.

"Can't you connect the dots?" Amanda asked.

My back hairs shot up. Billy might've been a lot of things, but he wasn't a killer. Murder would've been too messy for him. He hadn't even been able to make an effort with me, thus proving he didn't care enough to do something so unforgiveable. "Are you saying that you think Billy killed Jonathan?" I asked.

"He knew about the rape," Chelsea said. "And that's why my money is on Jonathan being your attacker."

"But I never pressed charges in addition to how I've left him alone," I said.

Amanda shook her head in a vigorous fashion. "Doesn't matter. He could still see you as a threat. Besides, some people aren't meant to be understood."

"I need an honest answer regardless of whether you think you'll offend me. Do you think Billy could be alive?" I reached for my water cup on the in front of me—which was connected to the gurney—when Freddie got up, grabbed the cup, and held it in front of mouth. So, I just concentrated on my lips remaining on the straw and slurping the remaining water.

Bless Freddie. Doing the right thing didn't make him perfect since any decent person would've helped an injured friend. But even the tiniest action defined someone's character. And I kind of needed any positive fact to hold onto that I could in light of Billy maybe being alive and almost dying. Those facts just couldn't be taken like someone forcing them to swallow a bitter pill which provided essential medical help.

"I wouldn't be shocked if Billy was alive. He's the type of person that could pull something like that off," Chelsea said.

I tilted my head. The blinds being open on the other side of the room meant the person sitting in the leather chair outside my room was visible. And in my case, that meant figuring out why the hell Dean was in the infirmary.

"Dean doesn't know when to quit it," I said.

"Don't be too tough on him. Not everyone would spend their free time waiting outside their crush's room. Especially when you hate him," Amanda said.

My eyes bulged. "Don't put words in my mouth. Anyway, you guys have to promise me that you won't tell anyone about my theory."

Nope. I couldn't take any risks, and that included leaving a question up to chance despite how some might've argued I should've known that they didn't even have to think twice about keeping my promise.

"We aren't that dumb," Freddie said.

"No offense, but I get the feeling you're kicking us out," Amanda said.

I yawned. "Sorry. My head still hurts in addition to how I wanna to sleep."

"Relax. We have homework we should pretend to be doing," Freddie said.

"But text us if you need anything," Amanda said.

Yeah. Her comment wasn't an error. I had my iPhone on me when I woke up, and one of the nurses gave me a spare charger since mine was in my dorm rom.

"Of course. And thanks. Don't laugh, but having you guys here makes a difference," I said. "Because I didn't know what I would do if I didn't have anyone to tell all my quirky thoughts too."

Chelsea pushed her sleeves up. "Yeah. It's a bummer that your parents are stuck in Colorado because of a blizzard."

Nope. Coincidences weren't unrealistic despite how some people would've argued that not having my parents visit me during this trauma was more than a cruel twist of fate. It actually happened. Although I hadn't cried about them being unable to visit me. Nope. Them not being here saved me from omitting, exaggerating, or lying about everything that happened to me since Billy "died." And that was a kindness whether or not I'd ever thank the universe for anything. A person could either deal with a medical issue or mold the truth to fit their story, not both.

"And you can't forget about my grandmother who is spending the next three weeks in Mexico," I said.

"Don't be hard on her," Chelsea said. "She deserves some tequila. In fact, we all deserve some, and I'm going to buy you the biggest bottle of tequila once you're discharged."

Amanda brushed her jeans off after standing. "Although you should give Dean a chance. We both know you can do a lot worse than him."

I feigned a smile. "Maybe."

"Anyway, you better get out of her ASAP because I'll kick your ass if you can't come to my photography debut next Friday," Amanda said.

Good for her. Amanda deserved her own hobby because the same would've been true if I always gave advice to a conflicted friend.

* * *

SUNDAY, OCTOBER 18, 2020

Dean hovered over my gurney while rays of mid-morning sunlight trickled into the infirmary room and a few birds chirped outside the window. "It was kind of you to let me visit."

"Only fair."

"I want you to know that I didn't come here to pressure you," he stammered "I just wanted to make sure you're okay. Although I still can't believe this happened to you…"

"I know, but the issue is complicated. And no worries; talking is fine."

"What do you mean?"

"Forget it. I'm concerned with why you're hiding your hands behind your back," I said.

Not mentioning Billy possibly being alive wasn't about keeping something from Dean. I needed a reprieve from him for one fleeting moment since Billy occupied too much of my time. Anyone could've told me how the dynamic hadn't been healthy in addition to how still thinking about him so much wasn't normal. There was also no telling how Dean would handle Billy being alive. Because he didn't have to be a mean person to panic about a revelation. Overreacting was a part of human nature. I didn't owe Dean anything either besides a thank you for visiting, thus further proving I shouldn't feel bad. Even if Dean and I would've been dating in a hypothetical world where Billy and I never met. Because that world looked pretty damn good as a result of the drama that wouldn't have happened if Billy never talked to me at that Barn party last year. Fuck. I'd never fathom how one event could have so much impact on a person's life. That just seemed so trivial.

"What are you thinking about?" Dean asked.

"Billy would never buy me a gift."

"I'm sure that isn't true. He must have cared about you in his own way."

"Must be the key word," I said.

Dean and I continued our eye contact, yet we didn't speak. Although no complaints from me. Someone's gaze being so intense that I would've melted in a matter of seconds if his eyes were lasers was problem enough for one afternoon. Because I couldn't fight my past interactions with Dean no matter how hard I tried. Despite his one moral lapse, he never did anything that made never being born more tempting than an automatic A on a final exam. And I wasn't referring to Jonathan; I was referring to Billy. No human should've loved somebody so much that death tempted them as a result of the passion being too intense.

"Wait," I said. "You still haven't revealed what your hiding behind your back."

Dean handed me an envelope, and I ripped it open. Inside it, was a FEEL BETTER card and a fifty dollar Starbucks gift card. In fact, the glitter on the card shimmered while sunlight beamed into my room.

"I hope you like it," he murmured.

"I love it." I put the Starbucks card, FEEL BETTER card, and envelope on the wooden tray, which was attached to the gurney. My eye contact with Dean resumed, yet silence wasn't an option. So, I did the only thing I could. I counted to ten in my head while another breeze trickled inside. Dean was neither Billy nor perfect, but he didn't have to be either of those things. Getting me a gift went beyond showing up since he took the initiative without anyone telling him what to do. "I want you to kiss me."

Dean kissed me, and my pulse increased, but a new romance wasn't the issue. From the corner of my eye, a person in a black hoodie hovered outside my room. Like the kind of black hoodie Jonathan's killer sported. The hood shrouded the person's face, though, which meant not identifying the creeper. Except the person in the black hoodie just trekked down the hallway before I could blink, and was soon out of sight.

* * *

WEDNESDAY, OCTOBER 21 2020

"Did you ever think that being on the rowing team would be helpful?" I asked.

A gust of wind whipped across the water while gray clouds stained the sky. But maybe, just maybe, there the tingling sensation in my stomach would go away. Checking my iPhone before Freddie and I went rowing meant believing it wouldn't rain, yet weather forecasts weren't perfect.

Freddie laughed at my comment while he continued as we sat in the canoe. "Never. But I'm glad it's providing you with amusement."

"This isn't a game. Billy is probably alive," I said.

"I know this isn't a laughing matter. Although have you thought about what you would say to Billy if you see him again?"

So much for Amanda being the one tough in the group. Freddie just had to ask me a difficult question. It wasn't as if my life was complicated enough by merely considering the possibility of Billy being alive. Nope. I also had to verbalize said thought.

He sighed. "I'm sorry. You don't have to answer the question if you don't want to. I'm not stupid, and know it was unfair of me."

Good save. I was so in the mood to respond to the possibility of Billy being alive. In fact, I hadn't thought about the issue enough. I'd now have to consider it every second of the day. Like when I stared at my dorm room ceiling at night while I should've already fallen asleep.

"I'm just thankful you remembered the fisherman. Although I hope he's there," I said.

Freddie rolled his eyes. "Please don't invent a problem that doesn't exist. He's always usually out on the water between two in the afternoon and eight in the evening."

"Do you really think Billy is capable of murder?" I asked.

Yup. I couldn't vanquish the thought regardless of

how negative it was. Billy might've been guilty of a lot, yet he couldn't have been a killer. That would've meant I was literally in bed with a murderer, which meant no number of showers would cure how unnerving being close to a demented person was.

"Where's that coming from?" he asked.

"You, Amanda, and Chelsea are the ones who told me about Jonathan…"

"And now I'm starting to think we should've never done that."

The wind picked up, making the salt water stench trickling through the air more distinct. Damn. It didn't matter how obvious the idea sounded, but I couldn't have been so obtuse that I forgot my boarding school was in a coastal town.

"The person in the black hood lurked outside of my infirmary room while Dean visited me," I said.

Telling someone about my near encounter with the black hooded stranger had to be done no matter how difficult doing so might've been. Freddie wouldn't be able to solve my problems, but he'd be able to listen. And that might've been enough. Just the prospect of someone else knowing something jarring meant not bearing the burden alone. I couldn't even speculate what life would be like if Billy just wasn't alive, but was also up to something ghastlier than I ever imagined.

"What's your point?" Freddie demanded.

"Billy better not be jealous."

"I don't think you want me to answer that question."

"You're probably right. But maybe, just maybe, this whole situation is a giant misunderstanding."

Denial wasn't only something people teased about being a river in Egypt. It was a real coping mechanism. Not doubting my intuition and sanity was one thing. However, a few seconds of pretend was okay. If Billy was alive, that meant figuring out why the hell he was okay with people thinking he died. That just wasn't normal since it was the type of thing that belonged in a spy novel.

"I just wanna remind you that the fisherman might not even know anything, so please don't get disappointed if you don't get the results you want," Freddie said.

Meaning well and not being condescending were two different things. Whether Freddie realized the truth or not, I wasn't a little kid who needing protection from the truth. On the contrary, the truth was more important than oxygen. Only then would I be able to know what to do with my life.

Freddie rowed up near the fishing boat a few minutes later. "Evening, sir."

The fisherman might've been in his boat, but he didn't seem like he would win any awards for his work ethic since he was just puffing on a cigarette while his metal fishing rod remained on the bloat's floor. Almost as if the cigarette excited him more than catching fish. And that idea was more than. The man could either relax or work, not do both at the same time.

"We were wondering if you'd be able to help us," Freddie said.

Letting Freddie do the talking didn't make me a coward. I was just being practical. I shouldn't have had to talk if I didn't want to. The only thing worse than public speaking was being forced to streak across campus. Because that activity wasn't on my bucket.

"It depends what you want." He took another drag, and a plume of smoke exited his mouth.

Freddie pulled out his iPhone from his pocket before placing this index finger and thumb on Billy's photo and enlarging it. He then turned it around for the fisherman to see. "We were wondering if you might've seen this guy a little over a month ago. His name is Billy."

"Save your breath, son," interrupted the man. "Everyone knows who Billy is."

"We think he might be alive," I touted.

Yeah. Public speaking might not have been my favorite activity. But that didn't mean I had to be completely silent. I had the biggest stake in the Billy situation, and that meant picking my balls up off the floor and pretending I wasn't afraid. Talking to the fisherman wouldn't kill me even though he had a skull tattoo under his right eye lid in addition how he had a gray ponytail and beard that extended several inches past his chest. And I couldn't forget about his yellow teeth. They were just charming. In fact, I'd have to ask him who his dentist was.

"And why the hell would you think that?" The man took a longer drag than before and smoke oozed out of his mouth. Then, he threw the cigarette butt into the ocean and grabbed another cigarette from his pack before groping through his jean jacket pockets and yanking out his lighter. One flick of the lighter later, and more smoke blew out of his mouth while the stench lingering in the air from his last cigarette became more amplified since he resumed smoking.

"I've seen him since his alleged suicide," I said.

Freddie gave me a look, yet I couldn't pay much attention to his possible disapproval. Revealing information wasn't always easy because I had to worry about whether the knowledge empowered someone in a good or bad way. However, I didn't have a choice. Not when Billy's behavior might escalate after killing Jonathan.

The man coughed so loud before taking a subsequent drag on his cigarette, that any reasonable person might've thought a piece of his lung should've fallen out of his mouth. "You're right. The boy didn't kill himself."

Bingo. I now had no choice but to focus. Having my mind be preoccupied with something random meant missing out on something important. And I couldn't have that—not when I might've been so close to getting answers. Giving me the opportunity for answers only to have the moment slip through my fingers was a classic dick move the universe wouldn't have hesitated over. Not even for a split-second.

"What do you mean?" Freddie asked.

"His body washed out with the tide, and I picked him out of the water." The fisherman lit another cigarette.

People might've been more than their pathologies in addition to how judging people for an unhealthy habit wasn't always fair since everyone made mistakes. But my jaw would've been down to my ankles if the man told me how cigarettes he smoked in a day. If he lit three cigarettes in such a short time, then betting he smoked more than a pack of day proved safe. However, that was where my imagination stopped. Contemplating his tar infested lungs would've only made my body shudder. And I couldn't have that—not when Freddie's glare meant having to coming up with another question ASAP.

"Did he drown?" I asked.

"No. He was floating on the water when I plucked him out of the ocean," the fisherman said.

"He was unconscious?" Freddie asked.

The man flicked the cigarette butt into the ocean. "Yeah. But he the guy was a little shit."

"And why would you say that?" I asked.

Anyone with even a little understanding about Billy would've been able to infer her wasn't perfect, yet I couldn't put words in the man's mouth. Letting him talk was the only way of finding out the truth. I'd never get my life back unless I finished sleuthing.

"He made me end my fishing early and take him to the motel near the marina." The fisherman took out the pack of cigarettes from his pocket. Except there were no more cigarettes for him to take. Instead, he cursed and discarded the empty pack in the ocean.

I wouldn't judge the man for littering, though. Not when his information offered more of a thrill than a police officer engaged in a high-speed car chase with a fugitive. I just had to hear the end of the story now.

"Why did you help him if you didn't wanna stop

fishing?" Freddie asked.

"The look in fear in his eyes couldn't have been faked." The man leaned over and picked up the fishing pole and casted the bait into the water. In fact, the bait even thudded when landing the water.

"Then what happened?" I asked.

The man shrugged. "I don't know. I dropped him off in the motel parking lot, and that was the last time I saw him."

"And you didn't consider going to the police?" Freddie asked.

Doing me a favor didn't mean Freddie escaped criticism. He wasn't, and should've known better than to be so confrontational. And my reasoning had nothing to do with bowing for the fisherman and thinking he was God. I didn't. He still just didn't seem like the type of person someone should anger. Not now. Not ever.

"I like to mind my own business," the man said, raising his voice.

"What about his head? Was he bleeding?" I asked.

The fisherman tapped his knees. "Yeah. But it was just a minor scrape in addition to how the cut had stopped bleeding when I got him out of the water."

Okay. Good to know the blood on the rock made sense from Freddie and mine's earlier sleuthing. Because I'd hate to think a rock with a little blood on it had just fallen from the sky. That would've been too bizarre even for me.

"Can we get the name of the motel you took him to?" Freddie asked.

* * *

THURSDAY, OCTOBER 22, 2020

I walked out of one of the academic buildings while not one single cloud floated in the sky. Apparently, the weather was unreliable like Billy since my former lover wasn't the only entity capable of changing from one extreme to the next without warning. Because I never considered how sunny weather was forecasted for today in light of the rain pummeling us on the way back to the rowing team warehouse last night.

Enough contemplating, though. Otto just approached me, yet an impromptu visit with someone I didn't know hadn't caused my frowning. His shaking body was what made me almost blink several times.

"Everything okay, Otto?" I asked.

"I owe you an apology."

Perhaps I wasn't the only sensitive person in the world. Expressing contrition without proper context was the type of thing someone who loved overanalyzing social encounters did.

"You must be mistaken, because I can't think of anything you did that might've offended me. And trust me. I'd let you know if you fucked up."

"It's all my fault," Otto said, stuttering.

"You're going to have to be more specific. I can't forgive somebody for something I'm not aware of."

"You know how Billy's father still hasn't cleared his stuff from my dorm room?" he asked.

I nodded.

"Well, Jonathan made me do it. Because you know him. There's no refusing Jonathan," Otto said.

Shit. No matter what I did, I couldn't escape Jonathan. I so loved talking about him as much as possible. It wasn't enough the image of him forcing himself inside me against the tree hadn't been etched into my brain enough times. Nope. More misery was needed.

"I'm sorry, but I still don't follow you," I said.

"I sent the iMessage from Billy, using his laptop. The iMessage that almost got you killed."

"Why are you telling me this?" I asked.

"I want to be a better person despite some of the

questionable decisions that Charity Now has made."

I dug my fingernails into my palms, struggling to breathe. I might not have wanted to be friends with Otto, but I still understand doing better and not wanting to repeat the same mistake over and over like I had by sleeping with Billy so many times. Yeah. I sometimes acknowledged my shortcomings despite how unflattering they were. If I couldn't be honest with myself at least some of the time, then I'd never be able to have a genuine interaction with someone.

* * *

FRIDAY, OCTOBER 23, 2020

Chatting with the headmaster wouldn't make my list of the most top ten epic moments of my life. However, at least our meeting meant getting an excused absence from my morning class. And I didn't have to be perfect to understand that missing a class was only a positive—even if I might as well have been trapped in a coffin while sitting in this chair. Because it wouldn't haven't killed the headmaster to open the blinds and two windows behind him. Anything that would've meant the air not being so hot.

"Thanks for coming on such short notice," he said.

"No problem."

His good intentions didn't mean laughing was bad. No reason existed for him to sound so formal. It wasn't like he was talking to the Queen of England.

He waved a bowl at me. "Candy?"

"I'm good, but thanks."

"No worries. Anyway, I should get to the point about why I called you here."

A jackass would've scrutinized him over semantics. He emailed me as opposed to talking on the phone, yet I wouldn't be the jerk. Because I would've pummeled someone if roles were reversed and someone fought about

170

whether I should've sounded literal or not. Like when an older creative writing teacher might've marked a student's paper in red when said student used the word flocked instead of walking.

He grinned. "I want you to know you aren't in trouble. I just wanted to make sure you're doing okay in light of your attack."

"I'm fine."

Yeah. Headmaster Martin's authority figure status didn't mean lying wasn't an option. I wasn't testifying in court. Besides, I didn't owe him anything. Because I would've had to have been out of been pretty naïve if I thought telling him about Jonathan and Billy maybe alive was a good thing.

"Good to know. But you don't have to filter because I won't think less if you swear." He grabbed a chocolate from the bowl and unraveled the wrapper in a matter of seconds before nibbling on the treat.

"I'm fine."

"Okay. But I also want to ask about Billy. I know you two were friends."

"Relax. I'm coping," I said.

No blinking required for my response. My response was technically true because I was coping. He just didn't need to know how I was coping. Like with convincing myself Billy's death wasn't a suicide in addition to how he might've been alive.

"That's great to hear. Teens will never make it in life if they don't have tenacity."

He didn't have to make a super offensive remark for me to almost frown. Even hinting at an offensive comment proved enough. Headmaster Martin needed to think about his next words carefully because there wasn't a much of a leap from what he said to believing that complaining about unfair things made someone weak. They didn't. It only meant someone was human. The obviousness of life being unfair didn't make the fact less true.

"It's surprising that the investigation about Billy's death wrapped so quickly," I said.

Touching on a sensitive subject didn't make me morbid. I just couldn't resist Headmaster Martin knowing anything, something that might've informed my understanding about Billy, anything I might not have known.

"There wasn't much to investigate. His sweater and suicide note revealed everything worth knowing. Although it stinks another student died so soon after Billy," he said.

Perhaps Billy wasn't the only topic I couldn't escape. I might not have been able to avoid the Jonathan issue either. Because he always came up like Billy. Almost as if I could never forget my past for that long.

"Yeah, it's a real shame someone pushed Jonathan off the astronomy tower." One quick glance around the room, and I almost laughed. Apparently, age had nothing to do with whether someone was a slob. A ton of papers and pencils were scattered all over his desk in addition to how the books in the bookshelf were piled on top of each other as opposed to being stacked. Dust also covered his bookshelf and desk. So much, that I should've thanked the universe for not making cough when I entered the room or while I continued sitting.

A vein surfaced on his head. "I mean, it's a miracle that parents haven't withdrawn their children from here."

* * *

Watching *Netflix* in my dorm room might've been more preferable than going to Amanda's photography debut, yet I couldn't be a jackass. It was my turn to be a good friend to her. Even if my head almost ached from the all the buzzing voices in the room in the admission's building where the art department was having the event.

Although Chelsea and Freddie were here me with.

Because I didn't know what I would've done if I had to stand alone in the corner of the room while Amanda was in the distance engrossed in conversation with several people about her photographs.

"I've been thinking about what we should do next," Freddie said.

Wow. Good to know I wasn't the only person who took initiative.

Obsessing about Billy and coming up with the next move was usually my prerogative, yet I couldn't complain. Not now. I could only think about the Billy situation for so many hours a day, proving Freddie took charge if he wanted-ed. It wasn't like I would start World War 3 if I wasn't in control.

"And what's that?" I asked.

Freddie finished his lemonade. "We should go to the motel the fisherman dropped Billy off at."

Okay. Maybe I had to complain after all. Going to the motel was the next logical step, and I should've come up with it myself. It wasn't like someone asked me to solve a Calculus question.

"I still can't believe Billy might be alive," Chelsea said.

I nodded. "I agree with you, Freddie."

"Good. Because that's the only thing I can think of doing." Freddie straightened his bowtie. "Although I can't believe that the motel person also wouldn't have gone to the police."

"I don't. Just look at the fisherman and how he kept quiet." I finished my last two crackers, then tossed the plate into the basket.

***

SATURDAY, OCTOBER 24, 2020

The motel's neon, red sign glowed while drizzling rain pattered against the ground. Because the weather just had to be shitty when we stepped out of the car.

Amanda shook her head. "What the hell kind of name is the Devil's Inn?"

"I don't know. But you can ask the owner if you want," I said.

"I intend to," Amanda said.

Okay. Maybe Amanda wasn't smart as everyone thought she was. She should've been able to pick up on my sarcasm since that trait was one of my defining characteristics.

Freddie opened his umbrella while the rain picked up, becoming louder and faster. "Let's stop talking and walk to the check-in building.

I turned to Amanda. "I was joking. I don't care what the hell this place is called as long we get an answer about Billy."

"I'm not sure what you expect the person to tell us," Amanda said while we shuffled towards the part of the building that had the sign CHECK IN plastered against it.

"We won't know unless we try," I said.

"Carson is right since there's nothing more that I hate than people who always talk about doing things, but never get around to doing them," Chelsea said.

I opened the door, and we stepped into the check-in office.

Pop culture didn't always have to be realistic. The point was some overdone ideas were true. Like a seedy person running a motel. Because the man sitting in swivel chair in front of his computer behind the desk counter didn't have to have yellow teeth, wrinkly skin, or body odor in order to be considered sketchy. Something unnerving just existed about his wide grin despite his hair being combed back and him also sporting a collared shirt.

"Can I help you?" asked the man.

I went onto the photo app on my iPhone and scrolled to the only picture I had of Billy. "We were wondering if you've ever seen this guy?"

The man squinted after taking my iPhone. He then started studying the picture—almost as if he thought I'd kill him if he didn't answer my question. Because Billy didn't even stare at me so hard when he eye-fucked me.

"I think I might've seen him one night during the first two weeks of September. But I can't be sure since my memory isn't what it used to be." The man handed my iPhone back to me. "Anyway, my name is Hank."

No offense, but I didn't ask him what his name was. Because his name could have been Mr. Horny, and I wouldn't have frowned as long as he gave me an adequate answer.

"This is important," Chelsea said. "Someone's life might be at stake."

Perhaps Chelsea had more in common with Billy than she realized. A quirky comment was the type of thing Billy would've done on an ordinary afternoon.

Hank stroked his chin. "Wait. It's coming back. I think I saw him. But he had a baseball hat on so I can't be completely sure."

Good enough for me. This conversation just wasn't the right time to complain about the universe always being ambiguous. It wasn't like my life depended on Hank being completely certain about seeing Billy. He only had to be reasonably certain.

"What did he want?" Freddie asked.

Thank goodness for Freddie. Because I would've bet my life savings on me staring into space and not come up with another question at some point during the "interrogation."

"He had to make a phone call," Hank said.

"Really? He couldn't have just used his iPhone?" Amanda asked.

"He said his battery died." Hank sipped his tea from the chipped mug next to his computer.

"Do you know who he called?" Chelsea asked.

"I don't know or care since I never say no to people in need. Everyone deserves to have their needs met," he said.

Jumping to conclusions might've meant a person making an ass out of themselves on the off chance of being wrong. But I couldn't lie to myself. My stomach might as well have been burning from Hank's comment. Helping someone was one thing, yet I couldn't forget about, "having their needs met" part of his comment. If I didn't know better, I would've thought the statement wreaked of sexual subtext. And I couldn't forget about his dopey expression since he hadn't stopped smiling. Because having a terminal disease cured was the only reason why someone should've been so giddy.

Amanda forced a smile "Do you have a copy of your phone bill?"

"Surely, you understand how I can't just give out my private information?" Hank asked.

Chelsea glared. "I can't emphasize enough how important this issue is."

"Fine. I'll let you look at the bill." Hank wobbled towards his filing cabinet, yanked open a drawer, and took out a piece of paper from a manila folder.

"Wait. I recognize the area code. It's from Flywood, which is the next town over," I said.

"Interesting," Amanda said.

"Anyway, would you like some tea or cookies?" Hank asked. "I don't often get visitors."

Okay. Any lingering positivity I might've showed Hank vanished. Offering someone food or a drink wasn't even the issue. I'd just have to take a really long shower when I returned to my dorm room from him revealing he didn't socialize much. That just wasn't the type of comment that qualified as social acceptable conversation.

"The guy and the girl didn't get a room?" Chelsea asked.

"No. She just picked him up, and I never saw him

again," Hank revealed.

Amanda quirked her eyebrows. "You do know the guy killed himself, right?"

"I don't pay attention to the news, but I'm sorry to hear that," Hank said. "Although at least I never talked to the police because I don't need them asking questions."

Yikes. The loneliness comment wasn't enough, and he just had to add to our negative impression of him. Because I wouldn't even ask Hank about what he meant with not wanting to deal with the police.

"I don't care if you guys think this sounds negative, but I would've died if we talked to Hank for one more minute," Amanda said several minutes later.

We were now back in Freddie's car. Chelsea was next to him in the front passenger seat while Amanda and I took the backseat.

"Agreed," I said.

Yeah. Life was too short to pretend how Hank couldn't have been related to Norman Bates. Because I could take the whole creeper issue one step further, and speculate about whether Hank wanted to give us tea so he could drug us.

"It's smart you looked up the address, Carson," Amanda said.

"You know me. I wouldn't rest until we checked out the lead," I said.

Freddie honked his horn at the driver in front of us. "And that's why I'm not complaining about investigating more tonight."

Chelsea played with a strand of her hair. "I wouldn't be surprised Hank killed his mother and has a necrophilia fetish."

Extra bonus points for Chelsea. She was the only one who I could think that wouldn't be afraid to make such a bold statement. Although it was a shame that an adult wasn't with us. Because I would have burst into laughter if Chelsea mentioned necrophilia in front of an adult.

"I never want to hear you mention necrophilia again," Freddie said.

Perhaps an adult didn't have to be present in the car for amusement to flood my body. Freddie qualified despite being a teenager since I couldn't forget about how his constant annoyance when Chelsea made questionable comments.

"We should start thinking of what we're going to say to the lady," Amanda said.

Shit. Amanda had a point even though she might've spent too much time with me if she now considered every possibility. It wasn't like I could bring up the weather. Doing so wouldn't have only wasted time, it would've made me look foolish.

"However, I'm still not crazy about going to a stranger's house," Amanda said.

"Then why didn't you just take an UBER back to campus?" Chelsea demanded.

"Selling a photograph yesterday means being a little impulsive," Amanda said.

"I hope you thanked the person for paying ten-thousand dollars for your photo," Chelsea said.

Good gracious. She had to mention that fact 1000 more times. It didn't matter how talented Amanda was, I would've never guessed that someone would pay so much for one of her photos. That type of good thing just didn't happen—at least not to me.

"I did," Amanda said.

The clunky sound of the ignition halted sometime later after Freddie parked his car on the curb. We then exited the car and walked up the grass while the wind picked up so fast that a dangling branch snapped and fell onto the ground.

"Let's pray the lady is nice," I said while we walked up the steps and towards the front door.

The wind blew even louder, and the swing on the

front porch creaked. I even almost recoiled. A surprise noise shouldn't have been the end of the world, yet I couldn't forget about the pitch-black night sky.

"Should we even bother? The person might not be home since the lights aren't on," Chelsea said.

"We didn't come here for nothing." Freddie rang the doorbell twice. But nobody answered the door. Damn. The universe still couldn't grant us a favor. Because I'd never move on with my life if I couldn't prove Billy was alive.

We all exchanged a glance, and Freddie knocked the door several times. However, nobody opened the door.

An icy sensation crawled up my back after I cocked my head. The upstairs bedroom light was on, and the faint silhouette of a guy with his back towards me remained visible. However, the person had blond hair, though.

But I would've recognized his broad shoulders anywhere, proving the guy had to have been Billy. The light from the upstairs bedroom clicked off after a lady walked into the room towards the guy, and started kissing him. Yet I didn't tell Chelsea, Amanda, or Freddie about how the guy might've been Billy. Getting closure was one thing, but not answering the door meant the person or people living in the house not wanting to deal with people. And that fact was fine. If Billy really was alive, then I'd think about what I'd say to him. Seeing him now wasn't the same as our encounter in my infirmary room because of no longer being on painkillers. And that meant risking vulnerability. Because I didn't have to be psychic to know Billy might disappoint me again.

THEN

SATURDAY, DECEMBER 7, 2019

"Did you ever think we'd go out on a date?" I asked.

Billy and I sat at a table in back of Della's, which was an Italian restaurant a mile or so from campus. And the place was worth throwing a parade over. This restaurant didn't have any questionable odors wafting through the air or dim lighting like one expected from a seedier restaurant. And that was why I hadn't question how this place got so many five stars on the websites I checked.

Yup. I was always researched where I ate my meals. Something comforting existed from being in control—even if the universe always fucked people over.

He pursed his lips. "No. But remember our cover. If we run into anyone from school, we'll say I'm taking you out to dinner to thank you tutoring for me."

Nope. I couldn't swallow the lump in my throat. Our date was another reminder of how the universe never gave people what they wanted even they technically got what they wanted. Because we just had to have a cover story—almost as if this was the nineteenth century, and lived in fear of constant judgement.

Maybe, just maybe, my mood would improve, though. The velvet cloth covering the table and two candles with flames flickering out of them added to the atmosphere since I'd never been to such a fancy restaurant before.

Billy lifted his gaze off his water glass. "What? Did you change your mind about the arrangement?"

I flipped to the menu's next page. "Just trying to decide what I want."

"Get whatever you want. My treat."

Damn. Billy had to almost make me wail one second, only to make me smile the following second. Not worrying about how expensive an entrée was showed Billy had class. It didn't take a genius to realize that some people counted pennies as if their lives depended on it.

"Thanks," I said. "Anyway, I might get the Fillet Mignon. I haven't had it since last Christmas."

"Go for it."

Wow. Perhaps Billy was capable of generosity. If someone asked if I thought Billy could give something without making the person work for said thing, then I would've accused said person of not being realistic. There was just no way Billy couldn't turn something into a big deal.

"What about you?" I asked.

"I'm not sure. I might get something a little less expensive."

So much for Billy and I having a nice evening. Because he had to contradict what he just said. It's not like I ate fancy food all the time. Besides, everyone deserved an occasional splurge.

"And what's that supposed to mean?" I asked. "I thought you said I could get whatever I want."

"You can. I just think Fillet Mignon is pretentious."

Billy had to have been in a bad mood. That explanation was the only reasoning I could think of as to why he'd be acting the way he was. He always through lavish party after lavish party at the Barn. Because doing so wasn't the type of thing simple people did. No offense to partying or anything.

I snorted. "Okay…"

"Enough about food. You didn't answer my question."

"It's kind insulting you think I'd out you."

"Don't put words in my mouth. I want to make sure we had an understanding." Billy gripped the sides of his blazer in addition to how more shock should've jolted my body. Sprucing up his image meant Billy might've cared about me in his own little way. At least in the alternate universe where we could date without drama. Someone should've showed me to how bend the laws of physics so I could travel to said alternate universe.

"The only understanding I needed is figuring out why you won't come out," I said.

"I told you," Billy spat. "Life is simpler being straight."

Perhaps arguing with Billy was a mistake. He was his own person, and I therefore couldn't change him not matter how tempting the desire might've been. Because it wasn't the end of the world for me to wish for simplicity.

"Whatever. It's your choice," I said through gritted teeth.

His elbows slid onto the table. "It'd be nice if you would respect my choice. Not everyone can be like you. Besides, being one of the few out kids on campus means you should have more sensitivity."

"I don't think it's a bullying issue. It's just a matter of people grappling with their identity."

My comment wasn't bizarre. Jonathan aside, I had never been bullied in addition how I couldn't recall one instance of bullying at my boarding school.

"Would you like Champagne?" Billy asked. "I bet bribing our waiter would solve the problem."

How nice of Billy to solve a problem with a bribe. Because not everyone got away with bribing people out of a debacle.

Champagne would've been nice, though. There was nothing like the combination of the sweet, tart, and carbonated flavors lingering on my taste buds. Yup. I was fortunate enough to know what Champagne tasted like since my parents let me have two glasses of Champagne last New Year's Eve. Yet I couldn't give into impulsive behavior all the time. Billy drove us here in his Mercedes, and he needed to be able to drive back to campus.

"Maybe another time," I said. "Anyway, if you're looking for something simple, I suggest the Spaghetti with tomato sauce."

"Don't be a buzzkill, Carson! Two glasses of Champagne won't impair my driving. In fact, it won't even give me a buzz."

Creepy. It was as if Billy saw right through me. And that wasn't a good thing in light of who Billy was. There was no telling if he respected vulnerability or would use it as a weapon to leverage something. Yet here I was sitting in a restaurant with him, which probably revealed more about me than him. Associating with Billy meant I was the type of person who was desperate enough that'd I let a questionable guy love me.

"Fine. Get the Champagne if you want." I let out a chuckle. "Although I'm surprise you don't have a fake ID."

"I actually have three fake ID's. I just forgot them in my dorm room."

Good gracious. I must not have heard him correctly. One fake ID was one thing, but three bordered on eccentric. The only person that I needed so many fake ID's was s fugitive.

"Do you know what you want to order?" asked someone.

A man with a mustache stood in front of us. Although he might've wanted to think about shaving the mustache off. The mustache's thickness was intense that not even one spec of skin was visible between his nose or upper lip. That was where my judgement stopped, though. Comparing our waiter's mustache to Stalin's mustache didn't seem like polite behavior—at least not while in the company of our waiter.

"Not yet, "Billy said. "But we'd like a bottle of your most expensive Champagne."

The man wove his arms together. "I'm going to need ID."

"I have something better." Billy slipped his wallet out of his blazer pocket before taking out a hundred-dollar bill, and handing it to the waiter.

The man scanned the room, but none of the other patrons or servers were glancing in our direction. He then yanked the bill out of Billy's hand so fast he might as well have been starving to death.

Billy grinned once the waiter left. "Never underestimate the power of bribery."

"You seem like you're enjoying this…"

"I can't help it if I love booze."

"I need to ask you something," I said.

Billy surveyed the menu again. "You better not be bringing up my sexuality."

Perhaps I wasn't the only person who needed to take one—or several—deep breaths. Insecurity was one thing, yet life wasn't a battlefield, and Billy should've trusted me. Or at least pretend to trust me. Because I'd never do anything that made him uncomfortable. A difference existed between having a thought and acting on it. At least for me.

"I wanna to know what you see in me," I said.

"What kind of question is that?" he asked.

"I'm serious. What's the point of this if we want different things?"

My question required an answer. I couldn't help myself despite some arguing I only had myself to blame for my current confusion. If Billy would never change, then we were wasting our time.

"I keep you around so I can get laid," Billy said.

I squatted his hand with my menu. "Are you serious?"

"I'm joking. But it really is nice having sex whenever I want."

"Forget I mentioned the issue."

"What are you doing here guys?" called out a voice.

We cocked our heads, then Billy's hands dug into the tablecloth. Otto stood in front of us with a brunette. But they might as well have been going to the Oscars. Otto didn't only just sport a blazer, buttoned down shirt, and khaki pants. He also had an argyle tie. And I couldn't forget about his date—whatever her name was. A crimson colored strapless dress covered her from the chest to a couple of inches below her knees in addition to how she had matching high heels and a purse.

"Carson has been tutoring me, and I thought I'd thank him by taking him out for a nice dinner," Billy said before I even thought about speaking.

The girl giggled. "That's so nice of you to spend time with someone who isn't popular. I don't think I'd be so benevolent."

"Wow. Look at you, Cheryl! You used an SAT word," Otto said.

She smacked him with her purse. "I can be both hot and smart."

Otto snapped his fingers. "I just had a thought. Why don't we join you?"

"That's a good idea. Because I don't have the energy to watch you wine and dine me in the hopes of getting laid tonight," she said.

Perhaps Cheryl should've been friends with Chelsea. Because they could've bonded over not filtering in social situations.

Otto hissed at her. "Cheryl!"

"I'm sorry, but it's true," she said.

Billy turned to me. "You don't mind if they join us, do you?"

On a superficial level, asking me how I felt appeared polite. Doing something without considering my feelings would've been rude. Yet I still called bullshit on Billy. It wasn't like I could say no. Doing so would've "violated" our agreement about how nobody could know about us. Not even if I could go the rest of the evening without talking because of adjusting tonight's expectations.

"Nope. That'd be great," I forced out.

"Fantastic," Cheryl said. "And don't worry. I promise not to make another condescending remark about how you're not popular."

"Have you been reading the dictionary?" Otto asked.

"I'll tell you one thing, though," Billy said. "You can't have any of the Champagne I ordered for Carson and me. It's just for us."

No. No. No. Dinner couldn't have been a time when the universe technically gave something while taking it away at the same time. I deserved to experience a real date once in my life.

***

SUNDAY, DECEMBER 8, 2019

"Sorry about last night," Chelsea said.

We turned left, and continued strolling along the south side of campus while a thick blanket of snow covered the ground. Yup. Somewhere between last night's disappointment and an hour ago, it snowed.

"No worries," I said.

She nudged me. "You don't have to pretend with me. You must be devastated."

"I'm dumb for expecting so much from Billy."

"You're not a fool. You're just idealistic."

Perhaps Chelsea had more tact than I realized. Chelsea didn't have to spare my feelings, yet she restrained herself. Because I wouldn't have struggled with doing the same thing if I were in her position. Nothing sexy existed from a toxic relationship. Yup. I hadn't minced words. A relationship didn't have to reach *Gone Girl* level toxic for squirming. Something unhealthy existed about my dynamic with Billy no matter how good the sex was. Relationships entailed equal footing, not contemplating when Billy would fuck me over again.

"Maybe I should stop seeing him," I said.

"How does that make you feel?"

Her good intentions didn't matter since I might as well have been a five-year-old being forced to eat fruits and vegetables. General honesty was important for friendships because Chelsea might as well have been a stranger if I couldn't be honest with her, yet that didn't mean she always had to be direct. I would've mentioned my feelings in more detail if I felt like it. Although I wouldn't have a choice with discussing my feelings now. Broaching the subject meant Chelsea wouldn't let the conversation digress until getting a satisfactory answer. And that might've entailed talking all day.

"Please don't play shrink," I said.

"I'm not your therapist; I'm your best friend. And that means it's my job to let you talk about problems. Even when I'd rather be anywhere else."

"I can't be that bad."

Her scarf sagged in the wind, and she tied it tighter. "Have you listened to yourself lately?"

I forced a laugh. "Good point."

"I might not lecture about who you sleep with him, but I can't let the shorts slide."

Chelsea should've known better than to criticize my fashion choice. It wasn't like I'd visit Antarctica in shorts. I just had to pretend it was summer all the time. Because maybe, just maybe, I could wish summer into existence if I never wore pants.

"I'm sorry. I can't help dressing for summer all year," I said.

"It's below freezing," Chelsea snapped.

Emotions might've meant people were human, but Chelsea wouldn't accomplish anything from harping on her disapproval. The current temperature shouldn't have been synonymous with the apocalypse. Because I could've thought about a dozen worse things that the temperature only being below freezing.

"Could be worse," I said. "Anyway, there's something else."

Chelsea stuffed her hands into her coat pockets. "Billy better not have given you any diseases."

There she was. Classic Chelsea. That was just the inappropriate comment I would've expected from her earlier in the conversation. Because if she even thought about making that comment in front of Freddie and Amanda, then I would have to reexamine why I was friends with her.

"I wish. But no. I was talking about Amanda. She didn't return my texts, and it might be because we kissed on Friday night," I said.

"That didn't happen?"

Permission granted for her confused expression. I would've had the same reaction if someone told me about a shocking kiss with a friend. That just wasn't the type of thing to happen in real. Ambiguity was a better fit for pop culture since at least then the consequences weren't real.

"It did," I said. "Anyway, my concern is if she's hurt that it was only one kiss."

She scratched the right side of her head. "You still haven't told me why you and Amanda kissed."

"It was to make Billy jealous."

"Wow. Everything always comes back to him."

Hopefully, Chelsea had no intention of becoming a writer. I would steal that line. Something profound existed from everything coming back to Billy despite how obvious the idea sounded. Because I couldn't escape Billy no matter how hard I tried.

* * *

TUESDAY, DECEMBER 10, 2019

My boxers traced the contours of my legs while I rushed into them after getting off Billy's bed. Then, I slid into my shorts in a matter of seconds—almost as if I wanted to run away from a crocodile.

And no. I hadn't lost my mind. Billy invited me to his dorm room since Otto was at away hockey game, and wouldn't be back for several more hours.

Billy's eyebrows knitted. "It's rude to leave your boyfriend when he's still horny."

Billy might've been a lot of things, but he shouldn't have insulted me. Regardless of how nice returning back to the part of my life during childhood when anything was possible, Billy would never be my boyfriend. He couldn't. And maybe that fact was okay since I might've eventually been able to live with said disappointment at some distant point in the future. Like the Tenth of Never.

"What's wrong?" Billy continued. "You should be glad I just called you my boyfriend. Besides, I'm the one with hurt feelings. Anyone would be lucky enough to cuddle with me."

"Can you please give me my shirt?" I asked.

"You're gonna have to sit back down on the bed if you want it."

Damn him. Nothing could be simple with Billy. I always had to work for every little thing—even something simple like taking my shirt off his bed.

Although I might've only had myself to blame for how Billy snatched my shirt, and now hid it behind his back.

And I did the only thing I could. I leaned forward onto the bed so far that my lips might as well touched. However, my shirt still remained behind Billy's back while his grip intensified. Even as I tried prying his fingers off my shirt.

"Think fast!" Billy tossed me the shirt.

"I want an honest answer. Are you hurt that I'm not cuddling with?"

Maybe I was more delusional than I thought. Only a fool would've asked the question I just did. Even if I couldn't help myself, and needed something concrete to hold onto. Something that revealed Billy cared. Something that revealed I wasn't wasting my time with him. Something that alluded to hope for our dynamic becoming more serious at some point in the future.

"Don't be ridiculous. I was only giving you a hard time," Billy said. "Besides, you should know that I'd rather die than cuddle with someone."

Perhaps Billy had a future as a writer—regardless of whether some people would've had a problem with his comment being melodramatic. His remark was still unique. Only Billy would've compared intimacy to death because not even my grandmother would've made that type of comment.

"I guess I shouldn't ask if you wanna grab lunch tomorrow," I said.

"I would, but I have a test I have to study for."

Extending myself couldn't be faulted. Perfection wasn't required for sharing a meal together—at least then I could pretend we were on a date.

***

WEDNESDAY, DECEMBER 11, 2019

Freddie gave me a look while he, Chelsea, Amanda, and I sat in the dining hall while numerous voices reverberated through the air. "It's good you ate your salad, but you could at least say something, Carson. Because you haven't made one comment since we sat down."

Yup. Now was one of those times I should've ditched hanging out with my friends. Billy sat a few tables away from us, engrossed in conversation with some of the guys from Charity Now. A couple of them even laughed once Billy stopped talking.

"It's just school stress," I said.

"Bullshit," Chelsea said. "That excuse isn't going to work on the girl who invented that line."

"I was being honest. I just want to be on Winter Break," I said.

Amanda glanced at Billy and then me and then Billy and then back to me. "What did your boyfriend do now?"

Good gracious. They just couldn't give up. Because I deserved some privacy in my life. It wasn't like I'd go to jail if I didn't give them a second by second replay of my life. Besides, I couldn't have known everything about their lives either.

"Nothing. I honestly just wanna crash from all the work I'm doing," I said.

Damn. Life could be so cruel—even a small way. My friends provided with me an opportunity to tell the truth, yet I chose lying over honesty. No reason existed why they should also have to live with my pain.

"I'm glad you asked Chelsea and Freddie to leave," Amanda said a few minutes later while we remained in our seats in the dining hall. "Because I want to talk to you."

"May I please go first?" I asked.

"Sure. What's up?"

"Are you annoyed we kissed just to make Billy jealous? Because you blew off my texts last weekend?"

Being direct was the only thing worth doing. I could tap my feet against the ground for one minute or ten minutes, yet it wouldn't change how difficult conversations sometimes had to be had—the type of conversation that might've been worse than a woman sleeping with a man she hated.

Her attention drifted to the napkin in front of her. "Don't be silly. I just had a lot of homework and chores."

Great. Amanda couldn't have used the homework and chores excuse. That remark was something Billy would say when he didn't want to be bothered, yet didn't have the guts to be honest. And I also couldn't forget about her looking away. The napkin couldn't have been so interesting that she would rather devote her focus to it then talk to me. Because that was just plain rude.

* * *

SATURDAY, DECEMBER 13, 2019

Billy pointed his right index finger at me. "I'm serious, Carson. I want an explanation about why you're blowing me off."

"I know you lied to me." I closed my dorm room door. "Because it wouldn't have killed you to at least lie better."

"What are you talking about?"

"I saw you the other day in the dining hall when you claimed to be too busy to hang because of having to study."

"Are you spying on me?" Billy nibbled on the inside of his lip. In fact, Billy bit down so hard on his lower lip that it was a miracle that he didn't bleed. "I know you're a lot of things, but I never thought you were a loser."

"How am I a loser?" I asked.

"I'm allowed to hang with my friends when I want. I only took an hour to eat."

Tolerating imperfection wasn't synonymous with buying snake oil. Billy's head couldn't have been so thick that he didn't understand the problem with not saying how he couldn't grab lunch with me because he already made plans to hang with his friends. Doing so would've been much simpler since I wouldn't have given the issue a second thought. But if he brought the chaos on himself, then that was a different story. Almost as if he wanted to make his life as complicated as possible.

"Not just the other day," I said. "I haven't forgotten about last Saturday. Not holding hands in public is one thing, but we could've had our meal alone. It's not like I even know Otto and Cheryl."

Mentioning our dinner date didn't make me petty. Doing so made me human. It wasn't like I wanted to kill Billy because I didn't get my way. Billy just had to know he fucked up, and that it couldn't happen again—that was if an again even existed. At this rate, I didn't even know why we were stilling talking.

"Do you realize how clingy you sound?" Billy demanded.

Maybe I'd buy Billy a dictionary for Christmas. Having standards didn't mean I was clingy. It just meant I expected great things in life. And that wasn't a crime. I still didn't anticipate the universe dropping a mansion or sports car in my lap. I just needed to stop feeling like I rolled in a pile of shit after every conversation with Billy. Because I could scrub my body all day, yet I'd never be clean.

"And do you realize how much of an asshole you are?" I asked.

Billy raised an eyebrow. "I give up. I don't know what you want from me. It's not like I'll become a different person."

"You're right. You aren't gonna change."

Billy zipped up his pants sometime later while I was in bed with the comforter wrapped around me, covering me from the chest down. I even panted, attempting to catch my breath. There was nothing like an afternoon tryst to cause sweating.

He whipped his body around after putting on his shirt. "I hope we made the right decision."

Someone had to give Billy a lecture about not being ambiguous. No good reason existed for him creating doubt, begging the question if a small part of him got off on fucking with people. A less patient person would've told him off a long time ago; not continue enabling his behavior.

"We did, but you should go," I said. "I wouldn't want Otto to become suspicious of you because of coming and going at odd hours."

"Relax. We both know I'm not afraid of lying."

"Just go," I said.

"It's okay if you've changed your mind," Billy said.

NOW

MONDAY, OCTOBER 26, 2020

"Grabbing frozen yogurt was a good suggestion," I said.

Dean and I sat at a table in back of the shop, which was a couple of blocks from the Starbucks I frequented when going off campus. However, someone should've given me a medal when Dean suggested this outing after we finished our classes for the day. I hadn't complained about the date's location. I just didn't understand why people liked frozen yogurt. And my opinion was confirmed because of the dull flavor of the frozen vanilla yogurt. My taste buds weren't electrified like when the mixture of the sweet, buttery, and vanilla flavor rubbed against my tongue when I ever I got ice cream with rainbow sprinkles. But at least Dean sported a leather jacket today since I couldn't lie to myself. The fashion choice polished Dean's soft image because something dangerous existed from wearing a leather jacket.

"Glad you think so," Dean said. "Anyway, are you still doing okay in light of your attack?"

Way to ask a loaded question. Sometimes a person's intentions didn't matter. I couldn't think about Jonathan right now. He was a close leap from Billy. And I just loved thinking about him. Because then my mind would've drifted back to standing on the porch Saturday night, discovering Billy involved in a passionate embrace while Chelsea, Amanda, and Freddie had been too preoccupied to notice.

I nodded. "Yeah, I'm fine."

"No problem. Although forgive me for being a jackass, but you have a little frozen yogurt stuck on your lip." Dean took his finger to his tongue, and wet it. Then, he wiped my upper lip and his eyes were also glued on mine, yet my body wouldn't shake from Dean touching me. Sure. Spending time with him might've been different than spending time with Billy, yet I couldn't be weak anymore. Even if that meant seeming more robotic. Nothing good ever came from vulnerability. "I hope that wasn't out of line…"

"Don't worry about it," I said.

My response was fair. Not putting my emotions on display didn't mean I had to punish Dean since I was still capable of distinguishing between minor touching and someone slipping their hand into my boxers and groping me.

"Writing anything new?" he asked.

"Nope. I haven't had a chance to, but I'd like to resume writing again soon. What about you? How's Charity Now?"

"It's okay. Although it gets old fast."

"I imagine," I said.

"Anyway, I still can't believe Jonathan is dead…"

"I don't mean to be rude, but would it be okay if

we didn't talk about Jonathan?" I asked. "Perhaps you can tell me more about your hobbies, likes, and dislikes."

Referencing Jonathan didn't mean lashing out against Dean even though he knew the truth about him. A part of me also still had small pangs of disbelief because my boarding school could only take so much negative publicity as Headmaster Martin articulated the other day when I was in his office.

"Sure. I'd love to." Dean scraped the sides of his cup with his spoon, and shoveled the last bite of frozen yogurt into my mouth. Except chocolate coated his lips just like I got the vanilla frozen yogurt over my upper lip moments earlier.

"Sorry, but I gotta help you." I extended my right index finger, and whipped away the chocolate. "There! All better."

"Maybe I'm clumsier than I realized."

"Don't worry about it." I pulled my hand away, then Dean grabbed it.

He gave me a quick kiss. The embrace couldn't have lasted more than five seconds, but the moment should've lasted for five thousand years. That length would've ensured never thinking or worrying about Billy again.

The kiss didn't mean Dean was a distraction, though; he wasn't. Dean would always be a better person than Billy. Real people didn't play games as a result of how I still had no idea what Billy's endgame was. Nobody did. That was how Billy liked it, after all.

***

TUESDAY OCTOBER 27, 2020

I walked away from the school's coffee cart after buying my Caramel Macchiato, and I almost thanked the universe despite how I never wanted to owe it any favors. Otto just grazed by the coffee cart, and I caught up to him in a matter of seconds while other students walked by too.

"Do you have a second to talk?" I asked.

"Sure. I can make time for you because Billy's father finally moved out Billy's crap."

"How did that happen?"

"I gave the headmaster an earful," Otto said.

"Anyway, I had a question about Billy."

Sure. No way existed for me to know if Otto could give me the answer I wanted. But I wouldn't know unless I asked. It wasn't like talking to Otto meant I'd die of some terrible virus.

"Shoot," He said.

I coughed into my free hand. "Did he ever mention an older woman he might've been seeing?"

"Yes, last spring." Otto paused for a second. "He mentioned seeing someone older, but I thought he meant the person was in college," Otto said.

"Cool. Thanks."

I was about to scurry away when Otto gripped my hand just like Billy did that day at the gay bar last April. "Thanks again for not telling anyone about me sending the text."

"Don't worry about it. I have bigger things to focus on."

* * *

WEDNESDAY, OCTOBER 28, 2020

I twirled a strand of spaghetti while sitting at table in front of the dining hall with Freddie, Chelsea, and Amanda. But my mind hadn't shifted focus from Billy's older woman since my friends and I arrived in here a few minutes earlier. Two instances of Billy's lady friend being mentioned hinted the issue wasn't a fluke, and I had to mention something to my friends. Not knowing what to say to Billy upon have a non-dopey encounter with him as a result of not being on the pain killers was one thing, yet I couldn't let the fear radiating through my body cripple me. I'd never move on with my life if the Billy issue wasn't solved.

Freddie looked up from his plate. "Something wrong, Carson?"

His question might've been considerate, but I couldn't forget about my Déjà vu. Because it seemed like Freddie asked me if I was okay every time we ate in the dining hall. And that was fact a little disconcerting. My life couldn't have been the equivalent of someone named Jane being nicknamed, "Calamity Jane."

"I lied to you," I said.

"Don't tell me you've secretly been in contact with Billy all along?" Amanda asked.

Not having time for contemplating Amanda's comment didn't mean I couldn't make a mental note of it later. How she could say something like that was beyond me. I might not have been perfect, but I wasn't Billy level eccentric. I couldn't imagine letting people think I was dead when I wasn't.

"I saw Billy in the window while you three were distracted and he was kissing an older woman before they turned off the lights. Except I only saw the side of the guy, and he was blond," I said.

"And you're just saying something now?" Amanda asked.

"It doesn't matter. The point is, Carson is speaking up now." Chelsea guzzled the rest of her lemonade before pushing her plate and cup to the side.

Thank goodness for Chelsea. No reason existed for Amanda criticizing me. It wasn't like I ran over her cat on purpose. I just sometimes had to process information myself for telling others what was on my mind.

"And it had to have been Billy." I finished the last of my spaghetti. "He made an off handed comment to me last April about being involved with an older woman in addition to how Otto said. And we also can't forget about Hank's tidbit about a lady picking up Billy the night of his 'death.'"

"What are you saying?" Freddie asked.

"We should go back to the house, but this time let's go in the daytime right after class," I said.

***

THURSDAY, OCTOBER 29, 2020

"It's now or never." Freddie rang the doorbell three times before footsteps from inside the house grew louder and louder.

The door opened, revealing a woman with curly hair that fell a few inches past her chest. She also had a nightgown on. But I wouldn't criticize her for how she should've put a bathrobe on when greeting company.

"Can I help you with something?" she asked.

Freddie handed the woman his phone. "We were wondering if you know this guy."

Props to Freddie for not needing a lecture. His initial question wasn't exciting, yet it accomplished what we wanted. Scaring this lady off was the opposite of what we needed. Although a part of me would've had to lift my jaw off the floor if I was a cartoon character. The wrinkles on her forehead hinted the woman must've been in her thirties. There was just no way a twenty-something year old would've had so many frown lines.

She pushed the iPhone back towards Freddie. "I'm sorry, but I've never seen this guy before in my life."

"Are you sure?" Chelsea asked. "Because this is important."

"I'd know if I knew that guy," she snapped.

Something banged against the ground, and the lady's gaze shifted to inside her home.

"We aren't trying to be mean, but we need answers, and think you might be able to help us," Amanda said.

Another banging noise echoed.

"I'm sorry, but I can't help you." The woman slammed the door.

Freddie, Chelsea, and I exchanged a collective sigh. And the universe should've been lucky I wasn't cursing it out of existence. I didn't care how dumb the lady might've thought we were. She couldn't have made the disturbance because she hadn't been holding anything in her hand while talking to us.

"We should just go. No use in forcing her to help us," I said.

***

"Are you sure okay? Everyone who I've watched *Pan's Labyrinth* with usually has a stronger opinion," Dean said.

We were currently seated on my bed with our backs against the wall and Dean's laptop between us. He had just hit the stop button since the movie finished in addition to how the sulky expression on his face must've meant I needed to come up with something intelligent to say about the movie so I didn't alienate him. No words left my mouth. Because I might as well have put my fists through my dorm room wall as a result of getting another goose egg about Billy earlier in the day when the lady failed to help us.

"Please don't mistake my silence for not being interested. I've just a long day." I pointed to his laptop's lid. "Although you're GREEND DAY: AMERICAN IDIOT sticker is cool.

"Thanks. But are you sure you're okay?"

"Yes."

"What do you wanna do now?" Dean asked.

"I don't know. What do you have in mind?"

My question had nothing to do with playing mind

games. Dean just needed to be clear with what he'd like to do. I yawned minutes earlier, and didn't have time to read his mind.

Dean slid his laptop to the side before scooting closer to me. In fact, we now must've only been an inch or two away from each other. He extended a hand, and stroked a lock of my hair out of the way, yet that was where the flirtation stopped. His gaze hadn't met mine like when Billy always eye-fucked me in the past.

I touched his free hand, and pulled him for a kiss.

And no. Fooling around with Dean didn't make me selfish because of how some people might've accused me of needing a distraction. I was still a teenager, and should've been allowed to indulge my hormones. It wasn't like I robbed a bank. I just stuck my tongue in Dean's mouth, which was harmless.

I pulled back after a beat. The image of Billy just couldn't leave my head.

"What's wrong?" Dean asked.

"I need to be honest with you before we get more serious."

"I don't understand."

Chelsea, Freddie, and Amanda might've debated the necessity of what I was about to tell Dean, yet I didn't have a choice. And I wasn't being idealistic. I could only take so many complications before my brain imploded. I still wasn't closer to finding out Billy's endgame, and I couldn't let anything bad happen to Dean. Not when all of his actions contrasted Billy's behavior.

"That was something." Dean rolled onto his back sometime later (as did I), and we even panted while the bed comforter covered us from the waist down.

"Agreed."

"I hope you don't regret taking our relationship to the next level."

"We're in a relationship?" I asked.

Dean laughed. "At least I thought we were."

My question wasn't about being cruel. Our dynamic required clarification despite Dean and I being on more honest ground then the day I first met in front of the coffee cart on the quad. Several kisses didn't replace defining our relationship no matter how good they might've been. Because physical intimacy was no substitute for an honest conversation.

I averted my gaze. "I see…"

"Why are you not ready for a relationship?"

"No. I just didn't realize we were in a relationship. But it's fine. I'd happy to call you my boyfriend. Although I can't believe we still slept together after what I told you."

Dean squeezed my hand. "It's not your fault Billy is still alive in addition to how I don't blame you for needing time to tell me."

***

FRIDAY, OCTOBER 30, 2020

"No offense, but I'm shocked you wanted to meet before class," I said.

The cashier behind the coffee cart on the quad handed Amanda and me our Caramel Macchiatos, and we walked towards a nearby bench. Gray clouds also lurched in the sky, yet I couldn't pay too much attention to the weather. Getting any type of free coffee this early in the morning outweighed any possibility of rain."

"We need to chat," she said.

"Did I do something wrong?"

She elbowed me. "Don't be ridiculous. It's nothing like that. If anything, you might be offended by what I'm about to tell you."

Shit. I just couldn't get free coffee without any complications. Because the universe just wasn't that nice.

"That issue stopped being important a long time ago," I said

"Very funny." She drank her beverage.

"What's up?"

"There's a guy in my photography class that I want to ask out, but I haven't out of respect to you and our fling."

Damn. Life was full of one complication after the next. Because we'd gone months without discussing how we had sex several times last April, and it would've been great if the momentum continued. Nothing good come from discussing how we saw each other naked.

"I appreciate the consideration, but you don't have to be formal. I never once asked if you minded me getting back together with Billy last spring or pursuing Dean," I said.

"It's fine because I know my brain works differently than yours. So, you really are cool with me seeing another guy?" Amanda asked.

"Yup. I have Dean now."

"How's that going?"

I took several generous sips of my Caramel Macchiato because there was no way I could tell Amanda what I was about tell her without more caffeine. "Good. We actually slept together last night. But that's not all. He knows about Billy being alive, and wants to be kept in the loop."

"Wow. I'm proud of you for being honest."

Perhaps I criticized Amanda more than I should've. No reason existed to assume she'd think being honest with Dean was a mistake. It wasn't like she criticized me just from the mere fact I was breathing. She just sometimes had intense opinions.

"I couldn't let anything bad happen to him," I said.

Amanda nibbled on her scone before speaking. "Now that the awkwardness is out of the way, I also had something else to ask you."

"Okay."

"Would you be up to going back to the house tomorrow afternoon? Because we need to end this once and for all."

"What if the woman doesn't take no for an answer?" I asked.

Yeah. The annoying version of myself returned. The Billy situation was one those situations when every type of variable had to be taken into account. Real life wasn't a battle of wits like a game of chess, it was worse. Because I would've never guessed something so convoluted was bound to happen before Billy "died."

"Then we'll be a pain in the ass until she gives us the answers we're looking for," she said.

"If you weren't interested in photography, I'd suggest you be a lawyer."

"And why is that?"

"Only an attorney would be so fierce." I finished the coffee before disposing of it in the garbage that must've only been a couple of inches away from me. And I didn't even fret at the squirrel peaking inside the trash can. Worse things existed than crossing paths with a squirrel because an ostrich would've been worse.

***

SATURDAY, OCTOBER 31, 2020

Freddie, Chelsea, Dean, Amanda, and I stood on Billy's girlfriend's front porch, yet we remained silent. Several blue slips rested by the front door. Like the kind of slips that covered a newspaper. And my mind just had to wonder why the newspapers were lying on the front porch. I didn't have to be the smartest person in the world to understand how newspapers were only around when people went out of town and were too lazy to have the delivery stopped.

Dean placed his hand on my shoulder. "Sorry. I

know how much you wanted closure."

"I'll just say it if nobody else wants to," Freddie said. "Why would Billy and his friend leave town? And what do we do now?"

Amanda snorted. "I didn't come here for nothing."

In one swift motion, Amanda took out a hairpin pinned to the right side of her head. She untangled it a little before putting it in the lock, then started fiddling with it.

"Are we really gonna break into the house?" Chelsea asked. "What if someone calls the cops?"

Wow. Time for everyone in the world to stop what they were doing. I would've never expected Chelsea to ever hesitate.

"Let them," Amanda said.

The lock clinked, and the door opened.

"What are we trying to find?" Chelsea asked.

Amanda shrugged. "Anything that might tell us where Billy and his friend are."

Several crows cawed after landing on the front yard. I grabbed my chest in a matter of seconds, and I shrieked. It didn't matter if anything bad hadn't occurred. I would never look forward to seeing crows. They were just spooky even if some people might've considered the fear irrational.

"Are we just gonna stand here, or are we gonna investigate?" Amanda continued.

We darted into the house, but we froze after shuffling only a foot or two inside. A blinking, red 1 flashed from the answering machine on the wooden table near the front door.

Exchanging glances might've been the obvious reaction, but we couldn't help myself. Or at least I couldn't (I couldn't speak for my friends). We'd have to decide whether or not we'd play the message.

"Fuck it." Amanda pressed the PLAY button.

"Hi, Ella, it's Kelsey. I didn't want to bother you since I know you and Marcus are in New York City till next Tuesday, so that's why I'm not calling your cellphone. However, I need to chat with you when you return to town. Anyway, I hope the Baylor Regency is treating you well. Ciao."

Wow. Perhaps the universe was sometimes capable of being generous. Whether I'd thank the universe, an answer fell into my lap. So, maybe, just maybe, I'd have fleeting gratitude. Any positive momentum was great.

"I guess we know where we're going tomorrow," Amanda said.

"What are you talking about?" Freddie asked.

Amanda gripped a strand of her hair, accentuating it greasy texture. Although I didn't need think about how she might've been forgetting to wash her hair and how similar it might've been to bacon fat. The point was, she was doing the work for me with our snooping. I was one person, and could only do so much.

"Let's end this once and for all, and go to New York City tomorrow," Amanda said. "I mean, it'd be foolish not. The train station near the school goes to Penn Station, which is only a couple of blocks from the Baylor Regency hotel."

Freddie folded his arms. "And how can you possibly know that?"

"My father goes there for business all the time," Amanda said.

Freddie's mouth gaped. "Oh…"

"Amanda's right. So, let's end this once and for all," I said.

We all nodded at each other, and my stomach lurched. Intellectualizing an idea and following through with it were two different things. There was just no telling what would happen when a situation involved Billy. Anything was possible with him, including something terrible.

THEN

MONDAY, JANUARY 13, 2020

Snow covered my school's once luscious grass while I clipped by several students flocking towards the academic buildings on the north side of campus. Although at least my body wasn't shivering since the air lacked a vindictive harshness that defined New England winters. Therefore, I sported shorts. Besides, the concrete ground had been paved, and I didn't have to think about snow soaking my sneakers and argyle socks. There was just nothing like wet socks to make me smile.

Except Billy just approached me. And now my pulse drummed loud enough in my ears that going deaf was possible. I so needed to run into Billy on my first day back from winter vacation.

Billy looked into my eyes. "How was your Winter Break, Carson?"

I must've been hallucinating. Billy couldn't have wanted to chat with me. Not causing a scene was one thing, yet no reason existed why we needed to pretend we were friends—even if we still had the short story class in common. The world wouldn't end if Billy and I never talked again.

"It was fine, thanks. What about you?" I asked.

Naming dozens of other places I'd rather be right now didn't make me a hypocrite for responding to Billy's question. He was the type of person that it was better to deal with then run away from. It wasn't like I just slept with him since some restraint was capable.

"Having almost a month off was good, but I can't help thinking of how we left things," he said.

"Billy, please!"

"I'm sorry we ended things."

Yup. Billy and I were finished. Just because my mind hadn't dwelled on the breakup, didn't make said fact less true. I just needed to move on with my life. After all, the definition of insanity was repeating the same thing over and over again while still expecting the same result.

A lump lingered in my throat. "Don't worry about it. Life goes on."

Billy's face drooped—almost as if someone told him he had to repeat a grade. "Getting one last goodbye was nice."

"I don't mean to be rude, but there's no reason to rehash everything. We slept together one last time, and that was enough."

"I wouldn't mind it happening again."

"Tell me something. Are you still determined to keep your sexuality a secret?" I asked.

He didn't wince. "That doesn't mean I don't want you…"

"Then nothing has changed."

Someone needed to throw a parade in my honor. I actually stood up to Billy without trembling. And that detail couldn't be forgotten about it. If I wanted better, then I needed to demand better.

"Don't be like this. I don't care how corny this sounds, but what we shared meant something to me," he said.

Damn. My demeanor must've been killing him. His didn't have to slouch for my inference. Anyone who met Billy could tell he craved attention more than oxygen. And that fact was sick. Billy was a person, not a dictator. So, need for a cult of personality. Yeah. I compared my ex to a dictator even if some people might've that analogy was too harsh.

"I don't know what you want me to say," I said.

"Just think about starting over."

Billy might not have forced himself on me, yet he should've known better than to say what he said. Accepting no for an answer was more than a little important to me in light of the Jonathan situation. Billy could accost me every second the day, and my answer still would've been no.

"Aren't you paying attention?" I asked. "We both want different things."

He licked his lips. "That doesn't mean we can't sleep together."

Okay. Billy had to have been a bigger fool than I realized. He couldn't have been that desperate to sleep with me. If I didn't know better, then I would've guessed that his current behavior almost resembled a someone being in love with their date before even having a first date.

I had to be honest about one thing, though. At least to myself. Getting Billy worked up was better than an orgasm. For once, I wasn't bowing since him begging for anything meant the dynamic flipped.

And no. The euphoria jolting my body from said conclusion didn't make me cruel. I just had to be truthful with myself. Anything was better than blaming myself for the agony Billy caused me, because I wasn't oblivious. All relationships—whether platonic or romantic—required two people. And I therefore played a part in my own misery whether I accepted that fact or not.

"Our relationship ended for a reason." I paused for a beat. "Please do me a favor, and don't speak to me during our short story class."

"I'm not sure what I did to make you this angry," Billy said.

One. Two. Three. Four. Yup. Pausing was the best thing to do in this situation. Ending my dynamic with Billy didn't mean require starting trouble. I just had to be firm. Even if doing so might've taken me more seconds than I realized.

"I'm not angry," I said. "I'm just done with you."

"You don't mean that."

He should've known better than to challenge what I said. I wasn't the same guy who he chatted up at the Barn party. Nope. Contrary to popular opinion, but I was capable of standing up for myself. If I didn't demand better for myself, then nobody would.

"Why are you so desperate for me to like you?" I asked.

Billy didn't answer my question. Instead, he darted through the crowd of students who were still en route to the academic buildings.

Someone clapped my back, and I turned around.

"Please don't sneak up on me, Freddie," I said.

Just because Freddie was my best friend didn't mean he could sneak up on me. He couldn't. I would never be okay with my heart beating even faster than usual. This was real life, not a movie, so I'd leave the drama to pop culture.

His eyebrows knitted together in confusion. "I'm just wanted to catch up."

"Did you have a good break?"

He rubbed his temple. "I did, but I'm more concerned about you. Your conversation with Billy looked tense."

"Everything is fine."

"Are you sure? Because you stopped talking about Billy before break. In fact, you've kind of stopped talking about him in general."

Ouch. The universe couldn't have been so sick that it provided me with an opportunity to confide in someone despite how I couldn't. Nope. No reason existed why I needed to display my vulnerability this early in the morning. Nothing good ever came from rambling about an issue I already solved. A point came when talking about a problem did more harm than good.

"It's all good," I said.

"Whatever you say. Just know I'm here for you if you ever wanna talk."

***

TUESDAY MARCH 3, 2020

Someone knocked on my door room door while I sat in front of my desk reading something on my laptop for one of my classes. I didn't answer the door, though. Not being bothered proved best because I deserved my own boundaries. It wasn't like my building was on fire and I needed to evacuate.

The knocking returned.

Shit. No choice existed in getting off my ass and answering the door. This situation was like Billy. Dealing with something unpleasant was sometimes best. If the person knocked again, then the person might do it a third time.

"What do you want?" I asked after opening the door.

Amanda strutted into my room. "You haven't been answering any texts."

"I've been busy." I closed the door.

"Sorry. But you'll have to try harder. Everyone is busy, but people make time for the important things."

Sure. Amanda's best friend status entailed giving her more latitude than the average person. But I couldn't be too much of a pushover. Having time to myself wasn't the end of the world as long as I wasn't a threat to myself or others. Because I wasn't. Not dealing with people, including my best friends, was sometimes more palatable than faking sincerity.

"What's up?" I asked.

"I want to know why you've been blowing us off, and I'm not leaving till you give me a real answer. I've got all night, and I won't hesitate to take advantage of said fact."

I shrieked. "Fine. You want the truth? I dumped Billy before Winter Break, and I just can't deal with anyone right now."

"I'm so sorry. But please explain everything because I need more context."

I drank water from my water bottle a few minutes later while Amanda and I sat in two chairs in front my desk. "Anyway, I hope you don't think I'm pathetic or foolish."

"No. I'm proud of you for demanding better. Because I wouldn't have the guts to do something like that."

Perhaps I judged Amanda too much. She could've lectured me more about the Billy situation right now, yet she hadn't. And that fact was worth holding. Some people weren't always able of self-control. One only needed to watch a television or movie to understand friends sometimes gave their friends an unfiltered opinion.

"Wanting more than I'm getting just isn't a healthy situation," I said.

"I was afraid you were still concerned about the kiss. Because I haven't been honest with you, Carson. I didn't kiss you at the charity function in December to make Billy jealous. I wanted to test the waters with us."

"Huh?"

"I have a crush on you," Amanda blurted.

Good gracious. The universe might've loved fucking with me, but Amanda couldn't have said what she just did. The kiss was one thing. However, a good chance existed that our friendship would become more complicated. Being polite and not making her feel bad for the confession didn't mean forgetting what she said. I couldn't. Her reveal was comparable to a child finding out Santa Claus wasn't real since some facts couldn't be unlearned no matter how much I wished the opposite was true.

"You what?" I asked.

"I'm sorry, but it's true. And I also know now that I shouldn't have taken advantage of our friendship."

"Mistakes happen."

Keeping my response brief enabled a simpler life. Any potential complication had to be squashed. I would be damned if I traded the Billy debacle for an even more challenging problem.

"I hope we can still be friends," Amanda said.

"Absolutely. And I'm sorry if I worried you, Chelsea, and Freddie."

"Don't worry about it. Although at least I stopped Chelsea and Freddie from contacting your RA or the counseling center to make sure you're okay."

Shit. Amanda hadn't only been ballsy because of her confession. She also had to pile on the emotional intensity more. Because Freddie and Chelsea's concern seemed more than a little extreme. It wasn't like I ever did anything that made them doubt my sanity.

"Do you still have a crush on me?" I asked.

"Yes. But why would you ask that question?"

"Some non-toxic person has to care about me as more than a friend." I lifted my gaze off the piece of lint on my shorts before making eye contact with Amanda. Neither one of us spoke as we kept looking at each other, though—almost as if our conversation resembled a nuclear standoff.

Amanda leaned forward, and kissed me. She stroked a lock of my hair out of the way in addition to moving her tongue inside my mouth. Except I didn't push her away or have an emotional outburst. For once, someone wanted me more than I wanted them, and my make-out session with Amanda was therefore better than getting everything I wanted on my Christmas list. Even if I should've known better than to complicate my life. Even if I'd punish myself in the morning if we went further than kissing. And even if I'd never make eye contact with Amanda again after today.

I continued holding the comforter over me sometime later while Amanda was in my bed next to me. "Wow…"

"My thoughts exactly."

"You have to promise me something."

"Anything," she said.

"Having sex can't ruin our friendship," I said.

"It won't; I promise. Although I'd appreciate it if you'd make the same agreement."

I held my palm up. "Promise."

Being genuine and following through with the promise were two different things. I wasn't a fortuneteller, and couldn't predict what would happen one hour, one week, one month, one year, or one decade from now. No explanation needed for people's good intentions sometimes going to shit. And that was why focusing on something positive—like Amanda's strawberry scented shampoo—was the only thing that mattered. Sure. Amanda might've smelled differently than Billy, but I could still latch onto a sensual detail. I'd need some souvenir of our tryst.

***

TUESDAY, MARCH 31, 2020

I sat at a bar counter of a local gay bar near campus that didn't card, except the earthly and sweet scent masking the air around me after the shuffle of footsteps meant chugging my Margarita and leaving. No reason existed why Billy and I needed to chat.

Billy grinned at me. "Fancy seeing you here."

"Did you follow me?"

"Don't be ridiculous. I can't help if we both frequent the same gay bar."

"Sure. Whatever." I grabbed my glass and finished the rest of my Margarita in a matter of seconds.

And no regret existed despite the mixture of the lime and bitter tequila taste making my lips pucker from the intense taste. My mental sanity was all that mattered. Besides, I could just have water when I got back to my dorm room.

"It just really sucks how you won't talk to me," Billy said.

"I'm sorry, but it's not my job to protect your feelings."

"I never said it was. It just would be nice if you gave me more consideration."

Okay. Billy had to have been high. Even he wasn't capable of being that much of a hypocrite. This was the same guy who never showed me one ounce of empathy, or if he did, I lost ten things in exchange for Billy's brief moment of kindness.

Billy gesticulated at the bartender, and the woman slid a Champagne flute in his direction. Interesting. Waving at the bar tender and getting a drink within several seconds of said gesture might've meant Billy was a regular. And I couldn't forget about Billy's baseball cap—almost as if wearing it was his lame attempt to hide his identity. But maybe, just maybe, I shouldn't have thought less for Billy wearing a baseball cap in door. At least he wasn't wearing it backwards like some pretentious douchebag. Someone's popularity had nothing to do with the issue—no good reason existed from wearing a cap backwards.

"I don't have time for this." I took my wallet out from my pocket, and threw a twenty-dollar bill on the counter.

Except Billy gripped my hand, and my body jerked. But not from the intensity of Billy's grip. Nope. The grip wasn't something someone expected from a wife batterer. If anything, the way Billy held my wrist resembled a child holding his or her parent's hand while crossing the street. Yet I couldn't allow Billy to think touching me was okay. Clear boundaries needed to exist because my palms couldn't have been sweaty just from Billy touching. I made a choice, and I'd stick by it.

I walked into the men's room with Billy a couple of minutes later. "I only agreed to chat in here so we wouldn't cause a scene."

"Understood." Billy flipped the lock on the door.

"Tell me what you want."

"I want a redo," he said.

"I'm sorry, but that's not gonna happen."

Wow. Someone needed to throw a party in my honor ASAP. I hadn't waffled yet, and might've had a chance with not caving. Because I didn't know what I'd do with myself if I returned to Billy

"Don't be stupid. I know you wanna kiss me." Billy trekked over to me while my back remained pressed against the sink counter.

I cackled. "Don't be ridiculous. Nothing could be further from the truth."

Yup. Even I was capable of sounding like the Wicked Witch of the West. Harshness meant creating the allusion that I didn't give a flying fuck about Billy.

"I might not feel like coming out, but you can still have everything else. I mean, don't you think second place is good?" Billy asked.

"Why can't you forget about me?"

"The sex was that good."

"I'm seeing someone…"

He rolled his eyes. "Please. I'm not falling for your fauxmance again. Even I'm not dumb enough to think all the times you've been hanging out with Amanda means you're dating."

"I'm sure you can find someone else to worship you."

"I don't want anyone else; I want you."

Wow. Perhaps Billy deserved a medal for his tenacity because anyone else would've just given up. But that just wasn't going to happen. Apparently, no still wasn't a word in Billy's vocabulary.

"That's not gonna happen," I said.

"I've been seeing someone too," Billy interrupted. "An older woman."

I placed my hands on my hips. "Then why do you care about getting back with me?"

"Being with her isn't as exciting as being with you." Billy brushed his lips against my ear. "Don't you remember how good I can make you feel?"

"Nope."

"Let me refresh your memory." Billy leaned downward after yanking my shorts and boxers to my ankles, but I didn't stop him from doing so despite how anyone could've figured out where his lips would soon go.

Billy studied my waist before making eye contact. I nodded, and soon let out a series of moans while my hands clutched the sink counter in an attempt to fix the kink in my back from my terrible posture.

Shit. I let Billy back into my life. Moving my head meant consenting to Billy's proposition, and I soon let out more moans. Loud enough that I'd pray the bartender or manager wouldn't break down the bathroom and kick us out.

My life would be okay despite my current bad choice, though. Fooling around with Billy didn't mean endangering my safety. It just meant drama. But maybe conflict was okay—at least for the small part of me that thrived off drama as a result of how it made life more exciting.

***

SATURDAY, APRIL 4, 2020

Amanda and I were in my dorm room bed with the bed comforter wrapped around both of our bodies, covering us from the waist down.

I exhaled the longest breath of my life. Having my speech planned didn't make what I was about to say any easier. If anything, life was more complicated. I slept with Amanda this afternoon despite how I had to tell her what I was about to tell her. Besides, I'd get over my guilt pangs at some point. We never said that we were dating. We were just having a little fun.

"We need to talk," I said.

"What's up?"

"We can't keep sleeping together."

"Don't tell me you're bored?"

"Nothing like that," I said. "I just don't want anything to ruin our friendship."

"Bullshit. I've seen you talking with Billy over the last few days."

"You don't understand..."

She ran her fingers through her hair, almost as if doing so created another reminder of her strawberry scented shampoo. Because I'd never get over how nice inhaling the odor was. "Relax, I'm not mad. If anything, I feel sorry for you. Billy will disappoint you again, and when he does, you'll come crying to me. Except I won't listen. So, if you really want to try again with Billy, then you'll have to vent to Freddie or Chelsea."

Ouch. Maybe, just maybe, I hadn't known Amanda as well as I thought I had. No way existed that she could be so mean. It wasn't like I wanted to hurt her. Being sixteen meant making mistakes was okay, though. Because I still stood by my original statement. Billy disappointing me didn't mean my physical safety would be jeopardized, it wouldn't. I just owed it to myself to see if Billy could change.

***

FRIDAY, APRIL 10, 2020

"Nice of you two to join me today," Chelsea said.

Chelsea, Amanda, and I sat in the auditorium in the admission's building while two tables—one on the right side of the stage, and one on the left side of the stage—were set up. A student occupied each chair in addition to how a bald man in a suit stood in front of the microphone between the two tables.

Amanda scoffed. "It's not like I had a choice."

"I know, but it's still important for us to cheer Freddie on," Chelsea said. "You've got no idea how important the debate team is to him."

Bullying us to show up might've qualified as extreme behavior. But she was right. Only a minute was left before the debate's start time, yet there couldn't have been more than fifteen people in the audience as a result of almost all the seats being empty.

"You dragged us here, and you need to live with that choice," Amanda said.

No need for her theatrics. Watching my school's debate team fight a rival school might not have made my list of favorite Friday night activities. But my life would be okay since a 90-minute debate was still shorter than a two-hour class.

"Something wrong?" Chelsea asked.

"I just don't approve of something Carson did," Amanda revealed.

"Don't tell me you're seeing Billy again?" Chelsea asked.

Amanda's nostrils flared. "More like screwing."

Okay. Fine. Amanda's disappointment meant not arguing with her today. However, conversation was her one free pass. She didn't have to like my choices, but she did have to respect me.

"It'll be different this time Just you see," I said.

Amanda took her sweater off, and put it on her lap. "Whatever you say."

Yeah. Amanda was right for criticizing me. Even I hadn't believed my farce. Billy would probably disappointment sooner rather than later.

***

TUESDAY, AUGUST 4, 2020

Sweat tumbled down my face while I was in my bedroom back home. And my current demeanor wasn't due to how Billy stopped answering my texts at the end of June. My AC was busted, and my parents wouldn't be able to buy a new one till Friday. Because there just had to be a heatwave when I didn't have air conditioning.

Fuck it. No harm existed in texting Billy again. Not responding was the worst he could do. It wasn't like I depended on him for an organ donation.

NOW

SUNDAY, NOVEMBER 1, 2020

The train screeched after halting, yet Dean and I didn't rise from our seats. Freddie, Chelsea—who happened to be seated in back of Dean and me—and Amanda (who happened to be seated behind Dean and me) didn't budge either. Instead, we remained in our spots while an unidentifiable stench filled the air as passengers flocked towards the open door a few feet away from us. And I had to dwell on one passenger—the person who just wobbled by. Because I couldn't not comment on her. Pastel blue hair wasn't the type of thing I saw every day. Besides, anything was better than focusing on what I'd say to Billy. No clever phrase could sum up the various thoughts racing through my head. Even if there was no one right way to feel.

Dean lifted his gaze off his book, and made direct

eye contact with me. However, I wouldn't laugh at how he packed his English book with us. Distracting myself was one thing, yet I couldn't knock my boyfriend. He hadn't done anything to hurt me.

"You can vent if you want," Dean said.

I fidgeted in my seat after my back started aching. "That's okay."

"Fine. Whatever you want."

Not sharing my feelings with Dean didn't make me a bad person. No law existed that said I had to tell him all of my wants, needs, and desires. There was such a thing as filtering and discretion. The same was also true for Dean since I was okay with not knowing everything he thought or felt. If anything, a little mystery made our relationship more exciting.

A chill trickled through the air while I walked down the city street. The Regency's neon sign glowed in the distance. But the five of us didn't pick up the pace because we were so close to the hotel. It was because Billy and his lady friend crossed the street, and were now only a few feet in front of us.

Sure. Billy's hair might've now been the same shade of blond as mine, yet I still would've recognized his broad shoulders anywhere.

Billy and his "friend" were too busy kissing each other to recoil from our presence.

I still put a finger to my lips. There was just no way Amanda, Chelsea, or Freddie would blow my opportunity for closure. Even if I still didn't know what I was going to say.

Billy and his "friend" detached from each other and darted down the street and towards the Regency. Then, I glanced in their direction.

Taking imitative might've made me bossy, but I wouldn't apologize. I needed to take control of my life so I wouldn't resemble some passive character from a boring novel. Or at least I could channel a façade by being braver than I was.

So, that was why I cleared my throat when we were closing in on them in front of the Regency's entrance while a man in a jean jacket dashed by us.

"Hello, Billy," I said, raising my voice.

Billy spun around before screaming. "What the hell are you doing here?"

"We need to talk," I said.

"I have nothing to say to you," Billy said.

The lady grunted. "You really are pathetic, you know that? You should let Billy go. He doesn't love you. In fact, he never cared about you."

For one fleeting moment, Billy and I exchanged eye contact, and his Adam's apple throbbed. Almost like he expressed contrition. But that would've entailed him being human, and that wasn't true. Not now.

My nostrils flared. "Did you know Billy and I were fucking last spring when you two were supposed to be together?"

Yup. I had no qualms about being tough. It wasn't like I wanted to turn into Charles Manson. Both Billy and his girlfriend needed to know I wasn't a fool. Besides, I was actually kind of proud of myself. Even if pride was one of the seven deadly sins. I deserved to defend myself, and that was what I'd keep doing. To do anything other than that just would've been dumb.

Billy furrowed his eyebrows. "What do you want, Carson?"

I rolled my eyes. "I deserve a real reason why you fucked with me so much."

"I killed for you," Billy said.

Oh, dear. My ears must've deceived me. Speculating about Billy killing Jonathan, and him actually killing Jonathan were two different things. No matter how awful Billy was, I couldn't think about sharing a bed with a murderer. Said thought would've meant wishing I was a snake and shedding my skin.

The lady tugged at Billy's arm. "Let's go, babe."

"One second," Billy said. "I wanna know how you found me."

Chelsea put her hands on her hips. "That's because we know how to pick a lock."

Smacking my hand over my forehead didn't make me weak. Doing so meant I was human. Chelsea could save her bluntness for later. Admitting to a crime and writing about it on our college essays was less than an ideal. I would've rather died than wear orange. Even if I enjoyed watching *Orange is the New Black* on *Netflix*.

The woman grabbed Billy's arm even harder this time, yet he didn't budge. Instead, Billy continued looking me in the eye before his gaze drifted to Dean.

Billy's lips curled. "I should kill you for what you did. You were there when I almost died."

"We both know the situation was a little more complicated than that," Dean said.

Go, Dean. And my praise wasn't about not wanting a weak boyfriend. There was just no reason why Dean should let my former flame have the last word.

Billy sighed at me. "You've clearly moved on, so that means there's nothing left to discuss. Anyway, have a great life."

I let out a laugh. "Wow. Good to know I mean nothing to you."

"Don't put words in my mouth," Billy piped.

Amanda glanced at Billy's girlfriend. "I'll give you some unsolicited advice. You should dump his lame ass before he leaves you high and dry. We slept together once, but he never spoke to me again."

The lady cackled. "Bitterness doesn't look good on you. Although it's good to know Billy traded up."

"Give me a real answer, Billy. Did you ever care about me?" I asked.

Billy's girlfriend screamed before he could respond. But I wouldn't criticize her—not this time. Beams of sunlight glinted against the metal gun that a man just waved at her.

The gunman shrieked. "Give me your purse."

"Never." She clutched the purse harder.

His hands remained on the trigger. "This is your last chance."

Billy sucked in a breath. "Just give him the purse; you can always replace material items."

The lady rolled her eyes. "Maybe you are a dumbass..."

A part of me almost snickered. And my reasoning wasn't from wanting to Billy's girlfriend to die—I didn't. It was just great knowing there was some justice in the world. Billy couldn't escape reality forever.

The gunman hissed. "This is your last warning, bitch!"

Amanda, Freddie, Chelsea, and I exchanged glances, yet did nothing. Being stereotypical bystanders didn't make us bad people, though. No reason existed as to why we should endanger our lives for someone we didn't know.

"I've had enough!" The gunman pulled the trigger three times. Then, the lady thumped against the ground, banging her head against the sidewalk. And the gunman grabbed the Gucci purse while Billy remained frozen.

A pool of blood oozed from both her head wound and stomach where the gunman shot her three times. Wow. I couldn't believe it. I was so concerned about coming face to face with Billy that I hadn't anticipated something bad happening to someone else. That was the universe, though. Fucking with me by making it appear something uneasy would happen, only to have nothing awful happen to me. Psychological trauma always left the deepest wounds. Although I probably wouldn't make that comment to Billy—even I wasn't that insensitive. Besides, he just leaned down on the ground and propped his girlfriend against his chest, and was now drenched in blood.

THEN

THURSDAY, SEPTEMBER 10, 2020

Some people might've thought I only had myself to blame for the annoyance raging through my body while I stood in front of the academic buildings on the south side of campus, yet I would've called bullshit. I was allowed to make a few mistakes as a result of being a teenager. Because there was a big difference standing between "dating" a bad guy and a downward spiral.

Billy handed me a coffee. "Thanks for responding to my text."

"I wanna know why you stopped texting me, Billy."

"It's complicated."

"That isn't good enough; not anymore. And you also better not eye-fuck me. Because that isn't going to work this time."

He took in a breath. "Doesn't chatting right now count for something?"

"You probably only wanted to hang before morning classes so I'd shut up."

"That's not true, and you know it."

"What I said last year is still true. I really can't keep doing all this back and forth. It's just not healthy." Throwing the Starbucks cup into the adjacent garbage didn't make me arrogant. I needed to do everything I could to defend myself. Flirting with me wasn't the only thing that wouldn't work. Buying me favors was all just a waste of Billy's time. Even if he went to the real Starbucks and not the coffee cart on campus. Because I didn't have to travel with Billy to know where he purchased the coffee. The cup's design proved he purchased the coffee or Caramel Macchiato.

"You aren't gonna succeed with picking a fight with me by acting childish," Billy said.

"Did you just accuse me of being childish?"

"Please stop arguing with me. I want to be with you."

Please. I was smart enough not to fall for his bullshit. Anyone with even an ounce of intelligence could've inferred how Billy was my school's version of the boy who cried wolf. There just came a point when no reason existed to believe him. Sure. Billy might change for a day or two. However, it'd only be a matter of time before he reverted back to his old ways. People might've been able to change if they wanted to, yet the key part was want to. Until Billy proved otherwise, he wasn't capable of acting like a human being.

"But only if it's by your rules. And that's just code for fucking whenever you get bored or horny," I said.

He scrunched his eyebrows. "There are things you don't know."

"And what's that?"

"I can't tell you, so you'll just have to take my

word for it."

Billy couldn't have said what he did. If he wanted the benefit of the doubt, then he had to earn it. I could list a million things that were more likely to happen than Billy becoming a better person. Like my father winning the lotto or me becoming a successful author.

"Do you know how stupid that sounds?" I asked.

"I'm being honest."

"I'm serious. This is it. We both want different things, and there's no reason to keep wasting our time."

"Don't be like this. I can change."

Billy might as well have once again had a bottle of snake oil in his hand. I would've been more likely to buy it then believe whatever farce he was trying to pull over me.

"What?" I asked. "Are you gonna tell me about some terrible event that happened in childhood that explains why you're such a jackass?"

Yeah. This conversation was one of those times when I could act like a jerk. My response wasn't an attempt to make light of people who might've experienced some horrific trauma like physical, sexual, or emotional abuse. That type of scenario was honestly the one thing that would've justified someone being so insecure about their life.

"You aren't as dumb as you look," he said.

"What are you talking about?" I asked.

Billy reached for my hand, yet I stepped backward. "If you give me a couple of more days, then I'll come out, and we can be together like you've always wanted."

"You're stringing me along."

"Not this time."

Billy might've deserved points for consistency. However, walking in dog shit would've been more exciting than having any positive will towards Billy.

"I don't wanna see you or communicate with you," I said.

Nope. My decision was the right one. Billy was given multiple opportunities to be a better person, yet he blew every chance. Almost as if Billy just couldn't help himself no matter how farces he put on.

A few students with backpacks strapped to their backs strutted by, and if I was a lesser person I would've punched them despite how they did nothing bad to me. There was just no reason to be jolly on the second day of classes. Because it was still a long time before Thanksgiving Break.

Tears welled in his eyes. "What do you want me to do? Kiss you right here in public?"

"I don't want a fucking thing from you."

Wow. No matter how many pangs of shock traveled through my body, I couldn't ignore the truth. I still hadn't caved to Billy's demand.

Billy threw his coffee cup against the ground before he continued wailing. "Damn you, Carson! You were supposed to understand me in a way that nobody else did."

"You never gave a shit about me. You just liked the attention."

"That's not true, and you know it. I might like the attention, but I genuinely care about you. Besides, it seemed like you enjoyed me sucking you off in the gay bar last April. Because you couldn't stop moaning."

Yup. He had to make me feel guilty for enjoying a moment of pleasure, which was further proof of the sick fuck he was. Life was complicated enough without making someone suffer for an orgasm.

"Goodbye, Billy."

* * *

SATURDAY, SEPTEMBER 12, 2020

Tear after tear rolled down my face. I also clenched my fists while sitting in front of my desk in my dorm room.

230

Billy couldn't have been dead. He just couldn't have. We were supposed to give things another shot—at least in the alternative universe where I pretended Billy was a good person and he'd treat me right.

Someone knocked, and I answered the door after standing.

"I'm so sorry." Freddie opened his arms, and I collapsed into his chest. His hands kept massaging my back while I buried my head in his chest.

Showing such vulnerability might not have been my favorite activity. But it was the only thing I could do. It was either cry or die. Although someone would pay for Billy's death. There was just no way a vain person like him would've committed suicide. And I'd therefore do something about Billy's death. Because if I lost the opportunity for a happily ever with Billy, then I could at least investigate my theory. Like starting with Charity Now since that was where Billy devoted a lot of time to when he was alive.

NOW

TUESDAY, MARCH 9, 2021

I sat in the dining hall at dinner with Freddie, Chelsea, Amanda, and Dean while the distinct chatter of numerous voices filled the air. And I couldn't forget about the seat in front of me—it was empty.

A guy strutted over to our table a couple of minutes later, walking slightly slower after glancing at the WET FLOOR sign. He put his backpack on the seat in front of me—the empty one—then kissed me.

I smiled. "Good to see you, Billy."

"Same. Anyway, I hope they've got something good for dinner," Billy said.

"I got the Chicken Fried Steak," I said.

Billy winked. "And?"

"It's nice," I said.

"Carson's right for once," Amanda said.

"Agreed," Chelsea parroted.

"I'll be right back." Billy squeezed my shoulder before walking away from the table and towards the part of the cafeteria where they kept the food.

Freddie shoved his empty plate to the side, then finished his water. "I still can't believe that Billy stopped playing games and you two are a real couple."

I chucked. "Same."

Chelsea glanced at Dean. "And I can't believe you're still friends with Carson."

"Some people are better off as friends. The breakup was also my idea," Dean said.

"A no drama breakup is something I can get behind," Amanda said. "And I want you to know that I completely support your relationship, Carson."

"Thanks," I mumbled.

Amanda gave me a look. "I'm serious."

A guy a few yards away dropped his plate, and it clanked against the ground. My mind then drifted back to that night several weeks ago when everything changed.

* * *

My boots crunched against the ice and snow-covered ground while the trees rattled in the wind and I went deeper and deeper into the woods. Although at least the moon provided a little extra lighting.

I came to an abrupt halt after I was within a few inches of a hooded figure.

"You took a big risk demanding I meet you—even if you used a burner phone," I said.

The guy whirled around before lifting off his hood. A tingling sensation even shot through my fingers and legs while my heart pounded faster and faster. Whether I accepted the truth or not, Billy was standing in front of me. And there wasn't a fucking thing I could do about said fact.

Billy gave me a weak smile, fear radiating from his eyes. "Hi, Carson."

I didn't respond. Instead, my jaw twitched. There was no telling what Billy planned, and I had to be prepared for any possibility.

"I'm not gonna hurt you," Billy stammered.

"I don't even know why I came."

"But you did."

I remained silent.

"Please say something," Billy pleaded.

The wind roared louder, and clumps of snow fell off the trees. A nearby owl even hooted before flying away.

"Something is really fucked up about you, and I'd love it if you'd tell me what it is." My teeth chattered. "But you're never gonna be honest with me because our entire relationship was a lie."

He pressed his hands together. "That's not true, and you know it."

"You haven't told me what you want," I spat.

"You're right. There's something seriously fucked up about me."

"Okay?"

"Do you remember that day in your room in early December of 2019? The day you saw the scars on my back?" he asked.

No. This conversation couldn't have been headed where I thought it was headed. People like Billy didn't have layers—they were just assholes with no redeeming qualities. Yet I couldn't dismiss Billy. Not entirely, at least. The look of dread hadn't left his face—almost as if he wasn't lying. Not this time.

"I never told you how I got the scars," Billy continued.

I forced in a deep breath.

"The reason why I was so adamant about helping you that night you revealed you were raped wasn't just because I sensed something fucked up happened," he said.

I stuffed my hands into my jacket pockets. "I don't understand."

"I'm a survivor of abuse," Billy revealed. "And I got those scars on my back because my mother burned me with cigarettes."

I choked. Some truths just couldn't be understood no how matter simply they were stated. No child deserved to be burned with cigarettes.

Billy looked away. "It started when I was seven."

"What about your sister and father?" I asked.

"I convinced my sister to attend boarding school in Switzerland when she was eight under the guise of being closer to our grandparents." Billy wiped the tears from his cheeks before sobbing louder. "As for my father, he was out of the picture a lot. And that made it easy for my mother to abuse me."

"And why was your mother so evil?" I asked.

"She hated my father and how he made her give up her career at a PR firm to be a doting housewife and mother," Billy said. "Apparently, she made good money."

"Okay," I said.

Billy stepped closer. "You must think I'm lying, but I'm not. I swear on my sister's life. If I was lying, then I would've concocted some story that day in your room."

"I believe you," I blurted.

"I hurt people because I'm so broken on the inside."

"You didn't only hurt other people, Billy," I said. "You manipulated me over and over again. And that fucking sucked."

He pressed his hands together. "I know, and I'm sorry. You didn't deserve that."

I huffed out a sigh. "And you didn't deserve what you went through."

"I don't expect you to ever forgive me. Just thought you should know the truth." He sobbed even louder this time. "I was never afraid of people finding out I liked guys. That was just a cover."

"Lying caused a lot of problems," I said.

"I know."

"Was the abuse ever sexual?" I asked. "Sorry. I shouldn't have asked that."

"She raped me with the end of a broom once when I was in the seventh grade. I got all A's except for one class where I got a C." Billy made a fist. "Apparently, raping me would make me wanna do better next time."

I gasped. "Fuck."

Billy coughed into his right arm.

"What's the deal with your mother now?" I asked.

"She died a couple of days before this school year started—drunk driving accident. Fortunately, she only harmed herself when she made the decision to drive drunk," Billy said.

"I see."

"My mother is the reason I ghosted you last summer," Billy said.

"Understandable."

Billy sobbed more while tears rolled down his face faster and faster. He even screamed.

"I'm so fucked up, and nobody will ever love me!" he exclaimed. "I'm sure people haven't forgotten about the hazing with Charity Now. Fuck. Everyone hates me, and I don't blame them."

"I don't hate you." I opened my arms, inviting Billy in for a hug. He collapsed into my body without another word and cried into my chest while I rubbed his back.

Billy pulled away after another beat. "Thanks for believing me."

"Do you wanna know how I'm certain you aren't lying?"

He nodded.

"It's not just your body language," I said. "You genuinely sound miserable."

"I want you to know I never stopped loving you." Billy gazed into my eyes, and I didn't look away. He kissed me, yet I didn't stop him. In fact, the kiss became deeper and harder while he shoved his tongue into my mouth and I inhaled the earthly and sweet scent of whatever deodorant he used.

"Wow!" I rubbed my lips, almost as if I hoped I could still feel the smooth, cotton like texture of Billy's lips on my mouth despite how the kiss ended.

"Sorry. I fucked up again." Billy shuddered. "That kiss shouldn't have happened."

"Not like you can hurt me more than you have."

Billy gave me a dirty look.

"I was joking," I continued.

My heart leapt out of my chest again. Disbelief still flooded me. One moment shouldn't have impacted me so much, yet it had. In one conversation, Billy transformed from monster to victim. And that was a concrete fact I couldn't ignore. Like it or not, Billy was a real human being like everyone else.

***

Billy's snickering snapped me out of my digression.

"Good to know some things don't change," Billy said before finishing the rest of his Chicken Fried Steak.

Chelsea ran her fingers through her hair. "Don't listen to him, Carson. You're daydreaming is cute."

Freddie drummed his fingers against the table. "I'm glad the cops believed you when you told them running away was a stupid prank."

Billy burped. "Let's not talk about it."

"Sorry," Freddie said.

Amanda made eye contact with Billy. "I'm sorry for what you went through."

"No big deal," Billy said.

"You don't have to put on a façade," Amanda said. "Your mother was a monster, and I hope she burns in Hell for what she did to you."

"I also owe you an apology." Billy sipped his water.

"For what?" Amanda asked.

"Not treating you better," Billy said.

Amanda let out a breath. "Sometimes sex is just sex. I also have an awesome boyfriend now, which wouldn't have happened if you and I started dating."

I cocked my head, then my pulse hammered in my ears. Sweat dripped down my back because of the guy who was fast approaching our table. Billy being alive was one thing, but a second dead person couldn't be alive. Stranger things happened all the time, though—lightning sometimes did strike twice. So, maybe, just maybe, my next nightmare was about to start.

I started panting while making a fist.

Billy lifted his gaze off his plate, then glanced at me. "Something wrong?"

"He's alive," I murmured.

"Who?" Billy asked.

I leaned closer to everyone. "Jonathan."

"Impossible," Billy said. "I looked online—the funeral was open casket."

Too late. The guy now stood in front of our table. "I don't mean to bother you. But I'm new here, and had a question," he said.

Amanda's, Freddie's, Chelsea's, and Dean's eyes remained glued to the guy standing before us. Fantastic. Good to know I wasn't the only one with shock pulsing through their body.

"Us first," Billy said. "Forgive us for being rude, but you have an uncanny resemblance to someone who used to attend this school."

"I know—I'm Joaquin Davidson. Jonathan Davidson's identical twin brother," he said. "I just transferred here this week."

Billy's mouth gaped. "Oh."

"What was your question?" Freddie asked.

"I was wondering if the dining hall had different

hours on the weekend?" Joaquin asked.

"It doesn't," Amanda said.

"Thanks for answering my question." Jonathan winked at us. "See you around."

Joaquin darted away without another word.

I gritted my teeth. "I'll say it if nobody else will. Do you think he's suspicious about Jonathan's death? Could talking to us have been a ruse?"

Nobody spoke. Instead, Freddie, Chelsea, Amanda, Dean, Billy, and I exchanged glances with each other. That was the thing about life. When one chapter ended, another began, and sometimes not for the better. So, I'd have to hope the truth wouldn't unravel about Jonathan's "murder"—not when I was finally happy.

Other titles by BLKDOG Publishing that you may enjoy:

Burning Bridges
By Chris Bedell

They've always said that three's a crowd...

24-year-old Sasha didn't anticipate her identical twin Riley killing herself upon their reconciliation after years of estrangement. But Sasha senses an opportunity and assumes Riley's identity so she can escape her old life.

Playing Riley isn't without complications, though. Riley's had a strained relationship with her wife and stepson so Sasha must do whatever she can to make her newfound family love and accept her. If Sasha's arrangement ends, then she'll have nothing protecting her from her past. However, when one of Sasha's former clients tracks her down, Sasha must choose between her new life and the only person who cared about her.

But things are about to become even more complicated, as a third sister, Katrina, enters the scene...

Cousin Dearest
By Chris Bedell

17-year-old Casey has opinions about everything. Like how his grandmother could have been a soap opera actress in another life. And his rantings only increase when his grandma is murdered the night of her 60th birthday party. Casey must also deal with his budding romance with the next-door neighbor, Logan. However, Logan's mother disapproves of their relationship because of Casey's grandmother being murdered. Disapproval be damned, though. Casey and Logan date despite Logan's mother's initial skepticism.

If life weren't complicated enough, Casey and Logan work together to investigate who killed Casey's grandma. But the killer is watching Casey and Logan. So, Casey and Logan must act quickly if they want to solve the case. If they don't, Casey and Logan might die next.

Sirkkusaga
By Kyt Wright

A saga — a long story of heroic achievement, especially a medieval prose narrative in Old Norse or a long, involved story, account, or series of incidents often named for the principal character.

Several hundred years after a world-shattering war, two of the surviving nations, the Reignweald and the Dominion, have fought themselves to a standstill, both remaining determined to control of what's left of it.

Sirki Vigsdottir, a songstress who performs under the name Freya in folk-rock group *The Harvest*, is a beautiful, self-centered woman who is fond of drink and a recovering addict to boot — not the sort of girl a boy brings home to Mother.

Following an attack from an unexpected quarter, abilities awaken within Sirki, who begins a journey of self-discovery. These new-found skills attract the attention of both the Psi, a mysterious group of telepaths headed by the fearsome Mina and an equally sinister government department – the ACG.

Sirki, learning the real truth of her origin, is dragged into plotting between the queen and the Government, finding herself in constant danger as Bren, fighting for the nation, becomes an important part of her life. As it becomes clear that her life of self-indulgence is over, Sirki wonders if her new-found powers are a blessing or a curse.

Arthur: Shadow of a God
By Richard Denham

King Arthur has fascinated the Western world for over a thousand years and yet we still know nothing more about him now than we did then. Layer upon layer of heroics and exploits have been piled upon him to the point where history, legend and myth have become hopelessly entangled.

In recent years, there has been a sort of scholarly consensus that 'the once and future king' was clearly some sort of Romano-British warlord, heroically stemming the tide of wave after wave of Saxon invaders after the end of Roman rule. But surprisingly, and no matter how much we enjoy this narrative, there is actually next-to-nothing solid to support this theory except the wishful thinking of understandably bitter contemporaries. The sources and scholarship used to support the 'real Arthur' are as much tentative guesswork and pushing 'evidence' to the extreme to fit in with this version as anything involving magic swords, wizards and dragons. Even Archaeology remains silent. Arthur is, and always has been, the square peg that refuses to fit neatly into the historians round hole.

Arthur: Shadow of a God gives a fascinating overview of Britain's lost hero and casts a light over an often-overlooked and somewhat inconvenient truth; Arthur was almost certainly not a man at all, but a god. He is linked inextricably to the world of Celtic folklore and Druidic traditions. Whereas tyrants like Nero and Caligula were men who fancied themselves gods; is it not possible that Arthur was a god we have turned into a man? Perhaps then there is a truth here. Arthur, 'The King under the Mountain'; sleeping until his return will never return, after all, because he doesn't need to. Arthur the god never left in the first place and remains as popular today as he ever was. His legend echoes in stories, films and games that are every bit as imaginative and fanciful as that which the minds of talented bards such as Taliesin and Aneirin came up with when the mists of the 'dark ages' still swirled over Britain – and perhaps that is a good thing after all, most at home in the imaginations of children and adults alike – being the Arthur his believers want him to be.

A Storm of Magic
By Ashley Laino

Being brought back from the dead is an impressive trick, even for magician Darien Burron. Now he must try and use his sleight of hand to swindle modern-day witch, Mirah, to sign her power away, or end up a tormented demon in the afterlife.

Meanwhile, sixteen-year-old Mirah is starting to lose control of her powers. After an incident at her aunt's Witchery store, Mirah is sent to a secret coven to learn to control her abilities. While away, Mirah meets up with a soft-spoken clairvoyant, a brazen storm witch, and the creator of dark magic itself. The young woman must learn to trust in herself before she loses herself entirely to the darkness that hunts her.

Weirder War Two
By Richard Denham & Michael Jecks

Did a Warner Bros. cartoon prophesize the use of the atom bomb? Did the Allies really plan to use stink bombs on the enemy? Why did the Nazis make their own version of Titanic and why were polar bear photographs appearing throughout Europe?

The Second World War was the bloodiest of all wars. Mass armies of men trudged, flew or rode from battlefields as far away as North Africa to central Europe, from India to Burma, from the Philippines to the borders of Japan. It saw the first aircraft carrier sea battle, and the indiscriminate use of terror against civilian populations in ways not seen since the Thirty Years War. Nuclear and incendiary bombs erased entire cities. V weapons brought new horror from the skies: the V1 with their hideous grumbling engines, the V2 with sudden, unexpected death. People were systematically starved: in Britain food had to be rationed because of the stranglehold of U-Boats, while in Holland the German blockage of food and fuel saw 30,000 die of starvation in the winter of 1944/5. It was a catastrophe for millions.

At a time of such enormous crisis, scientists sought ever more inventive weapons, or devices to help halt the war. Civilians were involved as never before, with women taking up new trades, proving themselves as capable as their male predecessors whether in the factories or the fields.

The stories in this book are of courage, of ingenuity, of hilarity in some cases, or of great sadness, but they are all thought-provoking - and rather weird. So whether you are interested in the last Polish cavalry charge, the Black-out Ripper, Dada, or Ghandi's attempt to stop the bloodshed, welcome to the Weirder War Two!

Click Bait
By Gillian Philip

A funny joke's a funny joke. Eddie Doolan doesn't think twice about adapting it to fit a tragic local news story and posting it on social media.

It's less of a joke when his drunken post goes viral. It stops being funny altogether when Eddie ends up jobless, friendless and ostracized by the whole town of Langburn. This isn't how he wanted to achieve fame.

Under siege from the press, and facing charges not just for the joke but for a history of abusive behavior on the internet, Eddie grows increasingly paranoid and desperate. The only people still speaking to him are Crow, a neglected kid who relies on Eddie for food and company, and Sid, the local gamekeeper's granddaughter. It's Sid who offers Eddie a refuge and an understanding ear.

But she also offers him an illegal shotgun - and as Eddie's life spirals downwards, and his efforts at redemption are thwarted at every turn, the gun starts to look like the answer to all his problems.

Father of Storms
By Dean Jones

Imagine losing everything you loved as well as the future you'd wished for so long to come true.

Seth was born with the gift to manipulate energy. Unfortunately his skills mark him as a target for one who wishes to control everything. So began a life running from those who would seek to command him, a life that spans over a thousand years waiting for the day when all will be once again as it was.

Captured in modern day London, Seth needs the help of his companions, the Mara, to show him who he is through dreams of his past, so he can save the family he has waited so long to have. A warrior bred for battle must fight once more – but this time the battlefield is his mind. Can Seth win, or will he finally lose who he is and become the weapon of the man who started his nightmare all those years ago?

www.blkdogpublishing.com